INCORRUPTIBLE

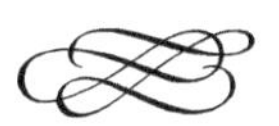

INCORRUPTIBLE

LILITH SAINTCROW

Noir comme le diable, chaud comme l'enfer, pur comme un ange, doux comme l'amour.

— CHARLES MAURICE DE TALLEYRAND-PÉRIGORD

Print edition ISBN: **978-1-950447-10-7**
Ebook edition ISBN: **978-1-950447-11-4**

For all the bad luck girls.

REGULAR GUY

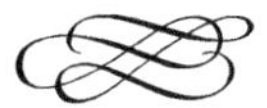

IT WAS A JOY TO KILL. To dive among the rebellious, flame following each wingtip and whipflick, the burning sword and the shield of faith singing as they were struck and striking in turn. Best of all was the knowledge of victory—they had won, they would always *win, and with each skirmish the conquest only became more total, more assured. Those they protected were safer with each wingèd unclean dying on his blade, with each scream of the agents of destruction smashed into dissolution—*

Michael Gabon woke, his pale cotton bedlinen thrashed out of recognition, prickling skin sweat-slicked. The warehouse groaned around him, electricity popping and sparking from outlets, bulbs flickering with a dull glow even though switches were safely off. The room with the heavy bag and weight-racks creaked and shivered, the bag swinging slightly, pushed by a feral current. Sheets gripped his hips like tentacles, and it took longer than he liked to work his way free.

Just a regular guy, on a regular night, bracing his elbows on his knees and dropping his blond head into his hands. Nothing much to see, especially in the dark.

Another dream. The entire echoing structure went back to its usual night-time dimness, and gradually his ribs stopped heaving. The two curved, vertical scars on his back hurt, a deep dissatisfied ache; the marks moved all over his body. Lines of dark not-ink, somewhere between black and blue, shifted as the shaking of adrenaline overdose faded, leaving only the thin metallic taste of battle filling his mouth.

The dreams, though infrequent, were getting worse. More violent. At least this one was a victory, and not the agony of defeat. Maybe he had suffered enough.

No. There are none left. That's why you're here.

It was a terrible thing to think. He pushed his fingers through sweat-stiffened blond hair, calluses rasping. The marks moved, tickling, and he discovered, almost as an afterthought, he had a hard-on. *That* was unusual, but maybe it was just a sign of grace leaving him.

Draining away, since the use for it was impossibly out of reach.

He wasn't going to be able to sleep, so he might as well get up. Practice a little, wash all his dishes, maybe even iron his jeans. Clean the bathroom grout with a toothbrush, like he had last week.

Had it been last week? He couldn't remember, only that he'd gone over the entire thing, gleaming white tile and bright nickel fittings, far too recently to be contemplating doing it again.

Maybe it was time to find another job? Something to keep him occupied, if he didn't want to do the fights anymore. The money there was good and he could be sure he was hitting someone who either liked or deserved it—but still, having to keep all his punches at fractional strength got boring, too.

Immortality was a tedious bitch when the reason for enduring it was gone. Or, if not gone, simply...absent.

The tall, solidly built man left the bed behind and set out, slowly, for the kitchen. His marks refused to quit moving and every scar, not just the ones on his back, ached with a deadly dull piercing.

It was irrelevant, like everything else.

At least by now Michael knew better than to hope. He padded into the kitchen, flicked the light on, and sighed.

BAD NEWS

When Jenna Delacroix rolled over, peering at her clock, the only indication it was going to be a bad day was the fact that her phone had fallen off the nightstand and somehow unplugged itself. When she managed to fumble the charger doohickey back in, the screen lit and after a few seconds of soaking up electricity, the palm-sized brick that kept track of her entire life began to ding over and over again. Her weekend, spent at home with tea and a stack of library books, was irretrievably gone.

At least she hadn't had any nightmares. Small mercies, right?

"Oh, *God*," she moaned, with feeling, then flinched. Froze, listening, her long dark hair webbed over her face. She'd slept rough, but deeply. If she'd accidentally kicked him in the middle of the night, there might be—

Then Jenna realized, as she did every morning now, that there was no need to worry. Eddie had never lived in this apartment, never slept in this bed, and definitely had never dirtied the bathroom here either.

And why? Because he was in prison, and she was safe. Her phone was blowing up for some reason, but she had to scramble if she was going to make it to work on time.

Jenna slid her legs out of bed and ran for the shower, hoping she could at least get some coffee on the way.

It was a sleet-gray, traffic-rattling day, and all the puddles were rimmed with ice. Tiny pellets at the heart of every raindrop made soft *pockpock* sounds lost under the bustling roar of passing vehicles, and she shivered at the bus stop for a good ten minutes before losing patience. The bus was late, the subway on time but packed, and the texts were mostly from Rachel, requests for Jenna to call as soon as possible. A ping from Bob, too, asking if she could come in early, but that ship had sailed.

Finally, when the uncaffeinated fog she was moving in lifted a little, she texted Rachel before plunging down the Ganter Street stairs. I just got up. Heading into work.

Rach must have been sitting on her damn phone, because Jenna's lit up almost immediately when she surfaced at T Street Station, Rach's message finally landing with an electronic thump.

Ohmygod are you okay???

Just fine, she typed back. What the fuck was wrong now? If Rach had broken up with Sam *again*, Jenna was going to have to listen to her moan and sob for a week before they got back together. On again, off again, the whole carousel running in circles until the engine busted, that was the Rach and Sam Show.

At least it was familiar. Neither of them dated anyone else, probably because they were both Leos.

Jenna hitched her mother's old, tawny leather purse higher on her shoulder, cut right to cross T Street, and begin working up. Three blocks was long enough to brace herself for whatever explosion Bob was having. They were down a cook since Greg had decided he didn't like their boss's bluff attitude. And if Sarah was having one of her episodes, that would mean a waitress down too. Went to bed, turned my phone off, she added.

The old familiar urge to over-explain. As if anyone cared, as if anyone who *did* care would accept such a faint excuse. Eddie certainly wouldn't.

Don't think about him, Jenna told herself sternly. A tinkling rendition of *I Believe in Miracles* was her reward, and she hit the "accept" button, plugging her other ear with a fingertip. "Jeez, Rach, calm down. What's going on?"

"Oh, Jenna." Long-limbed, black-haired Rachel sounded breathless even through the tiny speaker. "Sam was there, he saw it all. He saw him."

"What?" Jenna lengthened her stride. The crowd wasn't bad at this hour, everyone moving with their head down and shoulders up under a fine cold mist that promised yet more icy rain. The sleet was probably moving from the north. "Saw what?" Her heart began to hammer, and everything around her shrank through the roaring in her ears.

He'd seemed so sweet in the beginning. So contrite, too, when his temper occasionally snapped. *It's because I love you so much,* he used to say, and wasn't that a sign she was an idiot, lapping that bullshit up?

"Jenna, are you sitting down?" Now that she had her friend's attention, Rach wanted to draw it out. "You should sit down."

No thank you. If I stop moving I'll drown. "Hang on." Jenna glanced both ways and bolted across the street, her phone still clamped to the side of her face. If it skittered out of her hand and fell into the road, she might even be relieved. "How did he get out?" It wasn't really a surprise, not at this point.

"Something about appeal." If Rach was upset at Jenna guessing correctly, she kept it to herself. "Sam didn't catch much, it was loud and *he* was talking to Greg."

"Greg?" It was a good thing she had to keep going or be hit from behind by pedestrians. Jenna plugged her free ear again and lengthened her stride. "Which Greg?"

"The one with blue hair." Rachel, uncharacteristically somber, coughed slightly. It sounded like she was outside too, someone's horn was going off with an insistent, tinny bray. "Jenna, are you sure he doesn't know where you live?"

"Pretty sure." So it wasn't Greg-the-cook they were talking about, but Greg-the-petty-drug-dealer. Good news, even if Jenna's heart was pounding. "Unless someone told him. Rach, listen. Did he *see* Sam?" If Eddie had hassled Rachel's boyfriend, she might be pissed at Jenna for dating a guy who got them all in trouble.

Friends were great until you inconvenienced them. If Jenna had learned nothing else from the last eight months, she'd at least got *that* through her thick skull.

"Not sure." Now Rach sounded aggrieved at there being something she didn't know. At least there wasn't the telltale nasal burr of annoyance wending through her tone. "He got out of there, came straight home."

Shit. "I'm sorry," Jenna said, dully. Up ahead, a chrome-and-blue glow was the SunnyTime Diner, bobbing closer with every step. Maybe she should move again? She couldn't afford it, she could barely afford to stay still. Why on earth had they let Eddie out? It was a pretty open-and-shut case, for God's sake.

Now was a fine time to wish she'd watched more crime dramas.

"Why are *you* sorry?" Rach sounded honestly, instead of merely dramatically, baffled. "I'm just glad you're okay. Sam told me about it, and we both thought, well..."

"You thought what?" Jenna's neck began to ache. Well, she'd had a pleasant weekend, this was just the payment for it. If it was busy at work, she could ignore the incipient headache.

"We thought you should know as soon as possible." Rach was probably hunching over her own phone, cupping her mouth to whisper. Maybe she'd even dyed her hair some new fantastical shade; three weeks was long enough for her to get bored with cerulean. It was a wonder she had any curls left instead of just chemically processed straw. "Because of what he...did. To you."

"Yeah." Jenna winced, wishing she'd covered it up better. The scrapes, the bruises, the flinching, the embarrassment—if she'd been better at hiding, maybe she could have avoided some of this bullshit. The cold rainy breeze ruffled her hair. "I'm just glad I've moved, and I wasn't the one to put him away." No, Eddie had managed that little trick on his own, getting drunk and pulling a gun he wasn't supposed to have in a bar he wasn't supposed to be anywhere near, and to top it off, he'd shot a cop.

It was parole violation *and* assault with a deadly, there were a dozen witnesses, why, in God's name, would anyone let him out?

"I'll bet. Look, if you need anything—"

There it was again, the goddamn cloying *pity*. "I'm okay, it's just kind of a shock. I've gotta go into work now. Thanks." It was rude to hang up but Jenna did it anyway, flicking her phone to silent and swallowing a hot, slick wad of something too metal-tasting to be relief.

Or was it? Everything was out of her hands. He'd gotten himself into trouble, and she couldn't have bailed him out. It wasn't like talking the cops out of arresting him when the neighbors called 911 about the noise, or refusing to press charges. There was absolutely nothing Jenna could have done. She'd changed her phone number, moved out of the old place, and Eddie was firmly in her rearview mirror.

How much of a coward was she for being actually *grateful* it wasn't up to her? For once, a problem had been solved without her personal intervention; she should have known it wouldn't last.

The bell over the SunnyTime's door tinkled merrily; she glanced at the tables, gauging the damage. Not overwhelming, but not good, either. Three-quarters full, and it looked like Amy was the only one in. The kitchen hissed and clattered, but potbellied Bob was at the counter with the ancient, cranky cash register and his seamed, beaky face lit up when he saw her. "Jenna!" the squat, balding man bellowed across the diner. "Thank *God*!"

It was the most excited he'd ever been to see her, and she cautiously decided that was good. Jenna braced herself and threaded between tables, smiling apologetically at people waiting for their food. Who was in the kitchen, if Bob was at the register? Roberto? He was on vacation, Greg-the-cook was fired.

God, if Roberto'd been called in, *everyone* would be pissed at her for being late.

"So glad." Bob waved both hands as soon as Jenna got in range. His white T-shirt, radiantly bleached, clung to a physique best described as doughy, but he always had a sharp-ironed crease in his chinos, and changed his snowy aprons twice a day. "*So* glad to see you! Sarah, she called in sick. We got a new cook."

"That was fast." Jenna peered at the kitchen, saw nothing but the heat-lamp glow keeping plates for pickup warm and a haze of warmth from the grill. "Bob...we have to talk."

"What?" Her boss sobered, the smile dropping from his face so fast she all but flinched. "Oh. Let me guess. It's *him*."

What would it be like, to have a life where nobody could guess exactly what she was going to say? "One of my friends says he's out of prison." Her throat was dry. "I'm pretty sure he doesn't know where I live anymore, but..."

"Listen." Bob left the ancient cash register and edged around the counter. When he got close enough, he put a warm, broad hand on Jenna's arm. The chapping from constant hand-washing with harsh soap rasped against her coat sleeve. "It's gonna be all right, Jen. Promise."

Oh, yeah. Sure. How much trouble can he make here before you fire me to keep everyone else happy? "I don't know. I don't even know why they let him out, I just—"

"Hey." His fingers tightened, and she looked up into Bob's grizzled, familiar, florid face. Some people blushed every once in a while; Bob Stringman was perpetually flushed. "He shows up here, I'll throw him in the fryer. Nobody messes with my girls."

Well, wasn't that a kind thing to say. The wonder would be if he actually *meant* it. Still, Jenna suppressed a flinch at the proximity of a male—*any* male—and dredged up a smile all at once. "Yeah?"

"Yeah. So hustle up, cause we got hungry people, all right?" Bob winked one watery brown eye. His cheek twitched slightly, a sure sign of stress. "And I'm serious. Right into the deep-fryer."

"I might even help you," Jenna said, and summoned another weary smile as she hurried for the break room to lay down her purse and clock in.

HALLOWED AND BLESSED

The marks would not stop. A crescendo of prickling had driven Michael up and down the streets two days ago, and the only thing that made them abate was this tinfoil excuse for a diner set spitting distance from one of the city's busier corners, its neon sign blinking into life just as he rounded the corner at Ninth Avenue and R Street. He'd never seen the place before despite the bright, faux-chrome coating, but the prickling from the marks intensified to just short of pain when he attempted to turn away.

Of course he obeyed. Sometimes, though, he wondered if the marks were a faulty antenna, and he'd missed the important calls while it kept him in this city, wandering aimlessly. It could even have been warning of the presence of *diaboli*, except they didn't like this part of town very much.

Not enough prey.

So into the SunnyTime Diner he'd stepped, and the owner, a wide, mush-nosed pile of oily charm that could turn to aggression quickly enough, hired him on the spot. *You can cook?*

Yes, Michael told him. *I can learn*, was what he thought. It was a long time since he'd been in an industrial kitchen, but thankfully, not much had changed except the shapes of some implements. It was even easier now than it had been in 1939...had it been '39? Yes, it had. Right before the second war, and his last enlistment.

How many times had he gone into the military? He'd lost track. The structure was good for his kind; idleness did not suit a legionnaire at all.

A sharp-eyed Latino showed up to man the sinks. "I'm Ace, man," the boy mumbled, and though he moved slowly he managed to fit in a prodigious amount of clanking and scrubbing as well as prep. Michael worked, laying down stacks of pancakes, globs of egg, strips of bacon. A waitress, blonde and rail-thin, cautiously began to warm up to him when he didn't make a mess of the first orders, and after a couple days she was downright chatty.

Once the lunch rush began on the third day he was actually glad the marks had led him here. It was better than prowling the city or the warehouse hoping for something, anything to break the endless labyrinth of waiting.

And yet, dissatisfaction was a metallic tang against his palate, almost like adrenaline. Head down, Michael scrubbed the grill, taking a deep breath before the next flood of hungry customers. The marks began to prickle again, restlessly. Had they brought him here only to drag him somewhere else? The kitchen was too hot for anything other than a T-shirt; he could see the marks shift on his forearms, inked lines in a language older than Time scrolling over his skin.

An onlooker would only see thin blue tattoos that used to mean *felon* or *barbarian*; nowadays, the kindest term was *hipster*. The patterns were too linear to be truly tribal, more like a circuit map, and ordinary mortals wouldn't see their lazy movement, or the quick, fluid lines shifting when he was in battle.

It was when Michael looked up that the world stopped, threatening to slide from underneath him, a cat shaking an impertinent flea.

A flood of pale golden winterlight came through the front windows, the rainclouds parting for a bare second, and there was another waitress. When had *she* showed up?

Long wavy hair like dark honey in an amber jar, pulled back carelessly in a ponytail. Lucent, pale skin, slightly olive with golden undertones. He couldn't see her face, because she was turned away, one hip slightly out, already tired though her shift had just started.

It didn't matter, anyway; all that mattered was the *clarity*. Michael's marks ran with sweet hot pain, his knees turning to water, the smell of baking bread and all good things filling his nose along with the numinous, luminous musk of a piece of the Principle held in sweet, warm flesh.

An Incorruptible. Here. In this run-down flyblown diner, now hallowed and blessed among all places because *she* had appeared. Michael stared, and didn't realize what he was doing until Ace bumped into him from behind.

"Yo, man, be careful." The boy ambled away at a surprising pace, carrying a tub of dirties.

Michael snatched his hand from from the grill. He'd pressed it flat upon the sizzling-hot surface, and yet, he was unburned instead of quickly healing.

Walk through fire in the presence of the Principle. He studied his unmarked palm, wonderingly. The marks sang with high sweet pain, and the thin blonde waitress—Amy, her name was Amy—was suddenly at the counter. "You want to speed it up in here? I've got three full-tops, and you're gonna have more in a hot minute."

"Yes ma'am." Michael's lips were numb, as if he was a mortal meatsack half-poisoned with liquor. An Incorruptible, *here.* The marks ran over him like a waterfall, and he gazed at the spinner to find the orders glaring back at him, each one a puzzle full of promise, now. She was going to come up to the counter, and he was going to see her, perhaps even hear her voice.

He bent to work, every inch of him alive now. *This* was why the marks had brought him, this was why he'd dreamed. An Incorruptible. Here. In this very city, crossing his path.

So all hope was not lost, after all.

DAMAGED GOODS

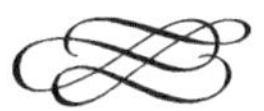

THE NEW COOK WAS BLOND, blue-eyed, and roughly the size of a Mack truck. Tattoos were visible above the collar of his white cotton T-shirt as well as down both brawny arms—vaguely tribal, not like Eddie's carnival-colorful sleeves, and the thought sent a sharp, quivering spear through her before she could push it away.

"Hey." Jenna decided that was an acceptable greeting, swallowing acid uncertainty along with a sip of overcooked coffee. She didn't care how long it had been in the pot, caffeine was caffeine no matter its form on a day like today. "Looks like we'll be working together. I'm Jenna."

"Michael." He didn't smile or offer his hand—not that he could have, with the order counter and its heat-lamps between them. His mouth stayed open a little, and he glared at her from under sandy eyebrows. Plenty of cooks had a chip on their shoulder, and if he'd been in the weeds all morning, his mood wasn't likely to be pleasant.

"Cool." She began clipping her first crop of orders on. "Let me know if my handwriting's bad, okay?"

He nodded, his mouth still slightly hanging. *Gonna catch flies with that*, Eddie would say, and emit a nasty laugh. Something hissed on the grill, and Ace jostled behind the new cook with a tray of clinking glasses, not a moment too soon. They were running out of clean 'ware, but at least with two waitresses working the floor and Bob at the counter they had a fighting chance.

It was so blessedly busy she didn't have to think. Just put the smile on, bring the kids tiny mason jars of crayons and the cheap coloring pages, suggest the special to the grandparents, smile and refill the coffee for the construction workers. The truckers weren't in until later when dinnertime traffic clotted the highway-arteries. Regulars made their regular jokes, said their regular things, and Jenna made every expected joke in return, her face aching but fixed in a public-service smile she sometimes imagined would engrave itself so deep she'd wear it in her coffin.

Her phone buzzed and buzzed in her skirt pocket, and the only time that smile was genuine was when she thought *jeez, should hook that up to my panties and have an enjoyable day.*

At least the tips were good. When Amy's shift ended the blonde hightailed it, switching her hips and lighting a cigarette the instant she got outside with a cheerfulness that made Jenna suddenly, vengefully wish she still smoked.

On the other hand, standing out in the rain with a cancer-stick would give her time to think, and that was the last thing she needed.

At least the new cook knew what he was doing. If some of the orders were a little slow, well, at least they were all *right.* Once, handing a high-top with goggles over the counter, he'd actually smiled, a tight strange expression under his buzzcut. He looked vaguely military, come to think of it, and his tattoos weren't quite *felon.* She couldn't think of another word that applied.

It didn't matter. Standoffish she could work with, as long as he did the orders right. At least Amy had been there long enough to cover the worst of the rushes.

The dead time near 8pm hit before she was quite ready. Bob appeared at her elbow, his combover ruffled and his iron-gray eyebrows pulled together; she tried not to startle-jump at his sudden proximity.

"You ain't taken a break yet," he said, gruffly, tying a fresh apron around his middle. Bleached cotton glowed, and a thin, wonderful smell of clean laundry brushed her nose before it was lost in fried food and industrial-strength cleaning supplies. "Eh, Mike! Make her something to eat!"

"Sure." The cook peered through steam rising on the other side of the order counter. "What would you like, Miss Jenna?"

"*Miss* Jenna?" Bob cackled, and his cheek had stopped twitching. He finished tying the apron and clapped his hands, a big meaty sound; Jenna tried not to flinch again. "Whatchoo want, honey? Club sandwich, fries? Get her a club, with fries. You can't live on no salad."

She would have preferred something a lot lighter, but Bob didn't like his magnanimity interfered with. When he set out to help, you got what *he* thought you should have, no more and no less. At least she was hungry, now that she thought about it. So she just nodded and put her head down, rolling clean silverware in fresh napkins, tapping them, securing the gummed band.

"Here." The new cook brought it out in record time, and the mountain of steaming, crispy fries was mind-boggling. He set the oversized plate gently on the counter, pushing it toward her with fingertips. He was pretty tall, towering even though she perched on a barstool, and his size made her nervous. "What do you want to drink?"

Was that an accent? Probably not. He looked about as Kansas corn-fed as they came, and that was local. Well, local-ish.

"I can get it, thanks." Jenna's gaze flicked up, down, a quick measuring of potential trouble. Hopefully her smile was placatory enough. He was *big*. "Wow. That's a lot of fries."

"You look hungry." A flash of white teeth was his smile, eager and very hopeful. He stood just a little too close, and Jenna curled up inside herself just in case he was getting ideas. "I just thought...you know."

You thought I needed eight pounds of fried and salted potato product? "Thanks." Her stomach clenched, gurgling. It would be a miracle if she even managed half the potato pile, not to mention the ungodly-huge sandwich. A dill spear the size of a breadknife was tucked onto the plate-edge, and the parsley sprig was more like a sapling. "You went all out."

"Well, you've got good handwriting. Makes it easier to do my job." He seemed to realize he was looming and took a half-step back, respecting her personal space at last. "Seriously, can I get you a Coke? Or coffee, or...?"

"I'm fine." How many times was she going to repeat that today, even to herself? "I'll get some water in a second."

"I got it. Ice, or no?"

"Either's fine." She darted another glance at his face. Anxious, bright blue eyes. He probably wanted to make a good impression. Pissing off a waitress could make a cook's life hell, and vice versa. "Thanks. Mike, right?"

He nodded, his shoulders straightening, level as an iron bar. "Yes ma'am." A small twitch, tiny as the one on Bob's cheeks, as if the new cook wanted to put his hands behind him.

Jenna's mouth tried to curve up at either corner; she hoped he didn't think she was laughing at him. *At ease, soldier. I haven't been ma'am'd in ages.* "Military?"

A short, sharp nod. He had a good face, even if his jaw was too strong and the muscle on him shouted *leave this one alone.* "Used to be."

The bell jangled and she spun to see who it was. Just a young couple, both in the standard office-worker's Monday gray-and-black; Bob already waving a hand and saying, *sit anywhere, we don't have a waiting list.* At the same time, the boss motioned Jenna back to her seat. She settled again, aware that her knees had hit the cook's when the stool rotated and that her heart was going a mile a minute again, throbbing in her throat.

"Expecting someone?" Mike's hands, denied parade rest, dangled at his sides like he didn't know what to do with them. He was, to make a bad day even worse, *paying attention*, and maybe he was getting ideas, too.

"More like dreading." Jenna braced herself to explain, again. God knew her status was probably common knowledge among every other diner employee. She could just get in on the ground floor now so someone else didn't tell him, and maybe that would warn him off. "Ex-boyfriend got out of prison recently." *Like, right before my weekend. And I didn't know.*

"Gotcha." Mike nodded, slowly, and for once, there was no flicker of judgment crossing someone's face when she tried to explain about Eddie. "He knows you're here?"

Maybe he was worried for his own safety. Jenna crushed a squirming tentacle of guilt somewhere around her solar plexus. "I was working here before he went in." *Since he didn't like me dancing anymore.*

"And..." The new cook trailed off and examined her again, those bright blue eyes distant but not judgmental. "I don't want to pry, but you think he might show up?"

"Maybe." *If he's mad enough.* Jenna also crushed the urge to cross her arms defensively. She could even cross her legs, body language shouting the way she refused to.

"Huh." The cook nodded again. For someone who had cranked out order after order all afternoon, he wasn't very spattered or splashed. Maybe he brought extra shirts, like Bob's extra aprons. "Well, don't worry."

Yeah. Sure. Easy for you to say. "I'll try not to." To prove it, she set the silverware tub aside and tried a French fry. Nice and crispy, just enough salt. Her stomach settled a bit, realizing it was hungry and nothing bad had happened yet today.

She'd need fuel for when it *did* happen, though.

"Yeah." The new cook backed up another half step, probably realizing she was damaged goods. Fluorescent light robbed his hair of its deep gold, but it would probably glow in sunshine. "I'll, um, get you some Coke."

She didn't want it, but she didn't bother saying so. What was the point?

Instead, she applied herself grimly to the business of consuming fuel, and got down a quarter of the sandwich plus a few more fries. Free food was nothing she could afford to miss, and she could even take the leftovers home.

Hallelujah.

PIECE OF WORK

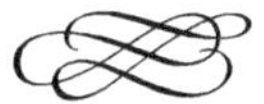

"Eh, Mike!" The diner's portly owner stepped into the kitchen, surveying its gleaming surfaces with a fastidious, proprietary air. A lord surveying his domain from a stone tower could hardly look as satisfied. "Looks nice, man. Looks nice."

Yeah, this is the cleanest it's probably been in years, so am I hired permanently? "Thanks." Michael swallowed impatience and irritation both, scrubbing at the grill with a palmetto brush. The dark-eyed Jenna—and yes, she was an Incorruptible, just standing next to her was enough to make his marks run with honeyed lightning—was wiping down tables with Ace and the other busboy, Henry with the dark pompadour and pegged jeans. She moved at a good clip, and every time someone got too close she all but flinched. No sign of bruises on her forearms or dancer-long legs under the uniform skirt, but every line on her, from her thin neck to her ruthlessly schooled expression, shouted *hurt*. He didn't even need the marks resonating with her nervousness to figure it out.

Ex-boyfriend, just out of prison. Well, she didn't have to worry about him ever again, but teaching her that simple truth couldn't be rushed. It took time for Incorruptibles to trust their legionnaires.

Time, and a few doses of hard proof. The fact that he was currently longing to provide said proof was irrelevant.

"I got somethin' else for you." Bob produced a toothpick from a tiny silver holder tucked into his breast pocket. He was fond of chinos and ruthlessly clean aprons, and while his place was small and the menu basic, it was also clean and he didn't skimp on supplies. Or, it appeared, his employees. "If you want it."

"What's that?" There wasn't a *this is a front* vibe to the place, but then, Michael hadn't been looking. "I'm gonna season this beast, by the way."

"Well, I'll tell you." Bob nodded and lifted the toothpick, lowered it as he visibly realized talking around it wasn't optimal. "See Jenna, there? Nice girl, good waitress, hard worker. She got this ex-boyfriend Eddie. Real piece of work."

Michael kept scrubbing. His short nod said *I hear you*. The marks kept moving, too, but this mortal man with his blinkered eyes wouldn't see.

She would, though. He'd have to be careful.

"She tells me Eddie just got out of the stir." Bob rolled the toothpick between blunt fingertips, his dark eyes narrowing. "He knows she works here. You got a car?"

"A truck." Strict truth was best, but not too large a serving of it. "Left it at home today." Parking was expensive in this slice of the city, and the poor man he was impersonating would avoid the cost.

"Well, she lives down Riverview way." Bob examined the toothpick like he thought he'd dug gold out of his interdental spaces. "Pay you to walk her home and make sure she gets there okay, until we figure out what the fuck with Eddie, right?"

Michael nodded again, his face a mask. Steam tickled his nose, and Ace passed with a plastic tub of dishes, safely out of earshot. Was it luck, or the Principle arranging events? Who knew, who cared, if this man was intent on smoothing a legionnaire's way? It would solve several problems at once. "You don't have to pay me. I've seen that look on a woman before." *Riverview. Fair ways away, that'll give me time. Get to know her.* He could even begin to soothe that anxiety.

If she'd let him.

"Yeah, well." Bob glanced over the order counter, blinking owlishly at the hot draft from the lamps. "I tell you, no funny stuff, all right? She's a good girl. You mess with her, I hold your head in the deep fryer."

Maybe the man even meant it. Trying it with a legionnaire—no matter how junior—would be detrimental to his pudgy little mortal health. Still, those who gave an Incorruptible their due were to be treated gently by any of Michael's kind. "Yessir." Michael decided that was enough of an answer. Short and sweet, nothing fancy to get him into trouble.

"All right, I'll go tell her. Get finished." He tucked the toothpick in the corner of his lips and ambled away.

"Yessir," Michael repeated, as if his pulse hadn't kicked up several notches. He watched the old man tack across the diner, straightening small things on the tabletops as he went and berating Ace and Henry, who both grinned and took it in stride.

Bob was, however, much gentler with Jenna, leaning on the other side of the table she'd just finished clearing, his tone dropping and the toothpick back in his fingertips. She listened, her expression unchanging, and when her dark gaze flickered over Bob's shoulder Michael felt it all along the marks even with his head down. Should he try to look unthreatening? Just threatening enough to handle a petty thug? Some women liked a breath of danger, but instinct told him this one might not.

He was about to find out where she lived. She'd survived to adulthood—had the Breath awakened in her yet? There were *diaboli* all around; he knew where they gathered in this city, feeding on civilians since rarer meat was denied them. When they met, he had enough grace and training to teach them the Legion still lived, if only in one place.

If only in one man.

Funny, Michael was thinking of himself as almost mortal. The marks moved over him, a dance invisible to the uninitiated. He could barely remember what came before his arrival, twin streams of fire down his back and the marks vibrating with distress as he landed on the hard, cold, inimical floor of an Eyrie thousands of mortal miles from here.

No, he couldn't really remember what came *before*, just the long sensation of hope draining away, grace weakening, the Principle turning silent.

Now, none of that mattered. There was an Incorruptible, alive and breathing out grace. Already he felt stronger, and the thanksgiving poured out in the secret chambers inside his chest was almost enough to deafen him.

THE HOSANNAS LASTED until Jenna set off down the damp sidewalk at a good clip, her head down, staring at her cell phone. Michael had to lengthen his stride—she moved quickly, for a woman. "Jesus," she breathed, dabbing at the phone's glassy, glowing face with her thumb. "Everyone knows."

"Huh?" Fortunately, there weren't many people around, so he didn't have to bump them out of her way.

"Everyone's blowing up my phone." She glanced up just enough to get her bearings, stretching those long legs as if she hadn't been using them all day. "Look, we're out of sight, now. You don't have to walk me home. Bob's just...well, you don't have to."

The marks drank in grace from her, but she didn't seem conscious of the pull. Her shoulders were tense, curved inward, and whenever his step brought him too close she half-skipped sideways, a habitual move that said a great deal about this ex-boyfriend. Michael watched the sidewalk in case she tripped, and the oncoming traffic as well. The *diaboli* clustered in the rougher areas of town, but they were drawn to Incorruptibles just as Michael's kind. How had she survived?

Not, it seemed, unscathed. "I'd like to," he said finally. *Keep it short and simple. You'll mess up anything else.* "Good exercise."

"Yeah." The faintest hint of an eyeroll stopped just in time and turned into a shrug, that dark gaze stuttering to his face to read his emotional status. She was painfully sensitive, far too hesitant. "I'll bet exercise is what you really like after a day of being on your feet."

As if *she* hadn't been on her feet all day, too. "I have a truck. Could drive you."

She shook her head, stopping so suddenly a man behind them let out a curse, veering wide. It would have been simple enough to take a step back and send the gray-suited businessman into the street, but instead, Michael simply froze, looking down at the top of her head. Her phone slipped back into her pocket, and when she tipped her chin back, dark eyes flashed in the glow from a leaning, half-cockeye streetlamp that had tangled with a veering car and somewhat won the battle.

Honeydark hair and velvety eyes, that beautiful skin with sweet clarity leaking through to fill the thin-etched marks on him with warmth and fresh strength—it was enough to make a legionnaire fall to his knees and beg the Principle for mercy.

"Look, Mike. It's really nice of you and all." Jenna glanced at the businessman, but he continued on his way, already forgetting the momentary inconvenience. Her dark eyes glowed, and this close faint reddening around the lids—and the tenderness of her nostrils—was visible. Maybe she'd cried in the bathroom. "But Eddie doesn't know where I live now. All right? If he cares enough to find out, he's going to be furious seeing me with a guy. He's got a bad temper, I don't want anyone hurt."

What, except herself? It was, as far as he could remember, typical of an Incorruptible to feel that way. The Principle guided them and gave them many a virtue, including kindness. "Isn't he your *ex*? I mean, him seeing you with someone else might make that clear." He knew, even as he said it, that he was getting fancy, and that was a bad idea.

Getting fancy only got a grunt in trouble.

Her chin lifted slightly, and those large dark eyes flashed. She could break a window with that look, if she really wanted to. "I didn't visit him in prison, I didn't get together the money to bail him out, so he might not *know* he's ex and that's not a discussion I'd care to have with him. At all. Okay?"

"Understood." Michael didn't move, the stinging awareness of every object, moving or still, on the street drawing him harpstring-tight. "All the same, I'll walk you home." Finding out where she lived, not to mention a good spot to stand guard, was his first objective. It was a relief, and a relaxation, to have a clear-cut mission instead of trying to fill time on his own.

Setting your own tasks was a good way to deviate, and no legionnaire wanted *that*.

"Look." Jenna's arms crossed defensively, her thin blue canvas jacket starred with tiny fog-gems. "I'm trying to be *nice*, here, okay?" Irritation, well-camouflaged, sharpened under her tone.

"Don't." He couldn't say it any more plainly. "There's no need."

"I really don't want anyone to get into trouble." An unwilling, unsteady smile tilted up both corners of her mouth, and the flash of relaxation turned her from almost-plain into pretty. Not that it mattered—as soon as she relaxed fully the Principle would shine from her. So much grace filled the air around her anyway Michael wasn't sure his marks could take increased intensity. Her force was all but visible.

One of the blessed, indeed.

"Then just let me walk you home." At least he had a subtle way of overcoming her objections. "Bob said he'd put my head in the deep fryer if I didn't."

"He's really fond of that threat." She still didn't move, studying his face. The deepening fog glistened on her cheeks, dotted her chapped lips. Her cheekbones stood out alarmingly. This close, you could see the stress and fine trembling in her, the way cords in her slim neck stood out.

Full of grace, yes. But that gift could be broken, and could burn the bearer from inside if not given proper care.

"Look at this." Michael brought his hands up. Folded them into fists, slowly, so he didn't spook her. The knuckles stood out, and the scars he'd chosen to keep crisscrossed the working surfaces. Each one was a reinforcement, and a reminder. "See those? Know what they say?"

Jenna studied his hands, intently; finally she looked up at him, her expression unreadable. The marks slid over the backs of his hands, too. Some paralleled the bones, reinforcing, strengthening. Did she see them move?

"They say I can take care of myself." Michael dropped his hands—but slowly, again, to avoid frightening her. If possible. "Okay?"

"Fine." Her shoulders sagged under the thin jacket. She needed a better coat, winter was on its way. "I'm too tired to argue."

"Okay." He doubted that, but he also knew a victory when he saw one. "So let's get going."

TYPE, BAD LUCK

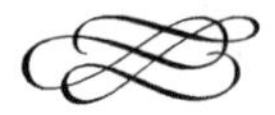

THE ONLY THING better than closing her own door and sliding her wet jacket off was checking her entire apartment, top to bottom, and making sure it still held not a single trace of Eddie.

Or any other man.

The new cook had seen her right up to the building door, watched while she unlocked it, and didn't try to come inside. Instead, he'd just watched from the other side, and no doubt he meant his smile to be encouraging. When added to the tattoos and the scars on his hands, the short hair, and how big his shoulders were...well, none of it was exactly *comforting*.

Nothing was.

Her phone was full of people texting to let her know they'd heard. Of course they had, Rach had done everything but send up smoke signals. She loved Sam, and she loved drama almost as much.

Jenna rubbed at her forehead, her fingernails bitten ruthlessly down. There was nothing in the fridge and takeout meant someone at the main door, knocking, wanting to be buzzed in. God, that was the last thing her nerves needed.

He won't show up. He's got other problems.

The thing about Eddie Rayburn, though, was that he liked to make his problems *other* people's problems. Spread the wealth, so to speak. He was generous like that.

Jenna, leaning against the kitchen counter, examined her right forearm. There was the scar, tracing up the underside, the little ladderlike divots where it had been sewn shut. Still there, big and ugly, a reminder—as if she needed one—that she was bad luck, and deserved it.

She deserved it *all*.

Still, the tiny studio was welcoming. It was even warm, because everyone around her had their heaters on. The end of summer had been awful, but she peeled out of her clothes as soon as she hit the door and got out a cheap spray bottle. Ninety-nine cents' worth of cheap mass-produced plastic bought a constant supply of artificial sweat, even when there was no breeze through the unscreened windows to make it worthwhile.

Like all blessings, the warmth was only situationally pleasant.

He was interested, Mike the new cook. She could tell by the way he strayed too close, and even by the way he just stood there and let the foyer door close on him, peering through the glass to catch one last glimpse.

Jenna could, she supposed, use that. Maybe if Eddie saw her with a guy who wasn't too weedy, he'd decide to go elsewhere. It was probably worth a try except it made her feel like a prostitute, and who needed that? Waitressing was honest, at least. So was working a pole; at least, that would *definitely* bring enough money in to move out of her current rathole. Still, exotic dancing was how she'd met Eddie, and the heatless fume of danger on him, like the shimmers over a hot grill or summer pavement, was all over the new cook, too.

It was no use. She had a type, and it was bad luck. Better to just keep her head down and forget about everything. Just do her job, and the cook would latch on to one of the other waitresses.

Probably Amy, she enjoyed notching her belt.

When the water boiled, she used a chamomile teabag. It was

supposed to be soothing. It just tasted like sticks and dandelions to her, but that didn't matter. She was committed to healthy choices now, *better* choices. The bad ones were easy, it was health and tofu and good boundaries that were hard. You had to work for it, and an instant of letting go could slide you back down the hill for miles.

Just like everything else.

Still, when she wedged her living room window open, settling on the sill and tilting so she could see a slice of glimmering citystars instead of the dark confines of the alley, something inside her eased. It wasn't bad, with a cold night wind slipping past full of grimy exhaust and cold rain. Even the thought that Eddie might be hiding in the darkness, looking for her or even making plans to stop by the SunnyTime, wasn't as bad as it could have been.

Sooner or later, things turned out all right—or so Mom had always said, and her daughter believed along with every other childhood truth.

The stupid, awful optimism that kept Jenna going instead of finishing the job and slicing open her other arm to match the first scar just kept returning, no matter how many times she tried to stamp on it, burn it, or pull it out by the roots.

Still, it didn't do any harm to think that maybe, just maybe, Eddie wouldn't show up at all.

As long as Jenna prepared for the worst, she could hope all she wanted.

Another night without bloodcurdling-bad dreams meant she was up early and feeling rested, for a change. The good feeling lasted until Jenna left for work the next morning. She spent a long while looking out the foyer's glass door, scrutinizing every visible bit of the gray street lingering under a heavy fog with pretensions at becoming wintry drizzle. When she finally darted out and set off down the street, her head down and the hood of an ancient black jacket pulled over her hair for insurance, an engine roused and crept closer, closer.

The low throbbing growl pulled up right next to her. Jenna whirled, her hands fists, her eyes wide, and her skin suddenly two sizes too small.

It was an ancient red Dodge pickup with an antique canopy, the outside looking too battered for its engine's buttery purr. The man behind the wheel wasn't short or dark-haired, though. Instead, Mike the cook's blue eyes blinked at her, and he smiled tentatively. His window, rolled half-down, showed her own pale cheeks and the black hood, her wide, distorted eyes, a mask of fear.

"Hey!" He sounded cheerful. "Want a ride?"

Her heart almost exploded, her knees turned to cooked noodles, and she almost fell down next to last week's garbage piled out near the curb by the building's silent, sclerotic super. As it was, she took two steps backward, her morning GrapeNuts threatening to exit in a spectacular breakfast fountain. If she puked, would the pressure behind it make it all the way across the street and splatter the truck?

She could try. There were animals who used projectile vomiting as a defense, and at that moment, Jenna thought they had the right idea.

"Jesus." In defiance of all acceptable traffic behavior, Mike the new cook popped the truck into park and opened his door, almost stepping out in front of an elderly but very well-maintained Cadillac that, predictably, laid on the horn.

Jenna bolted. It took her half a block to realize she was running flat-out, but she didn't stop until she'd almost tripped on the old, slick stairs of West Riverview Station and plunged into the morning commuter crowd.

NO WORRIES

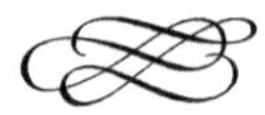

STUPID, *careless, brainless...* Michael had made his supply run to the warehouse, picked up what he needed to run close-guard on an Incorruptible until he could extract, and stood guard outside her apartment building last night without a whisper of the unclean showing up. He'd even been feeling *good* about his preparations—until he'd fouled everything up at the last second, like the dumb grunt he was.

The steering wheel creaked; Michael tried to loosen his fingers. Castigating himself wasn't an efficient use of energy, but he couldn't stop. Traffic wasn't helping either, but at least there was a cure for that—he could waste grace on opening chinks in probability, sliding through and snapping them closed to tangle other drivers in his wake. The exercise, with the fresh force granted him by a Lumina's nearness, was unexpectedly satisfying; wonder of wonders, he made it to the diner before she did. At least Bob was happy to see him, and even happier to get out from behind the grill himself.

As a result, Michael was already elbow-deep in prep when she arrived; the Incorruptible was breathless and flushed, her ribs heaving and her dark eyes so wide he almost curled his fingers under the grill to heave it skyward. Jenna didn't even glance in the kitchen's direction, hurrying for the dressing room. Her long flow of wavy dark-honey hair was a banner, her chin tucked and her shoulders bowed, she ducked through the employee door and was lost to sight but not his other senses. The throbbing of her terror along his marks shortened his own breath, and he was beginning to think he should set some of his resources to finding this ex-boyfriend of hers.

It would be satisfying, but against the rules. If others of the Legion had remained in this city, some could stand guard while others moved to bring the Incorruptible to safe haven. Since Michael had no backup, both duties rested on his shoulders. On the bright side, the amount of grace running through her would strengthen him immeasurably—a gift that renewed itself when shared, a hallmark of the Principle.

"Hey." Ace's face worked, a series of dynamic grimaces meant to express concern and trepidation at once. His damp hair was combed back from a ferocious widow's peak, and it suited him. "You okay, man?"

"Fine." Michael loosened his fingers, shook out his hands. The last thing he needed was to frighten his coworkers as well as the *lumina*. "Just thinking."

"Yeah, well, be careful with that shit." Ace rubbed at his right wrist, a quick, reflexive movement. Today it was a red and yellow plaid button-down over a black T-shirt and jeans—at least *he* didn't have to wear a uniform or cook's whites. "Only leads to trouble."

Wise, for a young mortal. "Don't I know it." Michael took a deep breath; the aggressive redheaded waitress was at the window, peering through and chewing a wad of gum big enough to dislocate her jaw. "Yeah, I'm here."

"Good," Sarah the soft-hipped redhead snapped, blue eyeshadow glittering on her lids. "Because I've got a crowd coming through the door and no time for bullshit."

Michael exhaled, softly. The Incorruptible was going to need whatever reserves of mortal politeness he had, not this woman. Still, there was no reason for anything other than strict reserve. "Better get them seated, then."

Sarah gave him a scathing look, one of many she no doubt reserved for people who talked at the theater or did not offer their bus seats to pregnant women; as if that could not express the depths of her irritation, the waitress did a military-smart about-face and marched off.

"Oh, man." Ace's *sotto voce* was pretty good, a thin thread of sound under the humming of a kitchen ready to be pressed into service. "She's gonna be pissed now."

"She always is." It was time to get to work, and at least the Incorruptible wasn't going anywhere this afternoon. "Been here long enough to figure *that* out."

He could begin soothing the *lumina*. The trouble was, he didn't have any damn idea *how*. At least when he was waiting for the inevitable end in an abandoned world, he hadn't been at risk of complete failure. The test had arrived, and he'd almost been caught napping.

A few minutes later, Sarah spun the wheel holding tickets, vengeful joy glittering in her gaze as paper fluttered. Jenna lingered nearby, tying her apron with thoughtless, habitual movements. Michael leaned forward, ostensibly to examine the orders.

"—fuckwad," Sarah finished, a venomous hiss. "I'm about to dump his ass."

"I'm sure it has nothing to do with your craving chocolate today." Jenna's smile, soft and pacific, lit her thin, wan face. She needed proper nutrition as well as a better coat; the black one she'd been wearing this morning was paper-thin. Her apartment building didn't look too shabby, clinging to the edge of respectability, but there were more fitting places for an Incorruptible to rest. "What was it this time?"

"Oh, he didn't want to go dancing because his *feet* hurt." Sarah glared over the shiny metal shelf under the heat-lamp. She had a generous mouth, pale lipgloss turned it into a landmark. "And *this* asshole's getting snippy with me too."

"Lay off, okay?" Jenna barely glanced through the window, her shoulders hunching. "Mike's a nice guy."

Had she really said that about him? Or were they talking about Ace? Michael froze, looking at the order slips but not seeing their cargo of scribbles.

"Pfft." Somewhat mollified, Sarah's gaze lit with mischief. "Well, I guess I know who's staked out a claim, huh?"

"Don't be ridiculous." Jenna made a face and the other woman laughed, tucking a pen in her reddish, hairspray-stiff mane before bouncing away, apparently soothed. At last the Incorruptible looked through the order window and essayed a weak smile, her dark eyes so shadowed with exhaustion they looked slightly bruised. "Hi. I'm, uh, sorry about that, it just kind of startled me."

"No worries." *No worries ever again, for you.* It wasn't anything the mortal man he was impersonating could say to her, but he could think it all he wanted, right? "I figured as much."

She studied him for a long moment, thoughts moving in those beautiful eyes. The marks along his arms and legs ran with sweet pain, and the ones on his trunk were padded whips of liquid fire. Even the curved scars on his back burned, a beautiful, strengthening ache.

"Really," Michael added. His hands moved independently, beginning prep for the clutch of orders Sarah had dropped off. "I was kicking myself for scaring you. Bob said to drive you to work, I figured he'd already let you know." Blaming the boss was a time-honored tactic, and of course, some almost-falsehoods were permissible in the service of the Incorruptible.

Anything that eased them or kept them safe until they could be closed in an Eyrie was acceptable, as long as there was no deviance or twisting in a legionnaire's motives.

"That explains it." Jenna settled her tied apron, smoothing her skirt against her hips. Michael's marks settled, sensing the draining-away of fear. "But it's not really neces—"

"I need this job," Michael said, baldly, and hoped his expression was suitably neutral. It wasn't quite acceptable to interrupt a *lumina*, and it wasn't quite accurate—he didn't need the job in the way she might think. The pay was a pittance, he had plenty saved.

But he *did* need, very much, to stay protectively near this piece of the Principle until it could be gathered into safety.

Social pressure, artfully applied, had its intended effect. "Fine." Jenna tugged at her ponytail, making sure it was secure, and glanced at the tables rapidly filling for breakfast. "When are you off?"

Another simple question he could answer simply. Michael liked those. "Same time as you."

"Bob." She shook her head, the wavy ponytail bouncing and spreading, and sighed. "All right. I'd better get to work."

"Me too." The hosannas were about to leap free of his skin and shatter on every surface. He had to be careful. Mortals might not *notice* a legionnaire, any display would make them turn instinctively aside. A *lumina* or *lumino*, though was exquisitely sensitive even without the Breath. "Thank you, ma'am."

That earned him a tight, mistrustful smile, still one to be treasured. "It's just Jen, Mike." And with that, she turned and set off, her sharp shoulders coming up to accept the weight of a burden she was probably unaware of carrying.

Michael allowed himself one last look at her hair, glowing with reddish highlights and fighting the elastic she'd confined it with, and got to work.

LITTLE SOFTLING

It was a normal day except for one of her periodic headaches, the kind that sent a jagged drill bit right through her temples turned her neck into concrete-fouled rebar. The bell on the door jangled its discordant welcome, the sound going right through Jenna's head, and she gritted her teeth.

Since she was deep in a five-top that couldn't decide if they wanted the special or not, the two men sat in Sarah's section. The redhead, her jaw working furiously—Bob didn't like her gum-chewing, but she flat-out refused to stop and raked in tips despite or because of it—smiled professionally as she swished her generous hips over to the new arrivals. A pair of businessmen, Jen thought, glancing at their suits and catching the gleam of a chunky watch on one thick, tanned wrist. Both of them were pretty broad in the shoulder, and Jenna sighed internally.

A surfeit of testosterone rarely tipped well, but Sarah had her ways.

The five-top finally settled on two specials and three burgers, each with something added or removed. Jenna made careful notes and escaped, retreating behind the counter to the pickup window.

She spun the ticket and rubbed at her temples, where the headache was just getting on the road bigtime. Maybe the barometric pressure was rising, and they'd get some sun—which would make the nights icy, but she was almost past caring.

It was time for a little light.

"Head hurt?" Mike peered out through a pall of steam. His tattoos almost seemed to twitch, but that was just her tired eyes. "You should sit down."

"I've got a bunch of people wanting lunch, I can't afford to sit down." She almost said *dipshits* instead of *people*, and wondered where the sudden irritability came from. Maybe she needed some of Bob's boiled coffee to get her through the afternoon. The headache was turning into a doozy, and her stomach was getting in on the act too. "You're going to need a break soon, though." He'd been at it since she arrived, and didn't seem to mind she'd made a complete idiot out of herself earlier.

"You worry about everyone, huh." Mike's smile, wide and seemingly genuine, almost managed to make her forget she was on her last nerve, too. "I'm tough, ma'am. Get some water, you look pale."

She *felt* pretty damn pale. Her shoulders were aching, too. Had she just not realized how tense she was? The bell on the door jangled again, the sound spearing her skull. "I think I will."

Bob spread his arms in exuberant greeting, welcoming yet more arrivals. The ice dispenser on the soda wall chugged, and she filled a paper cup before popping a cube in her mouth, her throat dry as baking glass. Was she coming down with a cold? That was the absolute *last* thing she needed.

Her chin jerked aside a split second before Sarah let out a short, sharp, wordless cry.

Jenna swung around, her hip bumping the soda wall's lower cabinet door, which was always just slightly ajar. Just enough to chip a knee in passing before you learned the swinging, loose step that would save you from a painful barking on the patella. The ice threatened to shoot between her teeth, lunging for escape, and she swallowed a cough.

At first what she saw made no sense. Sarah was bent over the businessmen's table, her uniform skirt riding up and showing the tender hollows behind her knees as well as her hamstrings tautening. At first Jenna thought it was a spill and took a step sideways, reaching for a stack of thirsty, over-bleached barmop towels. Her hand stopped halfway, because the guy sitting with his back to the second section pulled on Sarah's arm again, tugging even further her over the table.

"Hey!" Bob yelled, hurrying from the tables along the diner's left-hand wall. "*Hey*, now!"

The man holding Sarah's wrist bared his teeth. His wide, bland, tanned face crumpled like aluminum foil, and Sarah made another strange sound, a muffled scream.

A low, nasty hiss thrummed over every surface. The front windows, wide expanses of glass kept clean with immense effort and swearing on Bob's part, rippled a little as if they'd forgotten they were solid. Jenna's mouth dropped open and her pulse skyrocketed, her ears filling with damp cotton. The ice, crunched into two pieces because her jaw had snapped shut, went down her throat in a pair of cold, nausea-inducing lumps, hitting her cramping stomach and vanishing.

Thick silence filled the SunnyTime, even the fluorescents halting their buzzing, and every shadow turned black as ink, warping strangely at the corners. Panic poured down her ice-tickled throat, tinted with copper as if her teeth had cut her cheek again when Eddie's palm met her skin one breathless-hot August night.

Stay on the straight and narrow, Jen. His tone, oddly gentle when he was in the repentant phase. *Stay on the fuckin' straight and narrow, and we won't have any problems.*

"There it is," the one holding Sarah's wrist said, the words falling into that awful hissing and emerging from it with every edge polished to a razor gleam. "Look." And he raised one manicured, claw-twisting hand, pointing at Jenna.

Are they bail people? Maybe Eddie skipped out on... The thought trailed, off, patently ridiculous but less so than the way everyone in the diner had frozen, some covering their mouths and staring wide-eyed, the five-top she'd just gotten orders from in various attitudes of shock and dismay, two truckers at the counter twisting on their stools to see what the hubbub was, Bob near the door with one foot on worn linoleum and the other hanging casually in midair.

It was like the world had hit the pause button, but nobody had bothered to warn Jen and she couldn't find the remote.

The businessman facing the window rose, swelling upright in a fluid but hopelessly *wrong* movement, and Jenna's left hand snapped up to her face, cupping over her mouth. And yet, nobody else moved.

Hallucinating. I'm hallucinating. A clatter from the kitchen shattered the nasty hissing and brought both businessmen lunging fully upright. The one with Sarah's wrist made a casual twisting motion, and a hideous crunching noise was lost underneath the clangor.

The other businessman turned. His shape blurred, flickering between a tanned suit-wearing man indistinguishable from hundreds she'd brought food, soda refills, more fries, *honey I think I want a scoop of ice cream with my pie* and a high-shouldered, lean-nosed thing with dead white, ill-fitting skin and blazing yellowish eyes.

Jenna felt a fuzzy, faraway comfort that she was only hallucinating in the middle of a panic attack. When the terror receded she would shake her head, take deep gulping breaths, and do her best to cover up her lapse in sanity.

"*At last*," the bigger businessman hissed, and the throbbing scrape-noise returned, twisting the shadows even further. Jenna's red paper cup of crushed and cubed ice had left her hand somehow and was arrested halfway to the floor, just hanging there.

None of this matters. She stood very still, her ribs flickering as she tried to breathe through the asphyxiating noise.

"That's right," the thing in the businessman's body crooned. "That's right, little softling. It will all be over sssoon." The last word became a terrible, drilling hiss.

Jenna's eyelids turned leaden, fell. The blackness was sudden and very soft, not like the hurtful shadows outside.

The swinging door to the kitchen and the short employees-only hallway gave its particular squeak-thump. Her eyelids warmed, the darkness behind them turning crimson.

Light. From where? It didn't matter, it was a sign the panic attack was letting up.

At least, that's what Jenna thought before she opened her eyes again with a harsh, sweat-prickling effort, and saw Mike the new cook step in front of her, his broad back under a white T-shirt blessedly normal and proportionate. Hot water trickled down her cheeks, because he was glowing.

No, not really. A halo of clarity leaked from his skin and shirt and his worn jeans; his big, thick-soled boots placed lightly on the peeling linoleum behind the counter.

"No." Mike's voice rolled and boomed, rattling everything in the diner. Forks chattered, coffee cups jiggled, but Bob and the customers didn't move, frozen mid-frame in some mad movie that held *things* like the not-businessmen the cook was mercifully shielding her view of. "Leave now, *diaboli,* and I shall not pursue you."

Oh, God, Jenna thought. *He's in my hallucination. That can't be good.*

SLIPTIME

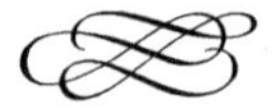

CONTRASTED with the painful uncertainty of coaxing a new Incorruptible into trusting him enough for summary extraction, this was a relief. Battle was, after all, what Michael was bred for, and it mattered little whether it was here or in a filthy alley at midnight. The Legion met the unclean wherever they were found—in penthouse suites, on rural backroads, or anywhere between.

The thought that the two unclean would have found Jenna unguarded a bare few days ago was almost as bad as the suspicion he'd somehow led them here. The city's *diaboli* had rarely challenged him, and he made sure whispers of more legionnaires circulated just infrequently enough to be true. For all Michael knew, he could be the only one of his kind posted here, a lonely outpost with an Eyrie barely within driving range—but there was no reason to make the unclean suspect as much.

So he simply stood, loose and easy, his hands relaxed but singing with grace, the half-sweet pain of battlerage throttled but still spreading from him in a haze. Behind him, the column of living light that was an Incorruptible emitted a soft chiming song of distress.

"*Legion.*" The smaller unclean made a spitting sound as it

hunched its misshapen shoulders, sinking its claws cruelly into the redhead waitress's broken arm. "*We thought your kind all fled.*"

It was the larger unclean with its frame smoking with glamour to fool mortal senses Michael worried about, because the fume drifting off it reached two high, quivering points above its malformed shoulders. Not very high, a handspan at most, but still...that was troublesome. If an Incorruptible didn't have the Breath yet, the wingèd unclean could sometimes cause something close to an allergic reaction. Which was the very last thing he wanted for tired, pale Jenna.

"*Give us the softling.*" The larger unclean's entire body twisted, and it shuffled forward. "*We shall leave thee in peace.*"

"*He won't leave good prey.*" The smaller sank its claws into the redhead's back, a meaty, crunching sound. "*They never do.*"

They meant only to lull him; the larger unclean darted forward in a skittering rush, leaving a boiling black streak on somnolent air. Normally, he would have simply moved aside and dealt it a glancing blow to begin the process of bleeding and maddening until he could kill it with little trouble. But the column of light at his back was achingly vulnerable, and narrowed his options.

They often thought, those unclean, that just because a legionnaire was economical with his force he perhaps did not have enough to overwhelm. Michael's fist flashed out. He didn't even bother to call upon a weapon, just met the clawed, smoking-hot paw with his broad, scarred knuckles.

He had a moment of clear sweet satisfaction that he'd gauged the force so precisely, and a static-laden howl rose from the larger unclean as its carapace shattered, spraying thick amber ichor. Michael's fist opened, wrist snapping up, and he grabbed the thing's arm, suddenly inside its strike range. The grace filling him turned slicing-sharp at his fingertips, and the thing howled as he ripped the appendage free of its shoulder-joint with an unholy creaksplatter.

It was another simple matter to pivot and strike the thing on its chest, flat palm colliding with cloth and carapace, a crunch like clay jars smashing. It went flying, streaking yet more ichor and a ribbon of smoking foulness, and Michael was already past, leaping after the smaller one.

Which had decided a member of the Legion was best left to its larger friend, but was not quite willing to let go of helpless prey. A shambling leap, and it thrust its clawed hands through the chest of a man at the five-top, bringing gristle-gobbets to its razortooth yawn and chowing down.

Michael collided with the thing, wine-dark fury filling him from crown to soles. Mortal bodies shivered in place as he flew, their cells absorbing concussive shocks, unable to flee even on an elemental level. The table went down, splintering as he ripped both life and spine from the small, thieving unclean, rising from its wreckage with a shake to splatter foulness away from the clear light of grace.

Sliptime blurred and flexed. The wingèd one bared its glassy, serrated teeth. It twitched in Jenna's direction, but Michael had already leapt, landing protectively before her with a jolt as the thing cackled in its hissing, brutish language and streaked for the door instead of attacking. Glass shattered outward, and as a final insult the *diabolo minoro* eviscerated Bob in passing, splattering gray-steaming guts far and wide. Blood sprayed, and the musical distress tolling behind Michael sharpened.

Of course. Without the Breath she would be trapped in sliptime, only able to see shutterclicks of disaster and mutilation.

The larger unclean had escaped. It would bring word to its fellows, and Michael wondered for a split second if he had moved to shield her instead of attacking because he *wanted* the *diaboli* to know the Legion was still alive and the Principle enfleshed, because he wanted the Incorruptible frightened and possibly dependent upon him...or both, perhaps?

He had been alone too long, away from his brothers and without the Principle breathing through him. Perhaps he had grown crooked, away from the pure path.

Perhaps he had *deviated*. The thought was a coldsweat nightmare greasing his skin.

Sliptime blurred, snapped into regular time with a subliminal click. The noise was incredible, soundwaves overlapping, bodies falling, glass tinkling onto indifferent pavement. A low rumbling settled under the skin of the world, a silent call quickening ear and mind and breath.

Jenna was broadcasting, the Principle within her plucking at invisible strings, the entire diner a resonating soundbox.

Michael's boots creaked as he halted before the Incorruptible, grace flaring to shield them both. His marks sang with sweet brilliant almost-pain, his arms closed around her, and she went limp as he dragged her down, debris peppering his back. The soda wall exploded, sticky sweetness spraying in a wide foaming fan, and Jenna shook underneath him.

Alive. Unwounded.

And now, she would be hunted.

PSYCHOLOGICAL VENTS

It was only a dream; only a nightmare from childhood bubbling up through psychological vents. It *had* to be. Jenna curled into a shaking, terrified snail-shape, a heavy warm shell against her back. The noise receded, an ocean wave of clattering breakage, and her breath was a series of tortuous gasps. Soft black feathers brushed at the edges of her vision, shadows of oxygen deprivation.

The weight behind her moved, sliding away to leave her unprotected. Jenna found herself crouching between the SunnyTime Diner's main counter and the soda wall, her hands over her ears, a heavy misting of carbonated water and soda-syrup settling against her hair and clothes.

A man's boots ground in broken glass, shattered dishes, and other detritus. "Are you hurt?" After the massive cacophony, his voice was a faint rumble. Jenna squeezed her ears more tightly. The soda cabinet door, pressed against her knee and shoulder, was spattered with syrup and other liquids.

Maybe the gas main. She blinked, her eyelashes heavy-clotted with dust and stickiness, or perhaps she'd been crying without meaning to. Eddie would be furious if she was leaking. *I had a hallucination, and something exploded? Maybe?*

"Are you *hurt*?" Someone's hand—warm, large, and hard—was on her arm, and pulled her to her feet. Gently, but with undeniable force.

Gentle or not, Jenna didn't resist. There was no point. Smoke-steam billowed from the kitchen. Water splashed, a musical counterpoint to the groaning of overstressed building materials.

The SunnyTime was *gone.*

No, not quite. It was only an empty shell; every table was smashed, the cake display in its glass casing was a mass of splinters and frosting, the truckers' counter had a hole in its middle the size of a dead body.

You could tell because the body was still there, flung so hard it was almost a smear, broken bones jabbing through deflated skin. It was the trucker in yellow-and-blue plaid, the one who took his coffee with half a sugar canister and liked his eggs over-easy.

Rancid, burning bile filled Jenna's throat. *Oh. My. God.*

The cook grabbed her other arm too, holding her like a wet towel, just about to drape her on a chair to dry. "Ma'am," he said. "Ma'am, Miss Jenna, look at me."

I can't. She craned her neck to stare past him.

There, at the front of the diner, was Bob. Or what was left of him, his stomach torn open, chips of white bone showing where his ribs had been wrenched aside. The five-top she'd just taken orders from were scattered like bowling pins, and there was a thick red flood on the floor amid stars of broken glass and the snow-falling grit of mulched ceiling tiles. Mired in the crimson puddle was a soaked mop of spray-stiffened coppery hair clinging to a shattered skull.

That's...it can't be, it's not...

It was Sarah. Or, like Bob, what was left of her. Just like in some of Jenna's more vivid dreams. She'd had one exactly like this just last week, but in it she'd been a bodiless observer instead of a terrified, frozen participant.

"You're all right." The new cook shook her. Not hard, just a gentle jostle to get her attention, but Jenna's head was too big for her neck and bobbled alarmingly. The rushing of another panic attack filled her ears, and the curious thought that maybe *this* was a hallucination might have been comforting if not for the petrifying terror. "You're all right. Look at me."

I don't want to. Jenna tried to breathe. The air had gone as hard as glass, pressing against her nose and mouth without condescending to come inside.

"*Look* at me!" Sharp and firm.

Mike's blue eyes were incandescent. His hair, military-short, was nevertheless mussed, and his white apron—wrapped around him twice, he was leaner than Bob—was gone. His T-shirt was splattered with strange colors, and the thought that some of the drops and spatters might be blood made her stomach cramp. She tried to free her arms so she could bend over, certain she was going to puke, but he held her up and studied her face. "You're safe. Okay? But we've got to get out of here."

Oh. Yeah. Sure. Her stomach rolled and contorted like a plastic bag on the freeway, caught in a passing slipstream. "I'll just go home," she heard herself whisper, six years old and deeply embarrassed at her cousin's birthday party again.

Wait, I thought her mom was the crazy one, one of her cousin's friends had said, very loudly, in a sudden hush, and Jenna had begun to cry. Uncle Jacques had taken her home, and spent some time in the living room with Mom—raised voices, and Mom's deadly paleness afterward. *I'll show you crazy, Jack.*

But Jenna wasn't a child. She was all grown up and in the middle of a disaster, her stomach revolving and her entire body cold with terror. "Home," she repeated, a dry-cricket whisper. "I'll just..."

"For a short while, yes." He eased up on her arms, and Jenna didn't want him to.

She had a sneaking suspicion she needed the support. Cold air whistled through the windows. All the glass was gone, blown outward, and something had happened on the street outside, too, to judge by the cries of dismay. In the distance, a ribbon of sound rose.

Sirens.

Oh, good. Someone called the cops. Or firemen. They'd show up, and ask what happened, and... Her brain gave a funny shiver, one she swore she could *feel* inside her skull, gray matter slopping around like a dog shaking away lake water. "A statement." She swallowed, dryly. "We'll have to give a statement, and...are *you* hurt?"

"It takes more than that to wound me." The cook's mouth pulled tight, a grim unsmile. He kept looking at her like *she* was the one with the answers. "We have to move, there could be more of them."

More explosions? "The gas main," she whispered. "Bob...*Sarah.* Where's Ace? First aid. We need the first aid kit."

"The kid went out the back, he might be okay. The rest...well, may they rest within the Principle." Mike cast a single glance over the shattered interior. A forlorn sunbreak pierced lowering rainclouds, glittering on window-fragments; it looked like a six-car pileup at the intersection of Tenth Avenue and R Street. Someone was yelling, a thin, lonely sound. Tiny, daylight-drained flames crept over the corpse of a blue Volkswagen beached on its side, one of its tires still rolling lazily. "Purse. We need your purse."

Oh sure, they'll want to check my ID when they get here. Sirens meant help was on the way. Jenna managed a nod. How were they even alive? Had the counter saved them? If it was the gas main, the entire kitchen was probably gone.

"Where's your purse, *lumina*?"

Jenna's gaze snagged on his neck. A faint gleam of sweat lay in the notch of his collarbone, but that wasn't what unnerved her. Rather, it was the marks leading under his T-shirt collar, spreading down his muscled arms past the sleeves.

The inked lines, a shade somewhere between blue and black, were *moving*. Crawling over his skin, melting together, separating, reforming.

All the breath walloped out of her again, and Jenna's legs buckled.

HAIL LUMINA

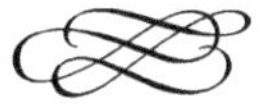

WHATEVER HE HAD EXPECTED an Incorruptible's home to look like, this was...not it. Shabby, anonymous, and painfully clean, the studio apartment had faded carpet, dingy walls, and the smell of food cooked on hotplates creeping under the door. Another tang of foulness told him the drains were probably indifferent at best.

Still, she had wanted to go home, and Michael was obeying the letter of that command instead of its spirit. He was fairly sure they weren't followed, but his nape tingled with the consciousness of danger. He paused, inspecting the secondhand bedspread—polyester, patterned with faded but still cheerful sunflowers, and smelling faintly of cheap fabric softener. The tiny kitchen held a few mismatched dishes and the bare pot-and-pan minimum, one of each; the bathroom was bleached and her towels mended with different-colored thread.

It was spartan even for a poverty-stricken waitress, and Michael decided she had perhaps left a great deal behind fleeing this ex-boyfriend. Even her closet was half-bare.

So he made another decision, this one easier than the last, and carried her away from that place.

THE INCORRUPTIBLE HAD ACHIEVED a soupy sort of consciousness as Michael lay her on his unmade bed, settling her head with care. The amber ichor all over his clothes was decaying rapidly; he longed to free himself of the stench. The warehouse resounded, its walls sighing as the invisible curtains and etchings of legionnaire defenses sensed the closeness of an Incorruptible. He backed away, suddenly bereft without living, breathing grace held against him.

She all but glowed visibly, a small woman supine on plain cotton sheets and the down comforter he rarely needed. It wasn't good enough for an Incorruptible, of course—they deserved silk, velvet, quiet luxury—but it was still a painful contrast to her stark little apartment. Her dark-honey hair fanned over pillows his own head had touched, and that vision shamed him too.

He should have at least pulled the covers up.

There were regulations about how to extract a new Incorruptible to safety under these circumstances, which meant he'd have to use the laptop. Her shock-slumber, reinforced by a mild *quietus*, should last some short while longer. Michael set off from the bedside, his hands still tingling.

A faint buzzing brought him around in a tight half-circle, his hands blurring with grace ready to coalesce into weapons. A faint metallic gleam filled his fingers, but he willed the blades away as soon as he discerned it was only a cell phone, vibrating inside Jenna's skirt pocket.

That roused her even through the *quietus*. She groaned, her small, soda-sticky hands patting at her hip. Her uniform skirt had ridden up, showing a generous proportion of pale, dancer-muscled thighs, and Michael averted his gaze for a few moments, taking a deep breath. The marks tingled, running with a sensation not quite heat, definitely not cold, and completely distracting.

"Oh, *fuck*," Jenna said, the soft slurred sound of a mortal surfacing from deep dreaming. "Ugh."

She rolled over, fishing in her pocket and exposing even more fascinating vistas of leg. Michael froze, dropping his gaze to hardwood floor. At least it was freshly polished, and though his lair was spare, it wasn't uncomfortable.

She did not belong here any more than in her apartment. An Incorruptible was to be pampered and served, cushioned and cloistered. He should have scooped her up, overridden any objections, and whisked her away before this. The very moment he saw her, in fact.

The trouble was, a modern woman wasn't likely to take such a thing calmly. Not that they ever had—the songs of defense were full of Incorruptibles lamenting luxurious solitude. Not that they were ever *alone*, either; legionnaires surrounded them, bathing in the Principle and safeguarding its bearers.

Still, the laments remained. And Michael realized, unsteadily, that he had not sought others of his kind in many a year, or heard the histories, spoken or sung.

It unnerved him that he couldn't quite recall just *how* many years.

"'Lo?" Jenna mumbled through cracked lips. "Rach?"

Tinny exclamations poured from the small rectangular thing pressed against her cheek. If he listened, Michael could hear the words, but she deserved a little privacy.

"Huh? No, I'm..." Cloth moved, her uniform scraping against the sheets. Both of them were filthy with construction dust. "I'm at home, I guess. Why?"

More tinny shouts. Someone was excited.

Jenna pushed herself up on her elbows. She stared uncomprehending at the walls, dark eyes wide and pink-rimmed from smoke and stress. Her cheeks seemed very soft, and Michael could have cursed himself into *diaboleri* because he was looking, after he had made up his mind not to.

Bare knees drew up, and the Incorruptible's head turned. She caught sight of him and froze, her dark eyebrows faintly lifted and her nose reddened. Was she about to weep? A high flush stood out on her cheekbones, and she blinked rapidly, no doubt trying to figure out just what the hell had happened.

"Rach?" Her lips shaped the word. "I'm, uh, I just woke up. What's going on?"

More babble. The Incorruptible moved, sliding her legs off the bed. Somehow, she'd lost one of her sensible shoes, and her blue under-ankle sock had a hole in the heel. The tiny flash of skin peeping through was a torment.

She didn't even have proper *socks*. He should have packed the few clothes in her closet, but there was nothing to put them in and Michael hadn't quite been thinking clearly, had he.

You'd better start, legionnaire. It wasn't an Authority's snap of command, but it was close. How long ago had he seen an Authority, or even a Principality? How long had it been since he'd seen even a centurion?

"I don't know." Jenna stared at him, dark eyes alive with furious thought. "Look, I gotta go. If something's...I gotta go, Rach. Thanks." A long pause. "Yeah, I love you too. Okay." She jabbed at the phone's face and her chin lifted.

At least she hadn't started to scream, or demand that her friend come find her. Either would have forced him into uncomfortable action.

Michael searched for something to say. *Hail, lumina* was traditional, but she would have no idea what that meant. Still, maybe he should started on the right foot? Tradition was tradition for a *reason*.

She dropped the phone into her lap. Her skirt was really, *really* high, and he tried desperately to look anywhere but her lap, her chest, her lips. Grace poured and prickled all over him, a flood of comfort.

"What," Jenna finally said, very softly, "the *fuck*?"

It wasn't an unreasonable reaction *or* question, he decided. "Uh." His throat wouldn't work quite right. "I, uh, suppose you have questions."

She licked her lips, a quick kittenish flicker, and grimaced. "Yeah, you could say that." Her voice broke on the last word and she glanced wildly at the window, then past him, at the door. "What the *fuck* happened?"

Gentle and easy, Michael. Where on earth could he start? He should have practiced what he was going to say. "I brought you here. It seemed...best. We need to move soon."

Jenna blinked, the picture of sleepy incomprehension. The grit painting her uniform, caught in the harsh fabric, turned into gems dyed by an Incorruptible's bright clarity. "I need to what now?"

"Move. To an Eyrie." He took another deep breath. What was most important, what would she want to hear? "Those things—the *diaboli*, the unclean—they'll be on your trail. We need to move you somewhere completely safe."

"Trail." She nodded, stray curls and waves worked free of her loosened ponytail bobbing with the motion, stiffened with cola syrup and starred with flying dust. "Safe. Uh-huh. Sure." Her knuckles whitened; she clutched at her phone like a lifeline. "Okay. Let's start with this. Where the fuck are we?"

"My place." He spread his hands, just a little, trying to look calm and relatively harmless. "Safe for now."

She rubbed her fingertips together; dropped her gaze to her hands. "Bob. Sarah. Ace." Quiet, and flat, as if she expected terrible news. Of course, it was hard to expect anything else after what she'd just witnessed. "Did they...what happened?"

He almost winced. "Pretty sure Ace got out okay." At least, the kid's body wasn't in the kitchen, and that was a blessing. "The others, well. The unclean, they don't take kindly to being balked." Was it merely bad luck, a pair of *diaboli* out hunting and just happening to cross her path? It was possible, certainly, but was it *probable*? Michael couldn't decide. "You can't help them now."

It was the wrong thing to say, he *knew* it was the wrong thing; he simply couldn't help himself.

She surprised him, though. A small, bitter sob-breath escaped her, and his marks moved uneasily, sensing fresh distress. "Oh, I know," Jenna said, softly. The hectic color had drained away, leaving her sallow but still poignant-pretty. "I can't help anyone. Least of all myself."

"You can." His throat wouldn't quite work correctly. "You are a piece of the Principle enfleshed. You are Incorruptible." To drive it home, he sank to one knee.

It was strange. The last time he had done so had been right after his awakening, when he had received his armoring grace. His weaponry, of course, had arrived with him.

"Hail, *lumina*," he said, helplessly, and waited for her response.

DEFINITELY NOT THAT

First she'd hallucinated through an explosion; now Jenna was in a stranger's house, covered in sticky syrup and rolled in the grit of crushed ceiling tiles. She should never have left her own damn bed, but then, that was true of most days.

A soft, resilient mattress cradled her. Plain white sheets, a plain white duvet, but the sheets were thick and the down comforter high-quality. The bed was a dark wooden four-poster, blocky and severe; the floor was mellow hardwood. Echoes bounced against a high roof, and bare, white-painted walls glowed under old-fashioned, unshaded bulbs hanging from thick wooden crossbeams. There was boxy cherrywood nightstand with an old green-glass lamp; across the room a wide, heavy wardrobe took up almost an entire wall, its closed face a secretive smugness. A half-open door to her left showed white tile and a flood of pearly natural sunshine probably from skylights; the other door, wide open, loomed behind Mike, full of more indistinct gray light.

The cook should have looked completely ridiculous, kneeling on mellow hardwood with his hair, like hers, full of sticky sugar and tile grit. Her skin crawled, a cheap polyester uniform turned into sandpaper; her skull was full of that strange roaring noise that inevitably accompanied catastrophes, even the small internal ones.

The problem was, Mike didn't *look* ridiculous. He looked intent, focused, and packed with muscle under his filthy T-shirt and dirty jeans. His blue eyes were altogether too vivid, and those tattoos—well, it went a lot better when she didn't look at thin dark ink-lines on a man's skin moving over flickering muscle and under sparse, wiry golden hairs.

As long as she didn't look at those, she could call the whole thing the product of an overworked brain, a mere neurological misfire, a goddamn stress-induced hallucination, and that was that.

Only it wasn't. That was, as Rach might put it, definitely *not* that. "Uh." Jenna decided to focus on the most pressing problem first. "How the *fuck* did you get me here?" Everything else would fall into place once she had that answered.

One of his brawny shoulders lifted microscopically, dropped. "Carried you."

Oh. Of course. A sensible, practical solution. "That's very nice of you," she managed, relatively diplomatically. The rushing in her head intensified. *Are you okay?* Rach had demanded, squeaky and breathless. *It's all over the news. Gas main or something. I thought you were at work today.* Some clear instinct had stopped her from telling Rachel anything—it had been a while since Jenna heard that small, still, irresistible voice inside her skull, echoed by the queer certainty in her ribcage, but she still followed it. "I, uh need to leave now."

He regarded her for a few electric moments, blue eyes narrowed. "No."

Well, that was simple, wasn't it? One small word. It didn't get much easier to understand than that.

"It wasn't a request, Mike." She didn't even know his last name. And how the hell had he *gotten* her here? Carried a sleeping woman on the subway? Loaded her into his beat-up red truck and solicitously buckled her in? She'd never passed out from a panic attack before, and doubly never hallucinated during one.

Well, first time for everything, her mother always said. It hurt to think of Mom, and Dad too. It hurt to think of anything, and now she could add Bob and Sarah to that list, and the trucker in the shattered counter, and...had Ace gotten out the back door?

Mike said he had.

It wasn't an explosion, Jen. That strange certainty was back, filling her chest. Was she just in shock? Was *he*?

He didn't *look* particularly shocked. "I know." Mike unfolded, rising with odd grace. Like a dancer, almost.

A dancer who had put himself between her and the hallucinations. Not to mention thrown himself over her, a warm protective weight.

"Great." Whether this was a nightmare or hallucination was academic, she decided. "I, uh. I should go home." *Don't antagonize him, don't ask for permission. Just think this through, then get moving.*

She didn't want to think about a good goddamn, as Dad might say. Jenna wanted to slide off the bed, march out the door, and not stop until she was safe at home. First she'd take a shower.

Then she'd burn her uniform and open up the want ads. It was a great plan, if she could just get started.

"That," Mike-the-cook said, patiently, "is not an option." He paused, perhaps to gauge her reaction, but Jenna simply stared at him. "They'll find you there."

Jenna swallowed, dryly. "Those things," she whispered. Wherever this place was, it was quiet. The door showing the bathroom had a lovely brass knob with a mellow gleam, the mattress was far better than her own, and the hardwood was seriously polished. What cook could afford this? "Those things are *real*."

She'd suspected for years, of course. But to actually see them when she wasn't asleep was...she couldn't think of a word other than *terrifying*. The only thing worse was hearing herself say it out loud.

Mike's shoulders stiffened, but he dropped his hands to his sides, carefully. "Have you seen them before?" As if he was talking about the weather.

How was he so *calm?*

"No," she lied. The old instinct to lie, to misdirect, to keep herself safe, was irresistible as well. *People fear what they don't understand,* Mom used to say. *And when they're afraid, they get angry.* "No, never. I just...panic attacks. It was a panic attack, I hallucinated."

"You can think so, if you want." Mike didn't shift uneasily, his tone—soft and reasonable—didn't alter. "But we've got to get you to an Eyrie."

A whatnow? "I don't want to go anywhere but home." She longed to pull her skirt down; at least he wasn't staring at her legs.

"You can't." He just *stood* there, hands dangling loosely, his hair filthy-stiff and small atoms of ground-up tile glitter-gleaming all over him. "They'll follow your usual trail from the diner, they'll be waiting for you."

"Who? *Who* will be waiting?" She had a sinking sensation she knew.

From his expression, so did he. "The unclean." A muscle flicked in Mike's cheek. "You saw them."

Is that what they're called? You learn something new every day. "It wasn't real," she tried again. "Right?" Maybe if she just explained that calmly enough, clearly enough, the bubble over her would pop and the world would get back on track. "None of this is *real.*" Certainly not nightmares come to horrible waking life.

It wouldn't stop; the absurdity just kept going. Mike simply regarded her, blue eyes cold and level. "Real or not, I'm here to protect you."

Boy, wouldn't that be nice. Even nicer would be a nip of bourbon, no matter how cheap, and her own bed. "You're a few years late," she managed, numbly. That sounded good, it sounded like the old wise-cracking Jen she'd been before Eddie.

"My apologies, *lumina.*" He even bowed his head a little, like a penitent child.

An overgrown, muscle-bound, penitent child twice her size. She slid her legs cautiously off the bed. "My name's Jen." *Great. I'm getting semantic.* She tugged at her skirt, trying to ignore the grinding and chafing. It was worse than getting sand in your bikini bottom. "I'll, uh, just call a cab."

"I'll be taking you to the Eyrie," he replied, as if it was the most natural thing in the world and he couldn't believe she wasn't jumping on the train, so to speak. "You don't have to worry about a thing anymore."

Oh, how I wish that were true. "I want to go home." *And shut my door, and crawl under the covers, and never think about this ever again.* Except she'd have to. She'd have to find another job, too.

And Christ, what sort of person was she that she'd just seen... what she'd seen, and she was thinking about a *job*?

"You can't," Mike repeated. Calm and flat, just stating the facts, ma'am. He would have made an impressive cop. Those yards of muscle in uniform could probably stop a riot cold. "They will be waiting for you there, and they will kill you, ma'am."

"You're crazy. *I'm* crazy." She shook her head, and stood up. Or tried to, her legs turned wobbly and she sat back down again, hard. The mattress was so good it didn't even squeak, just sighed, and it didn't help that she'd lost a shoe. *Dammit. I saved up for those.* "You saw them too?" An awed, little-girl whisper, one she couldn't believe came out of her own mouth.

"They burn, and trail in sliptime." He sketched a quick gesture, his fingers describing the odd, smokelike streaks following the creatures. "And they called you *softling*."

Oh, God. They had stepped out of the private chambers of her nightly terrors and invaded real life, again. *Give us the softling,* they hissed, and even in hazy memory the auditory wrongness scraped every inch of her raw, just like Sarah's hurt cry as one of them yanked her over the table.

Not to mention the hideous, unholy noises while Jen froze, eyes shut, swaying, waiting for the monsters to eat her. Because every child knows that's what monsters do, and she had been dreaming of those wrong, streaksmoke-fuming things all her life.

That, and the redheaded man wrapped in a pall of greasy black smoke, smiling his wide white smile perched on the crumpled hood of a serviceable secondhand black Volvo.

Fuck this noise. Jenna tried to stand up again. This time her legs simply wouldn't obey her. It occurred to her all at once, with stunning suddenness, that she was in a strange man's house. Or at least, he said it was his house, but it was too nice for a tattooed cook. The floor alone was too good. Maybe he was a slumming superchef? But why would he choose Bob's diner, of all places?

It hit her again, the diner smashed to bits and the body of the yellow-and-blue plaid trucker, thrown so hard the both corpse and counter had shattered. It wasn't Bob's corpse, or Sarah's, both nearly unrecognizable, that made the world start revolving around her again, it was that goddamn trucker's, and what was she going to do?

"I want to go home," she repeated, miserably.

"I'm sorry," Michael the cook said. "But maybe a shower instead?"

Jenna clutched her phone and began to laugh, a high breathless giggle with a raw slicing edge. It rose and rose until she finally found the strength to stand, and she tacked drunkenly across the hardwood in one shoe, the laughter mutating into a ribboning scream that started somewhere in her belly and rose on an escalator.

"*Quietus,*" the cook said, and he was suddenly *there*, looming over her. He didn't so much move as *blink* across the intervening space, and she hit his chest with a thud. He grabbed her wrists, Jen's phone skittered along hardwood with a crack she dismally suspected its case wouldn't stand up to, and she inhaled to scream again. Her shoulders hit the wall next to the bathroom door with a curiously soft sound.

"*Pace,*" he said, and her breath left in a rush. "*Tacium.*"

Thick, heavy silence dropped over the entire high-ceilinged room, a glass bell smothering the small creakings, whisperings, and other humming unquiets that made up a building expanding and contracting with the weather.

"Go ahead," the cook said. The words were muffled, but clearly audible. There were faint lines of silver in his blue irises, and this close, gold-tipped stubble on his cheeks poked through grit and streaks of syrup, plus a faint dewing of sweat. Both of them smelled of sugar, but only Jenna reeked of acrid, sweating fear. "Scream all you want. It's a natural reaction."

She did scream. Oh, she did. Smothering quiet ate the sound, closing softly and irrevocably around her. The cook still held her wrists, gently but firmly, strength thrumming through his fingers. Twisting did no good, and she was suddenly, painfully aware how *ridiculous* this all was.

"Who the fuck *are* you?" she shrieked. Or tried to, anyway. The sound was a cricket's chirp lost in deep snowfall.

His own voice wasn't subject to the deadening baffle. "Not *who, lumina. What.* I am of the Legion, a servant of the Principle. I am also your protector." He frowned slightly, tensing a little, and Jenna frantically pressed her back into the wall. "In other words, I'm your best bet of staying alive."

UNFAMILIAR TERRITORY

That went well. Michael exhaled sharply, rolling his shoulders. The Greater *Tacium* kept her subdued, a narcotic blanket he hadn't wanted to use once she was awake since an Incorruptible was not to be smothered. But the alternative was letting her damage herself with fruitless attempts to restore what she thought of as normalcy.

Sooner or later, she'd find a different definition of "normal." Until she did, he had to keep her in one piece, and as calm as possible.

He opened the laptop, glancing at her. Jenna sat at his kitchen table, straight-backed, her eyes heavy-lidded and her distress struggling with the *tacium*'s weight. "I'm sorry," he repeated. "But I have to." She was still dirty, he wasn't much better, and the prospect of leaving his home—a legionnaire's true home was technically wherever there was an Incorruptible needing protecting, preferably in an Eyrie—was no more appetizing than it had been when he arrived in this city.

How many years ago? It troubled him that he couldn't remember. Still, he had renovated this place from the bones up. A whole lot of work, and the unclean would piss in the corners and burn it down just for kicks.

"Stop it," she whispered. "Whatever you're doing. Please."

"It's called a *tacium.* I can teach you how to do it, just not right now." The laptop's screen lit and he tapped in the sequence of keys that triggered its hidden capabilities, hunt-and-pecking across unfamiliar terrain. A familiar winged glyph filled the greenish screen, and keying in the codes took a lot longer than he liked as he rummaged through mental storehouses to find the patterns.

The screen blanked again. He waited, trying a few calming breaths. Grace poured over him again, needles pricking along his skin. His marks moved faster now, drinking in the force she emitted.

"Your tattoos." Jenna's dark, drugged gaze lingered on his arm. If the way he was itching was any indication, she probably wanted a shower something fierce. "Why do they do that?"

So she could see them moving. Normally, that didn't happen until an Incorruptible had the Breath. Even the more sensitive of mortals could catch a glimpse, though, and Incorruptibles were nothing if not *sensitive.*

It was a nagging question—just how strong *was* she? The *tacium* should have turned her glaze-eyed and tractable, but she was still talking. He didn't mind; he liked hearing her. "To strengthen," Michael said. "To conserve. To remind."

"Remind?" Her lashes fluttered. Fighting a *tacium* after the day she'd had showed some some real grit, not to mention a disconcerting amount of raw power.

"I'm a legionnaire." Michael could even say it with a certain, acceptable amount of pride in front of an Incorruptible. "I serve the Principle."

A slow blink, her mouth pulling down at the corners. "You are seriously weird," she muttered.

You have no idea, lumina. He had to tear his gaze away from the fascinating shape her lips made when curved like that. The screen finally, blessedly, lit again with another familiar greenish graphic—the sword and the wings, straight and pure. Code flashed in falling rivers, and to his relief, he could still read the ancient symbols, glyphs turned into binary and back again. He managed to dredge out of memory the string of letters and numbers required to alert every legionnaire in a few hundred miles' radius that he had an Incorruptible, but instead of a flashing list of glyphs telling him to expect backup the screen simply blanked, background code falling in green rivers.

A cold thin trickle of unease worked down his spine. The warehouse resounded around them, full of creeping, stealthy sounds as a winter afternoon wended its way towards early dusk. This was taking too long. He should have put her under heavy *tacium* at the SunnyTime and done this first, instead of stupidly going to her apartment. The craving to see how the first Incorruptible he'd ever found lived had been all but irresistible, but he should have resisted.

Was he deviating? If so, he had to bring himself back to true in doubletime. He stared at the streams, his lips tightening and his shoulders tensing. "No," he breathed. "I don't...no."

"What?" Her alarm, dozy and faraway, prodded him. The last thing she needed was any uncertainty, especially from *his* quarter.

"Nothing." He tapped in a query; when the answer came back, he exhaled, hard, and closed the laptop. Then, with great deliberation, he brought his fist down on the slim silver case.

Metal crunched, plastic popped, and he mouthed a quiet but hurtfully spiked word. Smoke rose as the stinging *cursum* settled over plastic, metal, and glass, burrowing in. By the time it was spent, there would be nothing recoverable in the lump of slag; their electronic trail would be muddied past repair.

Jenna's dark, beautiful eyes were very round. She sat, frozen, and sweat dewed her forehead, clumping on the small particles of acoustic tile and the dust that always rose during demolition. Her struggling against the *tacium* grew frantic, and he cursed himself, again. It should have occurred to him what she'd take that little display as.

"It's all right," he said, dismally aware he was anything but soothing. "I just have to make sure nobody can trace us."

She made no reply. The *tacium* tightened, a protective thickening of invisible fabric, and her eyelids fluttered. Her lips parted slightly, and it wasn't just distress or unease radiating from her with the bright clear light of grace, it was outright *fear*.

An Incorruptible should fear nothing with the Legion present. "It's all right," Michael repeated. "I promise, *lumina*."

She shook her head, the slow rolling motion of a woman in a nightmare, and Michael pushed his chair back, equally slowly.

"We're going to have to move," he said, conversationally. "We'll get a shower and something to eat in the next city. Let's go." Sick knowledge thumped in his stomach. What he'd thought was the closest Eyrie, fifty miles to the west, was no longer there. But that wasn't the bad news.

The *real* bad news was that there was only one Eyrie left on the continent, and it was on the *West* Coast. Even the sliptravel roads were closed; there was no access point in easy range. Traveling by slip was hard enough on a legionnaire, it could make an Incorruptible violently, deathly ill.

Which could not be allowed, even if he found a forgotten access point.

"Please," Jenna whispered, pleadingly. "Please let me go. I'm sorry, please just let me go."

Now he'd outright terrified her. The fact that she sounded dismally used to pleading could be dealt with later when he had time to figure out who had taught her the skill—and just how he could teach *them* a lesson or two.

None of that helped him now. The unclean were on the hunt. They would swarm this place as soon as they discovered it, and with no Eyrie within range...when had the closest one been shuttered?

Michael hadn't known. Hadn't checked, either, since there was no reason to. He hadn't had a call from another of the Legion in easily three decades, probably longer.

"You don't have to worry," he said, aware it was almost a lie. Still, he was worried enough for both of them. "I know what to do, *lumina*. Don't fight me."

She did, but in the end it made no difference.

NOTHING TO SAY

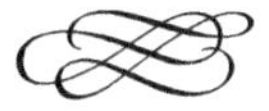

Rain splattered the windshield, the freeway was stop and go, and Jenna's skin crawled. What was even worse was the pressure weighing down her arms and legs, threatening to black her out if she struggled too hard. It was like swimming in deep mud, and the drying, sugar-sticky grit all over her didn't help.

The cook stared at the road before them, his lips a thin line. In profile, he was barely handsome, the lines and angles too severe; muscle swelled under his torn shirt. He hadn't even bothered to pack, just hustled her to the truck after he'd crushed his computer. He'd held the door for her, solicitously lifted her in when she tried to avoid it, even buckled her seat belt—and plucked her cell phone from her skirt pocket.

They can track this, he'd said, and folded the biggest expense of her current life into his big, scarred, callused fist. A flexing, his forearm swelling with corded muscle, and more noxious plastic-burning smoke rose from his hand. He dropped the resultant mess in the middle of his huge, echoing garage with its bright red tool chests and giant hoist like a giant insect rearing to strike, and there went her phone. There went her entire *life*. She had only her purse and her work uniform, and the latter was beginning to stink bigtime.

Nothing reeked like terror. Flat, metallic, creeping out of her pores in tiny, hateful drops—oh, she was stewing in the stuff, and had been for years.

"I'm sorry about that," Mike said for the fifth time, watching bright crimson taillights like he suspected they were about to start some mischief. "I didn't mean to scare you. We just can't be tracked."

From outside, they looked like an ordinary couple looking mistrustfully a screen of winter rain turning to sleet, maybe even a pair of carpooling coworkers. Just like every time she sat in Eddie's Camaro, her hands folded in her lap and her throat dry, listening to him calmly, pleasantly tell her that he was going to fuck her up when they got home if she wasn't careful.

Be careful, Eddie always said. *Stay on the straight and narrow, honey*.

Oh, how she'd tried.

"We'll stop in the next town big enough to provide cover." Mike leaned forward, hands easy on the wheel but his blue eyes narrowing, and a space opened up in the left-hand lane. He nosed forward, and another space magically appeared on the right. Somehow those spaces kept appearing, and though the rest of the freeway was in ruby-eyed gridlock, the truck crept forward at an idle.

Jen shut her eyes. The darkness behind her lids wasn't comforting; she opened them again. Even the inside of the Dodge's cab looked like it was wavering under pressure, or maybe it was just that her eyes kept filling with hot water. Tiny trickles laced her cheeks, cutting through crusted ick.

Bob. Sarah. All the customers, people whose only crime was the bad luck of choosing Jenna's diner to grab a quick bite in. She was a curse, she couldn't help it, and now more people were dead.

"Get you a shower, some food." Another space opened up, and Mike exhaled softly. The invisible wavering inside the cab grew more pronounced. "I apologize, *lumina.* I should have moved the moment I found you."

Found me? Even her brain was mud-swimming, maybe she was just as stupid as Eddie had always averred. "You just got hired," she said carefully, spacing the words out so they didn't slur. The draining lassitude retreated if she didn't fight. If she just sat quietly, it was even kind of pleasant. "But you didn't have to work there. Right?"

"I was looking for something to keep me occupied." Maybe he didn't mean it to sound so dismissive. "I didn't know...well, it's been a while. I've never run across an Incorruptible on my own before."

"In...corruptible?" If she concentrated, she could lift her arm. Maybe she could even get the truck door unlocked before he noticed, but she wasn't betting on it.

"It means—"

Dozy irritation sharpened inside her ribcage. "I speak English, Michael." *I even majored in it, after premed.* Then she almost flinched—it wasn't wise to piss off a guy who could crush a cell phone in his bare hand.

It wasn't wise at *all.*

"Yes. Uh." He coughed slightly, and another space opened up. The truck began to roll a little faster. "The unclean can't infect you, you bear a piece of the Principle."

"The whatsis-now?" If she concentrated on one thing at a time, she might even get through this.

Assuming there was an end to it. Assuming there would ever be an end to the violence swallowing her adult life. Maybe it started with the accident—the burning car, the sickly-sweet odor of roasting—or maybe it had started before, when Dad got sick. *Damn coffin-nails,* he'd said with a pained, terrified grin, and he hadn't bothered to stop smoking.

He'd probably wondered what the point was. *Diagnosis* didn't mean *dead,* but good luck getting Alan Delacroix to quit puffing on something so slender as a chance of survival.

"Strange things happen around you." Mike glanced at her, blue eyes dark. "They've happened all your life."

Jenna flinched. Was he reading her mind? *Be careful*, her mother's voice whispered in memory. *If anyone suspects...* Mom never quite said what, but then again, she didn't have to

"Life is strange," Jenna said cautiously. "I'm just an ordinary person, that's all." *Super normal. Nothing to see here, just move along.*

"Sure." Amazingly, the cook smiled, a tight curve of thin lips. His chin was too strong and his cheekbones too high, and his mouth hadn't relaxed since the world had veered off course and cola syrup sprayed everywhere. In the failing light he looked almost ugly. "Keep telling yourself that."

"You're crazy," she whispered. Her hands knotted against each other, sticky and sweating. "I won't tell anyone, I promise. Just let me go."

"Let's say I took the *tacium* off and you managed to elude me." The truck hung between two lanes for a brief moment, working its way to the far left. "And somehow you managed to get home with every *diaboli* in the city looking for you. They would be waiting for you, *lumina*. They won't just kill you, they'll try to rip the Principle from your flesh."

"Principal?" She had a mad internal vision of the petty ruler of her high school, florid-faced and football-crazed, waving his scarf at a pep rally. "I'm a *waitress*." She *had* finished college, but she'd never picked up the graduation paperwork. After Mom was dead, what was the point? Switching from premed to a literature degree had been yet another bad decision.

One among many.

"The Principle moves the world," he said, like he was quoting. "It is order, it is beauty, it is light."

"Wait. Back up." She took a deep breath, wishing she could roll her window down. Acceleration pushed her back into the bench seat. It was strange, traffic between the bridges and the curves on the uphill going west was usually a solid mass until well after seven, but great clumps were breaking free and rising, jewels of light against sodden cinder-gray. "Those things. In the diner. What...Jesus. What were they?" *How can you see them too?*

"*Diaboli.* The unclean." His fingers tightened on the wheel, scarred knuckles whitening, and Jenna's mouth turned dry. She could imagine the damage those big, capable hands could do. "They fear the Incorruptible, but what they truly hate is the Legion." He touched the accelerator, backed off a bit, and the truck slid through another sudden hole in traffic. "That's me."

Which told her almost nothing. "Okay." If she'd hallucinated, he had too, which was faint comfort. Jen decided to switch directions. "You're a legion?" It sounded faintly biblical, but Mom had never sent Jenna to Sunday school.

"A legionnaire." Mike's tone said he expected that to clarify matters.

Oh, for heaven's sake. "You don't look French."

"I was, for a few years." Eddie would have told her not to get cute, but Mike merely gave another pained half-smile. *He* didn't reek of fear, just of hot oil and sugar, with the faint rasping undertone of adult male adrenaline. "We like the military. Structure. A job."

"Your job isn't kidnapping strangers?" She couldn't help herself. Waving, rain-soaked shadows cast by moving headlights slid over her dirty skirt, touched her knees.

"I've *extracted* you." How could such a big lump of male sound so... so *pedantic*? "I'm here to protect you, too. If I hadn't been there, what do you think would have happened?"

Oh, she could imagine. She'd been seeing it in her nightmares for a long time. "I was doing just fine before you came along," she muttered, dropping her gaze to her lap.

"Were you?" He didn't sound sarcastic, just curious.

Oh, God. "No," she said, bleakly. There was no reason to keep lying, to him or to herself. At least it didn't seem like he got pissed off easily. "At least I'm pretty sure Eddie won't find me now."

"After we get to the Eyrie, we can send someone to track *him* down." He eased the truck to the right again, into another magically opening space. "If you want."

That sounded incredibly unappealing. Why on earth would she want anything else to do with Eddie, for God's sake? "And do what?" Jenna tried closing her eyes again, but they flew open when the Dodge lurched. It had a good suspension, but they were beginning to speed up.

"Whatever you want." He leaned forward a little more, windshield wipers marking time between the words. "Looks like it's clearing up. I know I haven't been exactly reassuring. But you're safe with me, and as soon as we get to the Eyrie you'll understand."

"I want to go home." She sounded like a querulous, overtired child, even to herself.

"That's not an option." Gently, almost kindly. The truck leaned forward again, and each spin of the tires took her farther from her apartment. It also took her away from the mess of the SunnyTime, and she was grateful for that, at least. "You got any family, ma'am?"

If I did, don't you think I would have said so by now? Jen stared out the window. Eddie would snarl at her—*don't ignore me, goddammit.* It was a surefire way to provoke him, especially on a bad day—and hadn't she wanted to, sometimes, if only to clear the air when the tension got too bad? Living on tenterhooks from one moment to the next, never sure when he was going to snap... sometimes Jenna just wanted it over with.

If *this* guy was going to, why not just get it over with, too?

On the other hand, he'd driven off those horrible things. Had hunched over her, a warm heavy shelter, while the world broke into pieces.

There was a strange relaxation in knowing the worst had happened and she was helpless in its grasp. Jenna leaned sideways as far as she could, resting her feverish temple against cold windowglass and watching the raindrops bead up, merge, vanish. Traffic was, indeed and bizarrely, clearing, and instead of crawling at an idle the truck was managing something akin to a slow jog.

Mike stopped talking. Maybe he knew there was nothing to say.

DEAD LETTERS

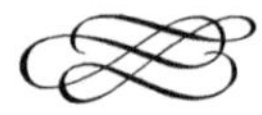

ONCE THEY LIFTED out of the bowl near the river they made good time, and Jenna was sound asleep when they hit freeway speed. The *tacium* helped, no doubt, and unconsciousness was the best thing for soldiers after a battle. It provided a buffer, and let the body try to forget. Of course Incorruptibles weren't precisely soldiers, but the basic principle remained.

At least, he hope it did.

Michael would be denied such release for a long while. A few days ago he'd been soul-numbingly bored; now he had too much to do. How could he have missed the closest Eyrie being shuttered? His bank accounts were filled from the common well punctually each month and the supply drops came like clockwork too. Someone had to know he was still operating in the region, right?

Or—and the cold trickle of dread down his spine intensified the more he considered it—maybe the Legion's bureaucratic machinery had become electronic, and no officer or centurion was checking the rolls. Worst of all was the prospect that there *were* no officers or centurions to check, that the Legion was moribund and his stipend hadn't failed because his needs were so modest.

He had forgotten some of his own personal investments over the years, too. They no doubt still existed in a ledger or two watched by no living eyes.

Dead letters. Wasn't that the term?

Grace filled the truck cab, mouthing his dirty skin and ripped clothes. He shouldn't have waited to extract her. What the hell had he been playing at? Mortality? Normalcy? Hoping Jenna would notice something unusual about him and approach, a thin, curious cat flinching at the slightest sound?

A centurion—let alone a higher officer—would find much to fault in Michael's handling of the situation.

You let a lumina be attacked. Not only that, but you allowed your temper to frighten her. He'd be lucky to be posted to some remote location once she was safely delivered, barred from any grace at all, much less the raw honey-soft power radiating from the other side of the cab.

And that was another thing. He was sure now, she had the Breath. No wonder she was powerful—but how had she survived its triggering? It generally took a Celeres or a life-threatening incident to loose the deep slow wellspring magnifying the Principle within an Incorruptible. After it awakened, they were slightly more durable, though not nearly as much as even a grunt legionnaire.

The Principle made them Incorruptible, but it was the Breath that made miracles. Without proper care and nurturing, those miracles could burn the mortal frame from the inside, grace eating up its fragile vessel. She needed an entire Eyrie around her, a hard shell around a glowing pearl.

What she had was one stupid, muzzle-headed legionnaire who had all but waved her in front of the *diaboli* and then been caught unprepared. Flatfooted, as the saying went.

There was no shame in a fault as long as discipline was accepted. Obedience to the Principle was true, and skewing away from that path made for *diaboli*.

"I will do better," he murmured. The wet road hissed underneath tires, icy pellets at the heart of sleet-drops stacking in patterns at the edge of wiper-range. He had time to redeem himself before they reached the Eyrie.

Hopefully. After all, she didn't know any better. That was a thought unworthy of a legionnaire, but...

Michael set his jaw and glanced at the dashboard clock. In another hour or two, he would start looking for a reasonable place to spend the night.

He hadn't been this far from his city in many a year, and it unnerved him. Not nearly as much as it unnerved *her*, though—his *lumina* woke when the truck's engine halted and peered at a towering granite-sheathed stack of a hotel, rubbing at her eyes like a maiden in an illustrated fairytale.

Did mortal children still read such things? He didn't know.

Jenna exhaled, shakily. "What the hell is that?" If she noticed the *tacium* had loosened its grip, she made no sign. Of course, she was calmer now, so its weight was a protection instead of sedation.

"Hotel." Michael eyed the shining lobby visible through water-clear glass doors, bellhops and valets hurrying about other guests' business with only a token glance at the truck. You couldn't tell, anymore, who had money and who didn't. Modernity had granted some small leeway; a rich man who traveled without ostentation might be simply eccentric instead of a miser. "Let me do the talking, all right?"

"Oh, sure," she muttered. "Can't have them knowing I'm kidnapped." The *tacium* did not flare, since she made no attempt to struggle against its grip. She did, however, dart him a small, mistrustful glance, clearly gauging his response.

"You're not *kidnapped*." Michael tried for a flat, informative tone. Of course she was upset, and tentative. It had been an upsetting day all the way around. He decided an encouraging smile would give her the wrong impression entirely, settling for a neutral expression and bare honesty. "I'm your protection. Consider me a bodyguard."

"Yeah, okay." She shook her head, reaching for her purse. "Sure. About ten years too late."

"I'm sorry," he repeated, dismally. It was all he could say. Michael popped the door, reaching for his wallet. Grace prickled and surged; a young carrot-haired man in a red-and-black valet uniform swallowed whatever he had intended to say. It wasn't a true glamour, just a little illusion to cover exhaustion, stickiness, and torn clothing.

And, incidentally, to send the subtle signal that Michael and his charge were a couple on vacation who tipped well if the employees hustled. There was a certain patina to those who made a service worker's time worthwhile, and Michael certainly had the resources to do so. Now would be a good time to start rectifying some of his mistakes by performing every expected duty with exemplary generosity.

"Sir." The valet's grin went from pained to wide in a single heartbeat as the illusion took hold. "Welcome to St. Armand's."

"Thank you." Michael glanced at the other side, where a bellhop was greeting his *lumina* with cheerful obliviousness. Jenna clutched her purse to her chest and stared over the truck's wide, sleet-speckled hood. Her eyes were huge, but the illusion turned her into a fashionably slim debutante in a brand-new greenish skirt and blazer. Illusion couldn't cover up the awful color, but it made the fabric look good and the cut even better.

"Luggage in the back," Michael said, and as long as he thought only of the next thing and the next, he could get her through the evening with little incident.

Or so he hoped.

INDIGNITY OF SURVIVAL

It was more expensive than any place Jenna could afford, even when she and Mom had pooled their resources for trips. The staff didn't seem to mind that she and Michael were disheveled and covered with goo, and honestly the instant a shower was possible, even in a great marble-and-glass cavern of a bathroom, Jenna longed to scrub the entire day away under a torrent of hot water.

This high up, city lights were a river of stars under a purple, sleet-lashed winter dusk. If not for the absence of the river, she could imagine she was back home. Except at home there weren't two full-size beds, each with foil-wrapped mints and a paper-wrapped welcome packet on the fluffy cream-colored pillow shams. There definitely wasn't a pleather binder on the dresser was full of plastic pages detailing amenities—massages in room or at the spa on the first floor, a truly staggering room service menu, a map to exercise rooms and *two* swimming pools as well as saunas, the list went on and on—in hushed, breathless prose at home either.

"Here." Michael dug in the smaller of two black canvas duffel bags extracted from the back of the truck, coming up with a handful of pale sweatshirt and drawstring pajama pants. "You probably want to clean up. There should be everything you need in there. You can wear these after, okay?"

They were obviously his, large enough for her to swim in; she couldn't tell if this was a comforting development. If he carried women's clothes around in that bag, it would be a sign he did this often. Jenna took the armful of material, holding it gingerly away from her stiff, rasping uniform. "They didn't seem to notice we're all messed up."

"Just a little illusion to make us look normal." *No big deal,* his tone suggested. The grit and sugar coating him looked uncomfortable, tiny pieces of acoustic tile glittering on his cheeks caught in rising dark-blond stubble. "You can do it too, with some training."

That sounded really useful, but it made her head hurt. Sleeping against a car window had given her a neck-ache, too, and her stomach would have been rumbling if it wasn't tied in knots. "Great." The hideous mental images—Bob, Sarah, the trucker in blue and yellow plaid—kept coming back now that she wasn't in a moving vehicle with a deep, buttery engine-purr lulling her.

"Go ahead." Michael stalked to the windows—huge expanses of glass, the heating bill for this pile probably went through the roof—and glanced at falling night, falling ice-pellets, and the wide, shuttered sky, only a faint venomous line of orange to the west showing where the sun had gone to sleep. "We're safe enough here tonight. I'll have to do some thinking about our route."

There's a route? "Where are we going?" She shifted uneasily; nobody had noticed she was missing a shoe, either. Her exposed sock was filthy, and rough nylon carpet scratched through the hole in the heel.

"To the closest Eyrie." Michael looked over his shoulder, electric light glowing in his blue eyes. The tattoos kept moving in slow clockwork increments, describing the edges of his muscles, crawling up his neck. "Maybe we can take the train. Not sure about flying."

Good luck getting a kidnapped woman on a plane. She bit back the sarcasm—it would be, in Eddie's words, getting off the straight and narrow. Besides, if Mike could keep hotel employees from seeing what they really looked like, could airline employees be any different? "So..." There was a bigger consideration, one she hesitated to voice. "Can those...those *things* fly?"

"Some of them can glide, but true flight is lost to them." He turned away from the window, regarding her somberly. With his weight balanced just-so and his hands clasped behind his back, he looked like a recruit at parade rest. "You have a legionnaire with you, Jenna. You don't have to worry."

Yeah, well. "I can't help it." She backed for the bathroom, awkward in one shoe. "I'm going to lock the door."

"Go ahead." He freed his hands and made a small shooing motion, muscle flickering under his torn T-shirt. "Whatever you need."

"I need to go home." There, she'd said it. Again. The heavy dragging invisible weight didn't come back, but she sensed it hovering just out of range.

"I know." Mike's expression—distant, listening—didn't change. Neither did his posture. "I'm sorry." Genuinely regretful, and just a touch weary. Any other inflection would have sounded ridiculous.

Jenna's throat had gone dry, and she fled to the bathroom's dubious safety without another word.

It was in the vast shower, with chevrons of rough plastic antislip on the sloped floor, that the shaking hit. She hugged herself under a spray of gloriously hot water, trembling so hard her knees vibrated against each other. She'd read of going knock-kneed from terror, and it was disconcerting to actually *feel* it.

Think about reading, Jenna. Think about watching movies. Think about something, anything, other than this.

Her library books were sitting patiently in the bag on the kitchen counter for her usual weekly trip. She was going to have a helluva late fine. Maybe they'd send the Library Police to drag her back. Wait—there were two weeks left on everything in the bag, because she'd had a whole two days off, plenty of time to get down to the library and carry her prizes home to her dull, cheap little studio that was better than anyplace else because Eddie had never set foot inside.

Rent wasn't due until the fifth, which was—what a coincidence—two weeks away as well. Not like she'd make it much past that, without a new job.

Bob. Sarah. Strange how she couldn't quite remember either of their...corpses. The one that kept showing up in garish detail was the trucker in plaid, thrown through the counter so hard flesh had almost liquified.

She got out of the shower, almost slipping because she hadn't set the bathmat, and her eyes stung because her hair was piled with shampoo suds. Which meant she had to put the goddamn mat down and restart the water, stepping in and wondering who was making that soft, broken moaning noise.

It was her. Jenna sobbed under hot water, her eyes watering furiously with salt and soap, until the tears dried up and the indignity of having survived reasserted itself, like it always did.

Because she was cursed.

THE SWEATSHIRT SMELLED like someone else's fabric softener, not the cheap harsh kind she used but not the fanciest either. It *also* smelled like dry testosterone and a faint male spiciness. Maybe he wore it to work out in, but there was no tinge of sweat or weird stains in the underarms, thank God. Faint smears of white paint smudged along the hem and his big warehouse home had white walls; maybe he'd done them himself.

The thought of big blond Mike carrying a ladder and paint buckets was blessedly normal, blessedly *sane*, but she was still in a hotel room a hundred-plus miles from home with a man she didn't know, chased by things that shouldn't exist—strange, smoke-streaming figures with nasty inhuman eyes and hiss-moaning voices, loping through alleys and lurking outside windows, ready to take a bite out of a child's flank or swallow a scream whole.

People were *dead*, but she was safe and showering in a fancy hotel.

Jenna edged out of the bathroom. Mike was at the suite door, glancing over his shoulder. "Room service," he said, cheerily. "You have good timing."

The flatscreen was on, local news turned down to a mutter. Jenna stopped and stared, riveted, as a duo of uniformed teenagers brought in a rolling cart gleaming with silver platters and covers, not to mention an ice bucket with a green glass bottle poking its tiny head over the rim, snug in a bleached white linen jacket.

Oh, my God, did he order champagne? The question died on her lips.

The news was full of fire. Literally. An apartment building was ablaze in rainy dusk, the fire spreading to buildings on either side. Jenna's heart gave a huge, thundering leap and all the shower's forgiving warmth drained away. Her hair dripped, curls tensing up and shedding water, and for a brief moment she couldn't remember if she'd wrapped a towel around her head to dry the mass.

Wait. Wait just a minute.

Mike tipped the teenagers, a flash of green and two young, grateful smiles. The suite door closed, the kids vanishing like genies. Back into the bottle, after bringing snacks.

Well, there were monsters in the world, why not genies? Why not unicorns, ghosts, or a rich man's kindness, too? All sorts of things could exist once monsters did.

"I didn't know what you'd like," Mike started, and pushed the cart gingerly over plush, scratchy carpeting. "So I got one of everything I thought might...oh. Yeah."

"That's my building," Jenna managed, numbly, lifting a trembling hand to point. *Don't be rude*, Mom whispered in her head, and her hand fell back to her side. "That's *my* building."

Now it was, a broken, blackened cup full of spreading, greasy orange flame. *Gas Main Explosions Rock City,* the chyron at the bottom said, and the footage was from a circling helicopter, its light stabbing down white and useless. It looked like half the block, including the corner bodega, was getting in on the act, a crowd of onlookers pressing against safety barricades. The inset was a reporter on the corner of Vine Street near the Riverview subway entrance, his mouth moving aggressively as he stared into the camera, damp slicking his dark hair.

"Yeah." Michael hunched so he could push the cart. The kids had made it look easy; he looked like a trained bear fiddling with a machine too small and delicate for its paws. "Pretty sure they'll find my place too. It'll just take them longer."

"That's...them?" *Who else would burn your house down, Jen?* Arson wasn't really Eddie's style, and she couldn't tell if the realization was a relief or not.

"Yeah. Looks like." Mike shrugged—it was an everyday occurrence, his expression said, just like being attacked by monsters or putting eggs on a grill. "It could be a coincidence. Listen, I'd like to wash up. You have something to eat, okay?"

Oh sure. They murdered everyone in the diner, my entire block is burning, and I should just have some cookies and milk before bed. "Uh." Her throat was dry, her hair was cold, and goosebumps rose all over her, hard and prickling. "I don't...Jesus. *Jesus.*"

The problem wasn't that she was just finding out the things were real, and that they wanted her dead. It was far deeper. She'd known all along, on some level, and had just been marking time until the nightmares found her again. She was a Typhoid Mary, bringing destruction to everyone within range, and now she had Bob, and Sarah, the customers, and everyone who lived on her block as well, on her conscience. If her neighbors weren't dead their home was gutted, and those apartments weren't for people who could afford a disaster.

At least Eddie hadn't found her, sure. But it might have been better if he had.

"Jenna." Mike was suddenly right next to her, taking the filthy, neatly folded uniform from her nerveless hands. "You're tired, you're hungry, you've been through a lot today. It's okay. You don't have to worry anymore."

She nodded, speechless, more to get him to stop talking than to agree with anything he said. The words were a jumble, they made no sense while flame licked over the shattered shell of what had been a reasonably decent, though desperately poor, apartment building.

It looked like a bad special effect. Why was it burning so hard while sleet came down in waves? Nothing made any sense. Just like the accident in San Francisco, that slick, hungry flame sending up billows of black smoke while the car bucked and the man on the hood grinned at her...

"*Tacium*," Mike said, grabbing her hands. The dragging, drugging quiet returned, wrapping around her like a blanket, and Jenna went limp underneath it, guiltily glad. She let her knees buckle, barely aware of Mike catching her on the way down. He moved with eerie, graceful speed, and for a moment she believed he'd fought off those terrible, smoke-fuming monsters.

Unclean, he called them. Well, Jenna was dirty too.

Mike set her in one of the white leather chairs, the cart right handily close, and turned the TV off. Its blank glass eye watched her while he disappeared into the bathroom, leaving the door ajar, and the sound of water running crept forlornly into the luxurious, impersonal suite.

Jenna's cheeks were wet. She sat, her hands folded in her lap, and wished with sudden and familiar vengeance that she was dead.

A LUMINA'S DISPLEASURE

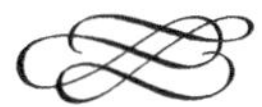

THE FOOD WASN'T BAD. He didn't exactly *need* it, but it was satisfying and would refuel him when there was no access to grace. Plus, it was camouflage whence went among mortals. And it probably helped a newly found Incorruptible remember that the normal world was still there, and required even their protectors to eat and shower, if not sleep.

Unfortunately, it didn't look like the reminder was going to do a lot of good in this particular case. Jenna sat staring at the blank television screen, and he wished he hadn't turned the damn thing on in the first place. It rotted the brain, but he needed intel. He'd been hoping for nothing, just the usual mixture of voyeurism and capitalism in a glass bowl spread over cable news and injected into the veins of the body politic.

Instead, not only had the *diaboli* fired her home, but it was messy and...public. It could be a coincidence on a slow news day, but something about it made Michael's nape tighten. Not quite gooseflesh, not an itch either, but the consciousness of something *wrong*. A break in the pattern, a splinter-twisting of the Principle, or just a predator's invisible gaze drifting over terrain and settling on another predator's unprotected back.

Alone, he could eat as if he was in a barracks. With an Incorruptible, however, manners were called for. He took a bite of steak—a little too well done, but not bad otherwise—and regulated his chewing. Jenna, paper-pale, her cheeks spotted with drying tears, stared bleakly at a plate containing a club sandwich and a pile of fries. The fries were a little soggy; whoever was running the kitchen either hadn't had the time or inclination to make sure they stayed otherwise.

It would hopefully be a long time before Michael worked a deep-fryer again, but he was tempted to go down to the kitchens and show them how.

"Try to eat." He glanced nervously at the ice bucket—the champagne wasn't his idea, but apparently it was complimentary when you ordered a triple-tier cart from room service. "It's still warm."

She shook her head, then reached slowly across the cart. The *tacium* hung from her in diaphanous veils, imperfectly masking the clarity of the Principle. She'd stopped fighting the protection, retreating into apathy. Her fingertips brushed the sweating-cold metal pail, frostflowers retreating from living warmth. "You ordered this?"

"Just the food." Michael shook his head, speared another reasonable bite of steak. Continental style was the only way to wield the tiny weapons required for eating. "But I guess they thought we needed it."

"Bourbon would be better." She blinked, fresh tears welling in her dark eyes, and each one was a sharp, precise pain in the upper left quadrant of his chest. "Don't you think?"

"I don't know." He'd get her a bottle if she wanted, but a hangover might make tomorrow more difficult. On the other hand, some Incorruptibles were fond of stating preferences and letting their legionnaires hop to obey. "It all tastes like paint thinner to me."

A flicker of interest stirred. She wiped at her cheek in slow motion, weighed down by the *tacium*'s grasp. "What about beer?"

The sweatshirt slipped sideways, the too-big neck showing a generous slice of her shoulder, the high beautiful arch of her collarbone—and the sweet, soft beginning slope of one breast, but he wasn't supposed to look.

He stared at his plate instead. "Beer's good." He was American at the moment, and they liked hops and malt. "It used to be thicker, though. Like bread."

"Used to be?" The flicker returned, curiosity overpowering fear. "Wait, no. The tattoos. Maybe you should start there."

"Oh." He laid knife and fork down, straightened his back. An Incorruptible deserved full attention whenever they expressed interest, no matter how small the subject. "Normal people just see tattoos, and they're similar, I guess. They move because they're protections. Like armor, and support." It was an oversimplification, but a reasonable one.

"Oh." She dropped her dark gaze to her own plate. Her hair, free of confinement and drying rapidly, was a soft honey-tinted halo, curls stretching and turning to waves. "What are those things? I mean, what are they *really*?"

"*Diaboli*." He pronounced it clearly, slowly. This was far better than numb silence. "You could call them demons, I suppose." Every mortal culture had names for the dark things that hunted—and those who fought.

She nodded, slowly. "And you're a...legionnaire."

"One of the Legion, yes." He sensed her newfound calm was brittle, so he kept his hands flat on the table, his gaze fixed on his plate, and the rest of him as hunched-small as possible. "I'm just a soldier, a kind of bodyguard. We're meant to protect people like you. Incorruptible."

"Huh." At least she wasn't screaming. What kind of bravery did it take for a mortal used to everyday, humdrum existence to compass the Legion, let alone the unclean? "So these things, they come from...hell?"

"Not as you'd understand it, I guess." Her courage all but shamed him. Michael studied the grill-marks on his steak, the piped mashed potatoes, the haricots. "Most of them were mortal once. Human, like you. Some of them—the wingèd unclean—were like me. But they're corrupted now."

"Corrupted?" At least she didn't ask *what do you mean, like you?*

"Yeah." Twisted by hatred or rage, the wingèd ones had a deep well of strength to draw on while their protective marks faded. They forgot what they were bit by bit, craving dominance, blood, murder, and other foul nourishment. A legionnaire served because otherwise a legionnaire *fell,* not the controlled, chosen First Descent but a spiraling into chaos and darkness. That was why the deviant hunted the Incorruptible, the Authorities said. To see what they had lost by turning away from discipline and obedience fueled the darkest of their rages.

Many a legionnaire sometimes wished to be Incorruptible themselves. It was only natural; the next best thing was serving the Principle enfleshed, but they were few. The Principle made its own path; a legionnaire's duty was to follow that line.

"God." Jenna closed her eyes. She didn't quite sway in the chair, but it was close. The *tacium* didn't flare, but that was probably close, too. "This is insane."

"Yeah, I know." Sometimes the Legion let mortals stumbling across the truth go upon their merry way, knowing that the vast mass of humanity preferred not to think about the dark things. Most of the stumblers ended up being considered harmless cranks; a few did desperate things to convince the world of their sanity. The risk of a gadfly mortal endangering an Incorruptible was all too high—mortal meatsacks were free to disregard the Principle in the way a legionnaire could not even consider. "You're doing really well, though." He'd expected more screaming and struggling, not to mention attempts to alert the hotel staff, as if he was a common kidnapper. "The important thing is, I'm here to protect you, and once we reach the Eyrie—" He almost felt her sharp, distrustful glance.

Fabric moved as she shifted uneasily. "What's this Eyrie thing?"

"It's a Legion stronghold." The clothes touching her now had touched his own body at least once, and the thought was powerfully distracting. "They're built to protect Incorruptibles, they're full of legionnaires and centurions and Celeres."

"Kel-ear-ees?" She had a good ear, putting the accent carefully in the right place.

"Cavalry, I guess you'd call them. Fast, well-armored. Principalities and Dominions, too—they're the heavy guns." It wasn't what he expected an Incorruptible to ask about, and he was in danger of overwhelming her fragile calm with too many details. "I mean it, you know. You're doing really, really well with this."

"I don't have a choice, Mike." Her gaze rose and rested upon him, a thorny pleasure with so much grace filling the air and filling his marks. They would turn darker as they drank. "You got a last name?"

"Gabon. Michael Gabon." He offered his hand over the table, careful to move slowly. "Pleased to meet you, *lumina*."

She watched his fingers like they might bite her, but eventually put her own against his palm. A brief, careful shake, and the contact poured hot grace up his arm, detonating in his shoulder, spilling down his back in pleasant, velvet-honey rivers.

"You're powerful," he said, hoping she would understand it was a compliment. "I don't know how you've survived this long on your own, but I promise, you're safe now. You won't have to worry about anything ever again." *At least, once we reach the Eyrie.*

"That's awful nice." She reclaimed her hand with a faint grimace, taking that warm, forgiving flood with her. "I've got to tell you, though, I'm worried about a lot right now. All my friends are going to be worried, too."

Or they'll think you're dead in a fire. That wouldn't cheer her up, though. "Once we reach the Eyrie you can contact them again. We'll get you a new phone, pay off all your debts, everything. I just couldn't have them tracking us while we get there." He wanted to check *her* expression, but that would mean raising his gaze past that slipping, extremely distracting neckline, and it seemed like tempting fate.

"I suppose." She sounded so dubious he ended up looking anyway, and found her gravely regarding her plate with a thin line between her sweetly curved eyebrows. "So where is this place, anyway? The Eyrie."

"West Coast." In other words, over half a continent away. There was no point in telling her the Eyries east of the Rockies were all shuttered.

"You're going to have to be more specific." His Incorruptible picked up a wilting fry, nibbled at it, and a curious look came over her wan face.

"California." Was that specific enough? He watched her expression for clues.

"Not San Francisco." Her shoulders hunched, and she dropped the potato straw as if it burned her. "I won't go there, I'm warning you."

"Uh, no." Interesting, but it wasn't his place to question. At least in this small matter, he could set her at ease. "Los Angeles. Is that okay?"

"L.A.?" A ghost of a rare smile touched her lips, and Michael's chest felt strange. "That's...really funny, actually."

In what way? But then again, you didn't question an Incorruptible. Not without a good, overriding, safety-related reason. "Yeah, well." He decided he could go back to eating. "When we get there, they'll ask you how I handled everything." *Handled you,* he almost said, but she probably wouldn't appreciate that phrase.

No, Michael decided, his Incorruptible—and the slight possessiveness in *that* term was a warning, too—would not appreciate the idea of being handled at *all*.

"Great." She tried another fry, staring at the plate with either dawning realization or horror. Some color returned to her cheeks, but her slim shoulders were tense. "God. How can I be hungry?"

"You've got to eat." Incorruptibles lasted a long while after they found the Breath, but they needed nourishment just like mortals. "It's normal."

Her chin lifted, and Jenna stared at him for a long moment. "Is anything about this *not* normal to you?" Her dark eyes flashed, and Michael suddenly found it very hard to breathe. "How many other women have you kidnapped? Or, uh, rescued? That's what you call it, right?"

"Extracted." Anger was a necessary part of the process. He knew as much, but it was still uncomfortable to feel a *lumina*'s displeasure. It was a disciplining blow all its own, and especially stinging. "And you're the first Incorruptible I've found by myself."

"Not the first one you've met?" Maybe it was the Principle within her, or maybe she was just that smart. A bright penny, this Jenna Delacroix—an old family name, and a proud one.

"No." Now Michael was wondering if the *lumino* he'd seen at his own long-ago arrival was still alive. He couldn't even remember that Incorruptible's name.

He'd been away from his own kind for far too long. Which meant he was vulnerable to twisting away from the true path. Deviance was to be guarded against.

She began to eat with feral caution, halting every so often to study him closely. Michael minded his manners, consumed the steak plate, and moved on to a chicken Caesar salad. They made the dressing onsite, he could tell, and he was almost ready to forgive them for overcooking the steak, though not for mistreating his *lumina*'s fries.

"Is it any good?" he asked finally, keeping the words soft and his gaze on his own dish. "The sandwich?"

She paused for a long moment. "Not as good as yours."

It could have been diplomatic, it could have been an untruth, but Michael looked up, the corners of his mouth bunching without any direction on his part. It felt good to smile. "Gonna count that as a win, then." Along with the bigger win of getting her out of the city and relatively safe for the moment.

"Sure," she agreed, and the *tacium* subsided as she relaxed a little, and a little more.

MANY AND MANY

THE MORNING WAS full of cold rain edging into gray sleet, and whatever Jenna had expected, it certainly wasn't a trip to a collection of factory outlet stores just over the state line. She'd further thought maybe they'd skip out on the hotel bill, but Mike glanced at the paper and signed it at the front desk while Jenna, bundled into a tightly-belted pair of his jeans rolled up so many times she looked like a twelve-year old playing dress-up, stood at his shoulder and attempted to look a little less ridiculous. His sweatshirt was way too big for her too, but it was all they had that might conceivably not fall off her shoulders if she shrugged too hard. She had to wear two pairs of his thick white cotton socks just so his spare sneakers didn't fall right off her feet whenever she lifted them.

The outlet malls were another hour away, and when they arrived Mike parked close to a luggage store. "I'm sorry there's not more options." He cut the ignition, and a warm, ticking silence filled the cab. "There's clothing, though, and a box store across the freeway for toiletries and anything else."

"This sounds expensive," she said, cautiously. Cold rain with ice at its heart plucked at the windows, ran down the windshield in streaks.

"Oh, money's not the problem." He had a black high-collared jacket over his heavy white T-shirt, both plain and functional as his jeans and boots. In fact, he looked like any other proto-jarhead or cop wannabe, a familiar type she'd served hundred of plates to in her diner days, and it was disconcerting to see how easily he blended in even with the tattoos. "Time is. We've got to get you what you need and move. I don't like how the air feels."

"It's just cold." Jenna eyed the luggage store. *SAMSONITE FOR FALL*, a sign declared, fabric boxes for lugging things around standing in tasteful window-groups under hidden floodlights. She'd had a job doing displays once, and liked it well enough. "It's winter."

She didn't even have a spare set of panties. Jenna was used to making do with very little, but now she'd scraped bottom. The only thing worse would be...well, best not to think about that.

Her nightmares showed her, after all.

"They made sure firing your building was on the nightly news." Michael kept his hands on the wheel. His profile was a statue's, the nose too long and slightly hooked, his chin set and his gaze soft as he stared through the windshield's glass curtain. "If that's a signal, I don't like what it's saying."

"Oh." Wasn't that a cheerful thought. Jenna's hands twisted together, her fingers aching. "Can I ask you something?"

A slight nod, his chin dipping but his stare fixed. "Of course, *lumina*."

"It's Jenna." *I wish he wouldn't call me that.* The word irritated her, not least because of its implications. "How many of those things have you fought?" What she meant was *killed*, and maybe he knew as much because he didn't answer right away.

"Many." Mike looked at his hands on the steering wheel. The thin white scars stayed still, the inked lines moved. Or were they ink? Who knew what was injected under his skin? He called the hideous malformed burning things *unclean*, but there was another word for it.

Demons.

Just thinking about *those* implications was enough to make her want to pop the door open and run screaming into the rain. The funny blurring around her had faded by degrees. Maybe he was sure she wasn't going to try to escape.

If so, he was smart. Where would she *go*? Her entire apartment building, not to mention her job, was gone. She didn't have any savings, barely a couple hundred in the bank. And the diner...

Her stomach flipped, cramped, and she was almost sorry she'd ordered a decent breakfast from room service. The orange juice had even been fresh-squeezed. How could she enjoy anything, or eat, or even just sit here calmly, after all that?

"Many and many," he repeated, softly. "Hopefully we won't see any more of them."

That would be good. Still, a nagging sense that maybe, just maybe, she would believe this more easily if more monsters *did* show up. It was the same urge that made a cat paw-push something off a dresser while staring directly at you, maybe.

Thank God she hadn't had a pet for years. She wouldn't have put it past Eddie to harm an animal, though he claimed to love dogs, and leaving a cat or dog behind would have been impossible. "How likely is it?" she heard herself say, numbly. Without the steady heat from the engine, the windshield was filming with fog, the cold creeping in. "That we won't see more of them?"

"Not very," Mike admitted. He kept staring straight ahead. "Don't worry so much. You're with me now."

It would have been nice to hear, except it came too awfully late to be any good. Besides, Eddie had said something similar many times.

You're with me now... stay on the straight and narrow, honey.

Jenna shivered.

"You want to shop for clothes first?" Did Mike sound, of all things, *tentative*? His eyes were very blue. Freshly shaven, his cheeks were roughened from the cold. He must have had his bags packed all the way back in his warehouse home, ready to leave at a moment's notice. Was he just that organized, or was he planning something like this?

Jenna suppressed a shrug. "I don't know that it makes much difference."

"It does to me." Quiet and earnest, he watched her like a puppy waiting for a treat.

You want your hostage to be comfortable, huh? Jenna swallowed the sarcasm. She wasn't a hostage; nobody would pay for her. Her nightmares had shown up in living color, and now she was trapped in them. "Okay." She reached for the door handle.

"Let me, okay?" He hurried to unclip his seatbelt and open his door, insisting on opening hers whenever they stopped.

Left alone for a few brief seconds while he came around, Jenna shut her eyes and took a deep breath. It was old-fashioned, and maybe another woman would have been charmed. Eddie, however, had done the same thing, unwilling to let her escape his control even in that small way. She shivered again, cold dread sliding down her back, and waited.

MORTAL CONCERNS

A FEW HOURS gained them a reasonable amount of jeans, T-shirts, undergarments, socks, a parka, slippers, two pairs of sneakers and a pair of boots in her size, pajamas that weren't his workout gear, and toiletries from the giant blue-and-yellow box store, all placed with solicitous care in a rolling suitcase and a smaller go-bag. She even consented to lunch at a small chain Mexican restaurant, though she didn't eat much.

He was hoping hunger would assert itself soon. You couldn't force a *lumina* to eat, but you could certainly *encourage*, and he intended to. Michael even had her pick out snacks and a cooler, since the box store had a grocery section. She kept glancing at him during checkout, as if she expected them to run out of cash.

It almost stung. Money was easy; did she think him so incapable?

The best on offer near Cedar Springs was a Golden Inn, but the shabbiness seemed, oddly, to put Jenna more at ease. At least, she waited in the truck when he got the room key, and didn't make a move to slip away even though there was no *tacium*. Keeping such a thing upon an Incorruptible for more than twenty-four hours was not advisable. Or acceptable.

Maybe he'd earned a fraction or two of trust. He certainly hoped so. And at least the towels in this tiny place were fresh.

Jenna curled up gingerly on the twin bed against the bathroom wall while he took the one near the window. He kept the television on for some short while after she fell asleep, watching images play in blue glow, checking local news for any hint of the unclean or their tricks.

He'd chosen the northern route even though it had tolls, and tomorrow they would be over yet another state border. The plains would steadily rise, and if they got to Denver without running across many more of the unclean, he could consider a flight to L.A. It would take less than three hours in the air. He could even *charter* a damn plane, but the thought made him nervous. Not because of having to justify the expense to a centurion or a Celeres accountant—any cost was acceptable where an Incorruptible was concerned—but because the *diaboli*, having found her apartment, probably had an electronic tattletale on her ID, including a previous picture to add to flagging software.

He had passport blanks, of course, all he had to do was get her photo on one and perform a minor work of grace to give her a whole new identity. He just wished he could figure out if such a move was safer or more dangerous for the Incorruptible breathing so softly across the room, scarcely audible even to a legionnaire's amped-up senses.

This was far above his grade. Michael wasn't even a centurion, just a grunt staring at a cheap popcorn ceiling in the dark after he turned the TV off, wondering and second-guessing his plans. A legionnaire didn't need much sleep, but he would have welcomed it tonight, even with the infrequent, vivid dreams.

Go over it again, Michael.

An Incorruptible. A *powerful* one, who had the Breath. Eking out a living in the margins, thin and nervous, avoiding notice with single-minded intensity. And the *diaboli*—had they found her by mere chance?

"There it is," one of them had said. So they had been sensible of her existence, but hadn't known enough of her location to collect her, perhaps. Who would think to look for a piece of the Principle in a shoddy little greasy-spoon diner?

Perhaps she'd survived by sheer chance and stubbornness. Just look at how thin and tired she was, how much grace she carried. Anyone might well bow under that burden, especially a *lumina* who hadn't been taught to control the welling within her.

take it from the top, Michael. The Eyrie closest to him, closed. *All* the Eyries east of the Rockies and all but one on the West Coast, closed. No backup, even a recon team, in range. Incorruptibles were always rare, but if the Legion had ceded half the continent or more to the unclean... well, it didn't look good.

Nobody had told him he was an outpost in hostile territory instead of a patroller in a city big enough to warrant at least five legionnaires and an Eyrie within range. Knowing your task and your place was paramount in war, each small cog within the whole working smoothly together.

This was not like the Legion *at all.* It bothered him more and more. He hadn't spent much of his stipend for years; the warehouse's property taxes were paid by one of the many shell corporations the Legion used. The money just *sat* there, piling up and earning interest, and that was not the way a business, even a multibillion-dollar one, was run. His account should have been drained once it got to a particular point, but he hadn't thought of that. No, he'd just assumed the Legion knew what it was doing and if he needed an opinion about how the officers ran their various affairs, they would issue him one.

Now he was in that most dangerous of positions, a legionnaire having to think for himself.

Supply drops had always come punctually, ammo and weapons plus other smaller items, all standard kit. Someone had to make the items, and someone else had to sign off on the purchase orders, right? That couldn't be *all* automated, especially if a legionnaire stopped taking delivery.

It made his head ache. That had to be purely psychosomatic; legionnaires didn't *get* usual mortal pains. The marks, channeling and containing the force of a thing not meant to exist on the mortal plane, also freed them of many petty human concerns.

The biggest worry, of course, was arriving in L.A. and finding just another skyscraper instead of an Eyrie. How long could he keep her alive if the Legion was no more? At least if there was a single Eyrie anywhere in the world, he had some hope of getting her there. A clear-cut objective was a comforting thing.

A soft sound from the other bed pulled his nerves even more taut. She was dreaming. He hoped it was something pleasant.

Michael lay on his back, interlaced hands under his head, staring at the ceiling, and thought long and hard that night. When slight gray touched the edges of the cheap taupe curtains, he curled upright and moved stealthily across cheap motel carpet to peer outside.

The walkway with its plain iron railing was just the same, and the parking lot, trailing into weeds at its far, crumbling pavement edge, held nothing of concern or interest.

Denver, he decided. When they reached Denver he'd do an intel run, if she could be induced to trust him a little more. It couldn't be that hard to find a public computer at a library, get in, look at a few things, and get out. He could also pick up a couple disposable cell phones. The important thing was speed and secrecy.

If he kept her moving, she was a more difficult target. His laptop had been unequivocal that L.A. was still operational. But Michael figured better safe than sorry, and if the worst happened, he would have planned for it.

Or so he thought, then.

FLAT-OUT UNAVOIDABLE

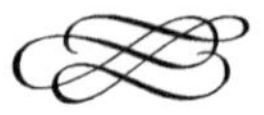

Her mother touched the brakes, keeping plenty of space between their battered but serviceable Volvo and the white, diesel-spewing half-ton pickup in front of them."This is an old place." Her heart-shaped tortoiseshell sunglasses made her look like a slumming movie star, and so did her clean, classic profile.

Jenna rested her heels on the hot dashboard."As America goes."

"Well, it's not Europe, but then again, what is?" Mom rubbed daintily at her forehead with her fingertips, massaging the vertical worry-line between her eyebrows. That line was showing up more and more frequently."As soon as we find the hotel I'm going to take a bath."

"Does it have a pool?" Jenna shifted uneasily, digging for her own sunglasses. She was going to get a headache if this kept up.

"It should, for what we're paying." Mom laughed, her honey hair lifting on the breeze through the open window as the half-ton finally began creeping forward. "Let's have dinner in Chinatown."

"I dunno, Mom." Jenna found her sunglasses, clicking their case open with a flick of her wrist. "There's a chocolate factory here somewhere. They probably don't have Wonka bars, though."

"That's for tomorrow." Mom's grin held a shadow of unease, but

only that—a single shadow. The light was still green and there was enough space for their car on the other side of the intersection, so they rolled forward, nosing from behind the stop line like a tentative, hungry dog. "I'm so excited, we're going to—"

Whatever she meant to say was lost in a giant crunching noise as the world turned over. Later, the cops told her it was a semi barreling through a stoplight, but Jenna was sure of one thing: the fire came first. A wump *of ignition, a sudden hot breath against her face, and her own screaming, an animal response bypassing conscious control of her own throat.*

The man crouched amid the flames on the crumpled front of the black Volvo, his short hair running with livid orange fire, and smiled. Jenna screamed again, scrabbling at her seatbelt, and her fingers found the catch just as the semi, its brakes shrieking in protest, plowed into the driver's side. Weightless, flung free, something tearing along her left forearm as the Volvo was broken like an egg...

JENNA SAT STRAIGHT UP, a scream dying in her chest, and almost cracked her forehead against Mike's. He was on the bed, his warm hard fingers braceleting her wrists, and for a moment she thought he was Eddie and she all but cowered, knowing how he hated to be awakened by her stupid, perennial nightmares.

"It's all right," a deep, quiet baritone said, and the relief of figuring out it wasn't her ex-boyfriend gave way to a sinking hideous sensation as she realized she was in a cheap hotel room outside a crappy little town called New Paris, of all things, with a man sitting on the edge of the bed. "It's okay, *lumina*. It's me, it's Michael."

Her cheeks were wet. The scream gurgled in her unhappy stomach; maybe she'd puke this time. Jenna's ribs flickered, giant heaving breaths filling her and escaping in turn. Her heart hammered, thudding not just in her chest but her throat, her wrists, her ankles, *everywhere.* She was one giant galloping heartbeat, and the sobs shook her back and forth.

"Jenna." He pulled on her wrists, gently, and the next thing she knew, he had his arms around her and she spilled almost into his lap. Warm, strong arms, he was solid and *real,* not a ghost with flaming crimson hair crouched on a crumpled hood and smiling, smiling like he was having a *great* old time. "It's all right. I'm here."

Oh, God. For a few moments she couldn't remember his name, or even where he'd come from.

"It's Michael," he repeated, his voice a rumble against her cheek. He was impossibly muscular, not wiry like Eddie, and there was a certain comfort in someone so solid. "Michael Gabon, *lumina.* You're safe, you're with me, whatever it is can't get you. I promise."

Nobody could promise anything like that, but oh, how Jenna longed to believe him. "D-d-dream," she managed, through the guttural sobs. "J-just a dream. S-s-sor-ry—" She couldn't even *apologize,* her teeth chattered the word into bits.

"That's right," he said, softly. "Just a dream. You're with me, it's all right. I'm not going to let anything hurt you."

"You c-can't promise that." It was retreating. Thank God it was only the accident dream, and not one with those horrible *things* in it. Demons. *The unclean,* he called them. Why did this have to happen to *her*? It was bullshit, all of it, and as the terror receded she was aware her new tank top and boxers were hopelessly twisted and she was clinging to a virtual stranger.

"I can." He sounded so sure. "I am of the Legion, Jenna, and I'm not going to let anyone or anything harm you."

"That's nice." She exhaled, shakily, and tried to let go of him. It didn't work. Some part of her was grateful for his solidity, grateful for the fact that he was built like a brick shithouse, as Eddie would say, and... "Did I wake you up?"

"Not really. We don't need much sleep." He was warm through the white cotton T-shirt, and his arms were gently but very definitely around her. She was practically in his *lap,* for God's sake. "Just take a deep breath, *lumi*—ah, ma'am. It's all right. It can't hurt you anymore."

It wasn't true, of course. She was old enough to know nobody could ever protect anyone else. If even your parents could die, one choking on his own lungfluid as cancer ate through his body, the other smashed to a pulp and roasted inside a burning car, anything could happen. Disaster, disease, death—it was all possible, and the possibility made it more than probable.

Made it, in fact, flat-out unavoidable.

Mom had never thought so. Jenna had inherited her mother's bone-deep, irrepressible optimism, and look where it had gotten them both.

Still, it was hard to feel anything but safe when a brawny guy had you in his lap, his chin resting atop your head, and he was the only familiar thing in a world that had skewed wildly off-course. And of course, resting where she did...well, it was nice to know he was interested. He made no other sign of it, thank goodness, but the body didn't lie.

After a little while, the shaking drained away. He let go when she moved restlessly, so Jenna had to slide into a nest of sheets and blankets smelling of industrial laundry and the faint ghost of however many people had passed through this small room. Michael stood, and in a few moments had the pillows plumped and the covers straightened, tucking her in solicitously.

If there was a moment that convinced her he was genuine, that was probably it. She hadn't been tucked in since Mom was alive.

"Try to get some more rest," he said finally, a tall, indistinct shadow with bright eyes looming at the bedside. "We're driving again tomorrow. I wish there was another Eyrie closer, but we've got what we've got."

"My dad used to say that." Jenna exhaled shakily. *What you get is what you get, baby girl.* "Michael?" It was kind of ridiculous to call him *Mike.* The nickname was far too young for his careful seriousness.

He didn't seem annoyed by her nightmares *or* her questions. "Yes?"

"Thank you." English needed different, deeper words to express gratitude, but those were all she had. "It...I mean, I'm sorry. Thank you."

"No need to be sorry. It's my honor, ma'am. And I mean that." His shadow merged into the dimness, his bulk passing in front of the window. He tweezed the curtain aside a fraction, peering out into the parking lot, and a slice of harsh sodium-arc light fell across his face. "You don't have to worry anymore."

"I'm going to anyway." She turned on her side, watching as he finished his survey and turned away from the window. If he kept calling her *ma'am* she was going to start checking for gray hairs. "It's a habit, you know. I can't stop."

"You can unlearn them. Habits, I mean." Did he sound amused? Secretly irritated? Or just sincere? "Just rest. When you wake up again, we'll go."

Normally, after a dream like that, Jenna just stayed up. It wasn't worth lying in bed and staring into the darkness, covers clutched to her chin, jumping at the slightest noise. Maybe it was sheer exhaustion, but she fell asleep within minutes, and mercifully, that night there were no more dreams.

None she remembered, anyway.

PROTECT AND CONSERVE

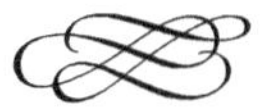

THE SLEET WAS TRYING for snow and melted halfway to the ground instead; the roads were sloppy but not bad, and they stopped just past Kansas City for something more substantial than the snacks packed into the cooler. Jenna appeared to be an old hand at road trips, and it was pleasant to drive with her in the passenger seat. She wasn't quite comfortable enough to make conversation with him yet, but she had stopped flinching when he moved quickly and even let him open doors for her.

It wasn't until they were seated in a red vinyl window booth that he saw how pale she was, and realized this diner shaped like an aluminum trailer probably reminded her of the SunnyTime. It was of much better quality, of course—he wouldn't take a *lumina* to a place like *that*, even though he could work there while waiting for her appearance. However nice the clientele, the place still smelled of fried food, salt, and a tang of bleach for cleaning, familiar and probably unsettling for her. The waiter, a young scruffy-bearded man with his curly hair twisted into a bun atop his head, glided away after filling their water glasses.

"We can go somewhere else," Michael said, setting his plastic-coated menu aside and folding his hands. "If you want."

"Wow, peanut butter malt-ball milkshakes." Jenna stared at her own menu before glancing at him quizzically. At least the new parka fit, and she'd stopped shivering. She no longer looked like a kid playing dress-up, lost in too-large clothes. "Oh, if you want we can. Is something wrong?"

"I just figured...another diner, you know." Now he felt stupid for drawing her attention to it and possibly causing unease. "You're awful pale."

"I think I'm just hungry." But she smiled, tentatively, pushing dark hair behind her ear with a swift, graceful motion. She looked like a college student on break, jeans and a black T-shirt under the fur-hooded coat. The circles under her eyes had eased too, despite early morning nightmares. "I've got a headache."

"Want some ibuprofen?" He could still feel her slight weight resting against him, shaking like a windblown leaf. Perhaps it was a memory of grace, but the way his flesh responded was perilously close to deviance, as far as he could tell. "Tylenol?" If she needed something stronger, they could visit a pharmacy.

Why did her smile broaden? "Got any in your pockets?" She regarded him over the table, cocking her head slightly as if listening to the forgettable pop song playing softly somewhere in the diner's depths.

"There's Tylenol in the truck, I think." And why could he not remember if he had? "If not, I'll go find some."

"I'm fine." Now the smile faded, bit by bit, while he watched and tried to figure out how to bring it back. Jenna studied him, a line appearing between her eyebrows. "What, you'd just run out the door and go on a quest for Tylenol?"

"If you needed it, of course." It was a worrying oversight. He should have planned, and packed some. "I should have thought of that."

"It's fine." The song changed; she touched the tabletop, running her fingertips along its metallic edge. "I'm not used to anyone caring that much."

Soon you will be. What could he say? It was up to him to teach her the basic, or at least introduce them. "You're Incorruptible. Your grace is our strength."

"I know you're speaking English." Jenna addressed the air over his head, lifting her chin slightly, and the fall of winter sunlight over her was wrong. She deserved a warmer light, a softer world. "But I don't have a clue what you're saying."

The waiter returned, grinning with porcelain-capped teeth; Jenna ordered a chicken Caesar salad. Michael, as usual when faced with any choice in the matter, went for a bacon cheeseburger. There was nothing even remotely as good in any other cuisine, as far as he was concerned. "And a peanut butter malt-ball milkshake, too," he added. Might as well start teaching her that even her casual desires had weight, and should be satisfied.

"Good choice, my man." The waiter scribbled on his pad, then tucked the pencil back into his bun. Long-shanked and sleepy-eyed, he looked like one of those mortals blessed with an eternally sunny disposition and a high-revving metabolism. "I could live on those."

"It sounds good," Jenna agreed, and gave Michael a curious look as the waiter left. "You like milkshakes?"

"It's for you." He studied the parking lot through the window, settling his hands on the table—very clean, the entire place sparkled. Hopefully the food was good enough. "Are you sure you don't want me to go get something for your headache? I can, you know. There's a gas station right across the freeway."

"It's okay. I'd much rather understand what you're talking about." She laced her fingers together and leaned forward, an eager student ready for a lecture, all that warm attention flooding him.

"Okay." Where was a good place to start? The breeze outside veered sharply, smacking window glass with wet palms. "You have a piece of the Principle in you. It's order, light, strength—all good things. The marks, they fill up from it. You're like a battery, kind of."

More like a power plant. It's a question of degree, really. The details would just confuse; what he had to express was her importance.

And, as far as he could, his commitment to her safety.

"So I'm useful." A short, decisive nod, her hair bouncing and a stray curl falling over her eyes. She shook it away with an impatient, habitual flick. "Good to know."

"Not just useful. Essential." What he told her now would resonate, so Michael chose his words carefully. He wished he was standing at attention to recite the lesson, so he didn't forget anything. "We fight the *diaboli,* but without something to fight *for,* we're just... it's just thrashing around, you know. It's just murder. We're supposed to protect and conserve, not just go out and kill."

"That's good." She rubbed at her temple with soft fingertips, turning even paler. "Ouch."

A warning rasped along his nerves, the marks moving uneasily. Michael turned his head, scanning the parking lot again. Nothing there. "Huh."

"What?" Now pale, she stared at him, those dark eyes growing even rounder.

"Something's wrong." Eventually, he could tell her not to worry and she wouldn't; eventually, he would have backup. For right now, though... "Stay here, okay? Right here."

"Michael—"

If she ordered him to remain, he would have to disobey. And if she could sense what he now did, it could also sense *her.* "I'll be back in a couple minutes. Okay? Stay *right here.*"

"Fine." Her chin set. "Whatever you say."

Michael slid out of the booth, the marks prickling with banked fury, and headed for the diner's front door. He waited until he was outside, stepping out under a cold gray cloud-lensed sky, to let the blurring weight of almost-invisibility settle over his shoulders.

It would keep the mortals from remarking upon a man darting across several lanes of freeway, but it wouldn't fool a *diaboli.*

It was a single, creeping minor unclean crouching behind the counter of a Shell station, the entire store full of its slip-fuming breath. No doubt there were rich pickings here, traveler and local alike presenting themselves for consumption. Everyone who drove had to stop for fuel, after all, and those walking in the neighborhood would be drawn in by bright gewgaws and flashing lights in the window promising cheap snacks, an easy drink, warmth in the winter and air conditioning in the summer.

There was nobody at the pumps, but it was only a matter of moments before a mortal was drawn in. He had no time to waste on subtlety, so Michael went through the glass front door at full speed, sliptime blooming around him in stinging petals. It was easier now, with so much grace filling his marks. The counter shattered, the thing behind it gibbering as careful protections and enticements stretched and snapped under the weight of a legionnaire's righteous rage.

The thing dropped the phone clapped to its misshapen head, its human-seeming shell blasted away by the force of a legionnaire's arrival. Metal filled Michael's palm; he lunged over the counter, the blade resolving in midair, piercing the thing's chest. He whipped it back and forth, opening the cavity, and stinking amber ichor sprayed.

At least he had not brought Jenna into combat, even though she was at risk alone in a flimsy tin can across the freeway. Michael resolved fully out of sliptime, glass shattering, the register imploding in a mess of melted plastic and pop-fusing circuitry. Gurgling and twitching, the unclean thing waved two malformed, tentacle-fingered hands, and a bubbling laugh escaped its crooked mouth.

"*Legion*," it whisper-hissed. "*We are legion too.*"

He did not bother replying. Great spiderweb-cracks bloomed over the front windows, and the neon *OPEN* sign buzz-blinked. The glass doors along the back wall, holding refrigerated air captive to cool overpriced drinks and perishables, had slivered into large jagged pieces.

Michael stabbed the thing again. If he'd brought the truck to be fueled he would have noticed the corruption behind the mask and moved directly, but Jenna might have been upset to see this. It was just as well, even if he had to leave her unprotected for a few minutes.

The unclean turned into a bubbling, slumping wreck, noisome fumes rising from its riven flesh and crunched bone. Michael exhaled, letting the rage slide away, and the marks tingled, scrambling any footage of him on the security feed. He glanced at the pumps—still deserted, he was fortunate. Perhaps the Principle, pleased he was caring for one of its bearers, was arranging things for him.

He stopped only to find an overpriced bottle of Advil in one of the well-stocked but now jumbled aisles and put his shoulder to the locked EMPLOYEES ONLY door past the restrooms. There was nothing lurking there, but the walk-in freezer held a mortal corpse wrapped in plastic.

Michael shook his head. There was no helping that victim. He had already left his *lumina* alone too long.

NEAR-DEATH EXPERIENCE

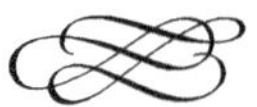

JENNA'S SILLY, stupid optimism was back, probably because the headache had eased tremendously by the time Michael also returned with a bottle of ibuprofen, the food arriving at almost the same moment. She was even feeling...well, *safe*.

That was the most exotic thing about this entire crazy road trip, she felt oddly protected. Which was a sure sign she wasn't quite sane —she was homeless, almost penniless, and there were monsters chasing her, but as soon as Mike reappeared through the diner's front door even though she hadn't seen him in the parking lot, she realized she hadn't even doubted he'd come back.

It wasn't like her to trust in someone else's permanence like that.

Jenna stared at rolling grassland outside the passenger window. Her heart beat, her lungs kept working, her eyes took in the scenery and she had a cup of Earl Gray from a coffee shop drive-thru cooling to a drinkable temperature. Her clothes smelled new, one of the better aromas available in the world despite the fact that the fabric was probably full of finishing chemicals. Pavement slid underneath tires checked every time they stopped for gas or otherwise—Mike even checked the *oil* at every fill-up, something Jenna had never thought real people did.

He also seemed almost-happy. Or at least, more cheerful than yesterday. After a few glances in her direction, he finally spoke. "We should reach Denver tomorrow."

"Okay." Long sere grass rippled, blasted by dry summer heat and not ready to green again under a flirting, unsteady rattle of sleet. Barbed wire loped alongside the freeway, strung between listing posts probably set in the ground several presidential administrations ago. The cold was following them all the way across state lines, the terrain was steadily rising, and maybe the Rockies would be difficult this time of year. "I have a question." It was her turn to steal a glance at him, checking his expression for any sign of irritation.

None was immediately apparent. He was just the same, big blond and almost bland, his hands surprisingly deft for their size. "You can ask anything you like." Long-nosed and serene, freshly shaven again, he flicked the wipers on when the sleet decided to thicken.

That doesn't mean you'll answer, or tell the truth. The reflexive thought was so natural she almost didn't register it, a hum of distrust under every breath. At least she could thank Eddie for that particular habit, and she had so many other problems now he wasn't even an issue. "So, if money's not a problem and we're going all the way to L.A., why are we driving?"

Michael nodded slightly, as if she'd said something profound. "Flying's kind of difficult. If the plane crashes there's not a lot I can do on my own to help you. Trains are safer, but we'd have to leave the truck behind until someone can be dispatched to bring it over the Rockies and I want to have options."

"Wait a second." Jenna turned from the window. Even the truck's defroster worked better than it had any right to, keeping the windshield crystal clear. This guy was a whiz at mechanical stuff. "You can survive a train crash? Is that what you're saying?"

"Oh, sure. Especially since you can choose a car that isn't statistically likely to derail." A small shrug, as if it was the most reasonable question in the world. "I can survive a plane crash too, but without another legionnaire or four around to take the hit, you might not. It's an unacceptable risk."

That put a whole new shine on matters, so to speak. A plane crash was probably small potatoes for someone who could fight monsters, but it brought up another question. "Take the hit for me?" *Is that even possible?*

In a world full of monsters and demons, what *wasn't* possible? The fenceposts alongside the road kept marking off their regular intervals, the sleet kept rattling, and her heart kept going, a fist-sized chunk of muscle unconcerned about anything outside its dark, cramped home. The possibilities seemed pretty damn infinite, right now.

"Legionnaires are tougher. We're *sent*." He paused as if he wanted to add more, shook his head slightly. The aggressive crewcut didn't do anything for him; if he grew it out a little, he might be handsomer. "But Incorruptibles are kind of fragile. Comparatively, that is."

Well. She certainly *felt* fragile. "Okay." The urge to pinch at the bridge of her nose like her seventh-grade English teacher was almost overwhelming. She couldn't even remember the man's name, just his expression at the end of a long day dealing with middle-schoolers. "Sent. From where?"

"Elsewhere." He hit the blinker, swinging into the left lane to pass a wallowing yellow semi hauling something refrigerated despite the cold.

She risked pressing a little further. "Where's elsewhere?" *If the monsters are demons, what does that make you?* It was ridiculous to even consider, especially with a cup of hot tea and her toes warm and dry inside new socks and creaky-new boots.

When was the last time she'd had *new* clothes, not thrift-store bargains or work uniforms? Was it bad to feel like she was better off now?

"Uh, we don't remember, and I never asked." He sounded honestly baffled. "Maybe an Authority knows, I don't. They're the ones who call new legionnaires. With your help, of course."

"Hang on." *What the ding-dang?* It was one of Dad's old expressions, and she almost smiled ruefully. God, she wished her parents were still here. "My help?" The idea that someone so competent and capable would need *her* help was outlandish at best.

"Well, an Incorruptible's help. Even an Authority can't move without your consent, that's the saying." He hit the blinker again, swung back to the right lane. Traffic was relatively light, strip malls blooming on either side of the freeway at odd intervals. "May I ask *you* a question?"

Here it comes. Of course there was a cost for the clothes, for the road trip, for rescuing her. The odd feeling of safety vanished in a heartbeat. "Fine."

"Have you had a near-death experience?"

"Other than recently? Several." She managed to say it with a straight face, added the stinger like old pre-Eddie Jenna would have. "I mean, I've dated a lot."

That earned several single sideways glances, very blue. "Uh." A crackling silence filled the cab.

Jenna's mouth twitched. He kept sneaking looks at her, and when she could stand it no longer she laughed, a soft forlorn sound. He followed suit, shaking his head and grinning, baffled but pleased. Their laughter sounded good together, she decided. If she had to be locked in a car with someone who shared her hallucinations and nightmares, he wasn't bad.

So she told him the truth. "I took a road trip with my mom, my last year of college." She tested a sip of her tea. It was now perfect temperature, go figure. "San Francisco. We...there was an accident. The car burned." Her left forearm twinged, the scar aching like it always did when she thought of that terrible day. "I got a cut up my entire arm, almost bled out next to the fire. I was trying to break the window and get my mom out." The greasy billowing smoke, the sound of traffic roaring by, and that horrifying, hideous thing she'd seen on the hood...

No. You didn't see that. Don't ever talk about it. To anyone. "It was too late," she continued. A couple in a blue Subaru had screeched to a halt, the wife already on her cell phone with emergency services, the man bailing out to drag her away from the inferno. The guy driving the semi had an extinguisher tucked in his sleeper cab, but it was like a garden hose trying to put out a forest fire. "*I* was too late."

"Ah." Michael nodded, as if confirming a private hypothesis. "I'm sorry."

"Those things...I *have* seen them before. In dreams. Nightmares." Admitting it again was just as hard as the first time. She chewed at her lower lip as they passed into a fringe of suburbia, houses and a mini-mall visible over a concrete barricade; the freeway signs proclaiming a town was just off the next exit. Her throat threatened to close up; she had to whisper, barely audible over the noise of wheels on pavement and the engine forcing them forward. "Since I was a kid."

Surprisingly, he asked the right question. "Did one of them cause the accident?"

Or at least, it would have been the right question if that soft, undeniable instinct didn't keep warning her away from mentioning what she'd seen. "I...maybe. I don't know." As far as she would ever say, it was bad luck—which was the only kind of luck she had, really.

Yet she hadn't burned to a crisp with Mom. She'd almost bled to death and half her hair had been scorched off, but she hadn't *died*. And sometimes, Jenna wondered why. It seemed pointless.

Other times, she hated the very thought of her survival.

"Don't worry." Mike watched the road, his jaw set. "I took care of the ones at the diner, didn't I? You're safe."

"Sure." And maybe she even sounded like she believed him. In any case, he smiled a little, and the silence turned almost companionable instead of awkward. He turned the radio on, but only to listen to the AM weather report.

They kept rising, adding altitude in steady increments, and maybe that was why Jenna could finally put a finger on the source of her unease. Michael had smashed his laptop and her phone, and they were driving over the Rockies late enough in the year snow was a real possibility. Maybe they weren't as safe as he wanted her to believe.

But that night, curled in a hotel bed, she did not dream.

HEADY PRIVILEGE

Denver rose in the distance like a half-eaten whale from the back of a great grass sea, sharp skyscraper rib-towers piercing a mound of smog. The sleet had retreated in long streaks and thin winter sunshine fell swordlike through the fringes; the road dried in great gray scabrous patches. Michael kept his gaze trained forward.

She seemed to find it easier to speak when he did, but each halting word turned him cold.

"We both had bad nightmares, Mom and me." Jenna's voice was soft with pain. "Dad said I must've heard her talk about them or something."

The father had died when she was thirteen. Cancer, she said, but her mouth drew down and he thought it very likely that wasn't the whole story. The mother had finished raising her, two women against the world. It was obvious the bonds were deep, and their breaking traumatic—especially the mother's passing. An accident, a car bursting into fire—maybe *diaboli* involved, but she wouldn't say more about that day, and Michael's guts turned to sharp ice thinking of how close it must have been.

He might never have met her, if she hadn't survived that day.

"Most of the time, I'm seeing something from outside." Jenna's knuckles were white; her hands clutching each other tightly to hide the shaking. It didn't work, maybe because she'd crumpled the drained paper cup in her palms and the material squeaked every time she clenched. "People going about their lives, and I try to warn them. I try to scream but I can't. Or if I can, they don't hear me. It's like I'm a ghost. I can see the *things*—those demon things—creeping up on them, and sooner or later they pounce. Then it's horrible. Blood, guts, screaming I can hear, and I have to watch every second of it. I have to *feel* every second of it."

Not all mortals were psychic, but every Incorruptible had more-than-mortal talents. It was very likely she had somehow pierced the veil of sleep and seen the unclean about their murderous business. Michael kept his expression carefully neutral. "That sounds awful."

"You think?" An uneasy laugh rattled out of her, and her hands tightened afresh. She'd finished her tea long ago; it was about time for a stop. "Is that normal, do you think? Do you have them? The dreams?"

"We don't need a lot of sleep, but yeah, we dream." Flying, winging through knots of similarly winged enemies, sword and shield and whip singing of destruction, the fury of righteous murder staining armor, hands, heart...oh, yes, he dreamed. Any living creature had to, or be driven insane. "Sometimes they're bad dreams, too." Dreams of defeat were the worst, holding the line with his brothers and knowing all was lost but they had to stand. Victory was better, and he'd had *those* dreams with increasing frequency before finding her.

Perhaps he had sensed an Incorruptible's approach, and just been too stupid to realize it.

"This is crazy." She freed her hands from each other and played with the paper tag of the teabag, folding it with slim, sensitive fingers. Her restlessness matched his own. "The whole thing."

"Yeah. The songs all say most Incorruptibles have a hard time with it, at the beginning." Then there were the laments, the loneliness of those set apart and longing to make the broken whole receiving only pain and terror for their kindness.

For some reason, that caught her interest. "There are songs?"

"Yeah, plenty of Incorruptibles write music." The dark-eyed *lumino* who brought Michael through had been a composer; he seemed to remember the plucking of a gittern and the man's voice wandering through a soft Provençal melody before Montségur fell. So long ago, trudging wearily through the years to end up here. "Legionnaires, though—we just sing."

"Like choirs?" Jenna had turned slightly, all her attention on him, and the sudden soft bath of warm, forgiving grace threatened to turn his arms and legs to molten iron.

"Chants, more like." *It would be terrible if we couldn't sing.* Michael suppressed a shudder at the thought. The city in the distance didn't seem to be getting any closer no matter how long they drove. "They help us remember, especially if we're alone. Legionnaires might twist away from the Principle if they forget."

"Forget what?" She opened her hands, seeming almost surprised to find the crushed remains of a paper cup.

"Anything important, but mostly good behavior." He checked the blind spot and swung out to pass an arthritic brown station wagon driven by a clean-shaven, middle-aged cowboy whose mouth moved like clockwork, maybe singing along with the radio or cursing other drivers. "There's rules."

"What are the rules?" They drove through a band of sunshine, and her hair glowed with honey highlights.

He ticked them off in sequence, lifting a finger slightly from the wheel for each one. "Protect the Incorruptible. Kill the *diaboli*. Keep unstained and untwisted."

A long pause—did she expect a longer series of objectives? Those few were more than enough.

Finally, she spoke. "That's a big list."

Michael glanced sideways and found out she was smiling. It was a small, restrained curve of her lips, but it was genuine, and beautiful to see, especially under the gilding of sunlight. "Simple, but not easy. That's one of the sayings."

"You guys have sayings and songs." She leaned forward, stuffing the crumpled cup in the litter bag hanging from the open, bone-clean ashtray. "And you also hide, right? Why don't you tell people what's going on? I mean, normal people."

Sooner or later, every Incorruptible asked. It was only natural. "Mortals don't want to know." Which was also natural, though Michael privately thought the Principle could have arranged things a little better. Still, secrecy kept its bearers safe, and he was just a simple grunt. Certainly his own tiny intellect wasn't fit to provide a solution if the Principle itself had already decided a different one was acceptable.

"Mortals. Okay." Jenna laced her fingers together, crossed her legs, and rested her hands on her slim knee. She still looked like a college student, maybe on a winter break trip. "So, uh...I'm human, right? I mean, I have to be. I was born."

"Incorruptibles are born, not made." *Mortal, yet more.* He didn't know the finer points. An Authority could probably explain it to her, once they reached the Eyrie. "That's another saying."

"Great. So, were my parents..." She shifted uneasily. "They couldn't have been, right? They'd have told me."

He wished he could turn the radio on. Or anything, really, to distract her from such thoughts. "I don't know, *lumina*."

"It's *Jenna*. Please. Or just Jen."

Addressing a *lumina* by name was a heady privilege. Michael swallowed, dryly. "Yes ma'am."

"That's not better." She turned away, staring out the window.

The sign appeared like a gift, *Rest Stop 3mi*. "There's a rest stop. You want to stretch your legs a little?"

"Sure." She bent to fish her tan leather purse out of the footwell, its scruffiness now a mark of habit and affection instead of poverty.

She hadn't wanted a new one, though he would have bought anything at the luggage store if she'd expressed a preference. "Michael?"

His full name, instead of *Mike*. Was she feeling formal? "Hm?"

"Thank you. For, uh, saving my life." A soft breath-catch, a hot flare of grace roiling along his skin. She was emitting more and more as she relaxed. "This is crazy and I'm not sure I believe it, but...thank you."

"Disbelief is easy." It sounded stodgy and unhelpful as soon as it left his mouth, and he hurried to add more. "You're very welcome, Jenna. It's my honor."

If she only knew what an honor it was to be an Incorruptible's sole hope. Still, he wished he had backup. Even just another grunt to stay close if he sensed another unclean drawing too close.

"When we get to this Eyrie place, what happens?" She clearly wasn't looking forward to it, but at least she seemed resigned.

"Well, they'll get you settled in quarters, get you everything you need." The immediate luxuries might well take his *lumina*'s breath away, and that was as it should be. Michael's shoulders were tight with nameless tension. "Ask you how I performed, if I twisted from the Principle. They'll teach you how to control the Breath. Once you're strong enough, you can call more legionnaires to help us. That sort of thing."

He thought she'd ask about the Breath, or about calling more of his kind. Instead, Jenna opened her purse, rummaging in it with a distracted air. "How you performed?"

"If I was respectful, if I kept you safe." He hit the blinker and moved over, easing up on the accelerator. The rest stop lunged for them at the end of its pavement tether. "That sort of thing."

"Well, you *have* been polite, I guess." That smile was back, and this time it lit up her velvety dark eyes. "You're not bad, Michael."

"Thank you, Jenna." He had to tear his gaze away and pay attention to driving, and he was grinning like an idiot.

He just couldn't help it.

❧

The long low concrete building housing restrooms was not overly clean, but it wasn't downright filthy either. With the horizon drawing away on all sides even the smallest building was a relief from empty space, and Jenna disappeared into the ladies' room with a nose-wrinkle but a determined step.

Michael fished out the disposable cell phone he'd bought in New Paris. Then, before he could talk himself out of it, he flicked it on, spent a few moments waiting for it to power up, and keyed in a number he never thought he'd have occasion to call.

Two automated menus and a long string of numeric code later, there was a clicking as the relays picked up. He headed for the corner of the building, stepping out of sight and looking down a long weedy slope that ended with a listing barbed-wire fence barely able to keep itself upright, let alone hold back the shallow sea of long yellow grass. The wind made a low mournful sound, licking every edge it could find.

The phone crackled against his ear. His throat was dry. *Please,* he thought, unaware of his free hand curling into a fist. So much grace pouring into him from close proximity, teasing and tempting, strengthening and solidifying. Her fragility was a temptation all its own, and his body was acting like a mortal man's. It was yet another worry he had no time to entertain.

Finally, he was rewarded with a success, however small. "Report," a crisp, almost-familiar voice barked.

For a moment, he couldn't speak.

"Report," the legionnaire on the other end repeated. "Hello?"

"Michael Gabon, legionnaire." He gave his serial number and coughed slightly, freeing the blockage in his throat. "I, uh, have an Incorruptible with me. We're an hour from Denver, and I could *really* use some help."

The Legion wasn't moribund at all. That was the good news.

The bad? They hadn't even known Michael Gabon was still

alive, let alone functioning. At least, the Celeres on pickup duty hadn't. And though it made little sense to him, the officer said Michael and his *lumina* would have to wait for a day or so in the Mile-High City to be collected, hoping the unclean wouldn't scent her nearness.

YOU GET NERVOUS

Despite all the warnings, the altitude wasn't bad. At least, Jenna didn't *think* it was, but then, she wasn't trying to run a marathon. Mike didn't seem to feel it either.

Maybe it was his tattoos.

The hotel had a glassed-in rooftop pool, and under other circumstances the idea of swimming a mile above sea level but under a wide Great Plains sky had plenty to recommend it. She didn't have a swimsuit, so she settled instead for stretching out on a luxuriously soft queen bed and wiggling her sock-clad toes as Michael spread a roll of woolen material out on the table holding an electrical strip, a lamp, and another fake-leather book with plastic pages full of amenities and room service. He began digging in his huge black duffel, too, and various metallic implements gleamed as he lay them out, his hands moving with the speed of habit. A handful of brightly colored paper came out too, bundled with an arthritic rubber band.

Warm air soughed through vents, sunshine through the window made rectangles on the carpet, and Jenna's throat was dry. "What's all that?"

Eddie would have snarled at her to mind her own damn business, if he'd been in a mood. Michael, however, glanced over his shoulder, the light gild his short blond hair and stubble. "Maps, just in case. And a few other things. I don't normally go around armed, but I think I should start."

"Armed?" She rolled onto her stomach, propping her chin on her hands, and studied his shoulder, his back. He was almost too big for the office chair he'd dragged from the small desk tucked in a corner. It was meant more for rotund businessmen or harried vacationing parents than a brawny, very fit tattooed cook.

Except he wasn't just a cook. It boggled the mind, how she could have mistaken him for *normal*. There was a subtle glitter in the air around him, and those marks...the lines shifted on his skin, like moving circuitry diagrams.

"Most of the time, we can call whatever weapons we need, with grace." Gleaming metal shapes filled the table; the larger black duffel bag sat next to the chair, an obedient dog. "Except guns. Those we need to carry, if we're going to use them."

"You have a gun?" Why on earth that should bother her, after all this, Jenna had no clue. She should have been more concerned about the single bed in the room. Were they going to share?

Michael's head was slightly cocked, as if listening to her was more important than paying attention to the table. "More than one, *lumina*."

"Oh." It should have frightened her; she didn't like guns, and a man holding one was even worse. Instead, it was almost comforting, and it was the comfort that scared her, she decided. "So, uh, you're going to Terminator it up?"

"What?" His hands kept moving, though his head was still at that same listening angle.

"It's a movie." Her throat was dry; she cast around for a distraction and lighted on the flatscreen bolted to the wall. "You ever seen it?"

"I don't watch a lot of TV." He picked up something heavy and metallic, examined it critically.

"I never did either, but it's here." Jenna rolled over, searching for the remote on the chunky, dark-veneered nightstand. She pushed a button and a documentary filled the huge screen, grainy footage of old planes diving over a massive ship. Probably World War II. Another button-press, a highly polished chef with bright white teeth and a shock of bleached hair was drizzling chocolate syrup over cheesecake. There was no sound, thankfully; whoever was in here last had muted the idiot box. "Might as well use it."

"Oh, yeah. I just haven't seen a lot of movies, I mean." There were tiny metallic clicks; muscle moved in his shoulders and down his back. "Sitting there in the dark with strangers makes me nervous."

"You get nervous?" Jenna pressed the button again, and a talk show host was listening thoughtfully, one finger pressed against his cheek, to a red-haired woman in a black flowered dress who looked vaguely familiar.

"Yeah. All the time."

Funny, he seemed almost preternaturally calm. Jenna pointed her toes, flexed her ankles, pointed her toes again. It was strange to not worry about going back to work, doubly strange to travel with someone who simply paid for everything as a matter of course. And he hadn't snapped at her yet, or even sounded *close* to snapping at her.

Then she realized the redhead on the screen looked like Sara, and a chill went through her. She pressed the button again. "Mike? I mean, Michael?"

"You can call me what you like."

As long as it's not late for dinner? "I was just going to thank you." *Again. Hope you don't get tired of it.*

"For what?" Baffled, he set down what he was working on and spun in the chair, regarding her across a sunny hotel room. He didn't seem upset at being interrupted, though.

"You're just a good guy." Jenna kept her gaze on the screen. Another daytime talk show filled the screen, a manicured host resting his chin on fingertips while his blow-dried celebrity guest waved his hands, laughing with the audience.

He was quiet for so long her throat closed up, too, and she started thinking she'd finally made the misstep that would push him over the edge. When she gathered the courage to glance at him, though, he was smiling. "Thank you, Jenna," he said, gravely. "I'd like to be a good guy."

"Well, you're pretty much there." If he did want to share the bed, she could be reasonably sure he wouldn't try anything. If he wanted to, he would have by now, right? Relief loosened all her joints, and she pressed the remote button again. Another cooking show, a pair of disembodied hands sautéing onions in a wide, luxurious pan.

He turned back to his work, and Jenna let out a soft, shaky breath. She pressed the power button and the television died, its electronic eye closing. Instead, she watched his back, slight movements as his hands did whatever they were doing, and the vulnerable paleness of his nape above those wide shoulders.

It wasn't a bad view at all.

SHADOW IN SLIPTIME

Michael watched the lamp-starred streets spread below the window, the city's orange stain fighting with starglow and what moonlight could reach through smog. Height was always an advantage, and if he had more legionnaires at least two would be on the roof keeping watch and another few stationed in a widening net, as well as more inside the hotel at chokepoints. There would be another three in the room with him, too, close-guarding a *lumina*. Eventually, two would sleep on either side of her while the other two stood ready at window and door...but that was for much later, once he'd brought her safely to rendezvous and the Eyrie. Four was the absolute bare minimum for guard duty.

He wondered, almost idly, how she would react to that development. She hadn't mentioned the single queen-sized bed, but he was certain she'd noticed it—and also noticed his careful avoidance of that piece of real estate, too.

Having to wait in heavily infested territory bothered him, but he didn't want to risk the mountain passes, or even the Eisenhower Tunnel, if it could be helped. They should have sent a chopper immediately, but his wasn't to question why. His was to hope that tonight would be quiet, that any local *diaboli* wouldn't sense an Incorruptible, and that tomorrow's pickup would go smoothly. And also to hope that when they reached the Eyrie and they asked her how he'd done, she would be kind enough to repeat that he was a good guy.

As performance reviews went, he could do a lot worse. Maybe he'd even made up for bungling her introduction to his world.

Her world too, now.

Michael shifted a fraction, cycling through a slightly different stance to keep his muscles from stiffening up. Motionlessness wore on you, and you could cramp up if the need for sudden motion arrived.

Jenna made a soft, sleepy sound, moving in the bed. He liked hearing her breathe, it was as soothing as sleeping himself.

More sounds of shifting cloth. She was in a tank top and boxers, he knew because he'd seen her pad from the bathroom to the bed's embrace and her bare legs—not to mention her arms, and the tank top's low neck—all but riveted him. The songs hinted at the effect a *lumina* could have on a legionnaire, but they hadn't prepared him for how deep and instant—or distracting—it would be, just when he needed a clear head most.

"Ow." Jenna sat up, and he turned from his post, dark-adapted eyes piercing the gloom. She rubbed at her face, her hair a dark silken tangle down her back, and blinked.

"You're safe, *lumina*." Low, calm, and quiet, in case she was disoriented. "Another dream?"

"No." She slid her feet out of bed, pushing the covers aside as a throat-filling yawn swallowed the last of the word. "I don't think so, at least. My head just hurts."

Huh. He tensed, muscle by muscle. "Are you dehydrated? It could be the altitude." Telling her what he suspected wouldn't help, he decided. The Principle was sensitive to disharmony of any kind, and her last sudden headache might have been triggered by the attention of the unclean across two parking lots and several lanes of freeway.

"Could be." She gained her feet in one lithe motion, and he tensed a little more. Pulling at her tank top's hem, she padded across the hotel room on delicate bare feet and halted next to him, rubbing at her temple with graceful fingers. "You really don't sleep much."

His marks moved uneasily and Michael extended his arm, gently pushing her away from the glass as he turned. He inhaled to say something soothing—*away from the window, lumina*, or perhaps, *I'll get you some water*.

The door shattered, splinters flying as he threw himself atop her, both of them landing hard on texture-patterned carpet. The window trembled uneasily in its casement, glass remembering it had been liquid once. Jenna's high, unsteady cry broke as his weight drove the breath out of her, and when the window shattered a bare half-second later, thin daggers buried themselves in his back with tiny popping noises.

His marks lit with fury, running over curves and flat planes of muscle, grace igniting in the stove of his belly. Michael was already up, booted feet thudding on either side of his sprawling *lumina*. Training and practice mixed, a metal hilt filling his palms as the sword resolved out of thin air with a high sustained note of bloodlust. His back twitched, ridding itself of splinters that could have punctured the sweet softness of his Incorruptible; he threw his weight sideways, spinning to bring the sword in a solid silver arc almost before it finished coalescing.

The blade bit deep. Amber ichor sprayed, and the spiderlike unclean attempting to scrabble through the window howled, its hairy cup-feet digging wildly for purchase. Sliced almost in half, it fell into the night outside and a cool clean draft of midnight air scoured the room, curtains belling wildly.

Instinct told him the window was clear for now so he pivoted again, uncoiling in a leap that took him well on his way to meeting the ones boiling through the door. He could hold them bottled near the bathroom—the flatscreen on the wall spiderwebbed with cracks as he met the first with a crash echoing through sliptime.

"*Michael!*" Jenna screamed. He had no time or breath for reassurance, the fuming streaks of unclean would flank him if he paused. As long as there was only one spider at the window, he had a chance.

Sliptime folded around him. His blade swept laterally, biting unclean flesh; one of his hands left the hilt and coruscating grace filled it, throwing dappled shadows on the walls. His own shadow stretched in front of him, which was wrong but he had no time to think of why. It was too bright—was he shedding grace?

The flatscreen exploded, fragments hanging in the air as sliptime flexed and shivered. Michael stutter-stepped through hardening air, his fist meeting an unclean's twisted face and crumpling it into oblivion. Soundwaves overlapped, intersecting rings rearranging dust, drywall exploding with coughing sounds.

Jenna screamed again, a rising note of pain and bafflement that nevertheless was full of harmony. Even an Incorruptible's fear was beautiful; the light shrank, a darkening before dawn.

They pressed through the shattered door, a tide of unclean moving so fast he hadn't sensed them. *She* had, though—the evidence was clear. Nobody had ever told him that an Incorruptible would get a headache when the *diaboli* pressed close and he would pay more attention in the future if he could just get through this battle. The wall on either side of the aperture crumbled, more piling into the breach. *Too* many. It wasn't like them to gather before striking, unless—

A shadow in sliptime. A hideous, crunching impact. He was thrown back, his boots digging deep furrows, carpet peeling aside and the floor underneath smoking under his heels. It screeched, compressed air pushing at Michael's clothes, and there was a hideous tearing sensation as the *hazazel*, one of the Greater Unclean, coalesced fully behind its foot soldiers and Michael realized there was a very real possibility of dying.

The *hazazel* crouched, smiling its perpetual glasstooth smile, six arms waving as its strangler's hands contorted into figures or traced twisted power-sigils. It was humanoid, but unlike other *diaboli* it did not inhabit a human host.

Legionnaires were *called*, and so were the higher orders of unclean from whatever twisted place bereft of the Principle they spent their long lives twisting in the tortures of. A legionnaire could twist away from grace and *become* unclean, but there was no shortage of other types.

No shortage at all.

The sword—heavy golden pommel, clawed crossbars, straight pure length of Principle-blessed steel—was a solid silver arc twisting through a blurring figure-eight as Michael bent sliptime and a hot flood of grace to his will. Ichor sprayed afresh, and his shadow was an ink-black shape with razor edges.

It was still in *front* of him, that shadow, and he wondered if Jenna had turned the lights on for a bare split second before the *hazazel*, grinning its fixed hideous grimace, lunged forward. Michael's blade was tangled in a knot of unclean, their weight of numbers telling. There were so *many*, and their chief's teeth dripped with scarlet and amber as one of its long extra-jointed hands filled with a short curving poisonsmoke blade.

"*Michael*!" Jenna screamed again, and a hot draft streamed past him.

She's emitting. Well, she has the Breath.

The point touched his chest, and Michael let out a hideous coughing cry. The *hazazel*'s blade bit deep, sliding between ribs, and *twisted*, searching for his heart.

Pain. A river, a flood, a sea of agony, swallowing him whole. He pitched forward, meaning to spit the thing—maybe Jenna might escape them if he could kill the greatest unclean—and the consciousness of defeat was his nightmare again, all bad dreams a preparation for this single moment. The tip of the curved blade twisted once more, seeking for the engine of muscle, gristle, and grace that fueled his seemingly-mortal body.

Kill it. Don't worry about anything but killing this thing, even if—
A great breathless calm descended, and his shadow became not ink but a black hole. He fell into it, and a warm draft touched his back with impersonal hands.

"No." Jenna's voice echoed like a golden bell, smashing sliptime into fragments. The light paled, liquid gold heated to the point of fierce combustion, intensifying in a single, shattering pulse. An Incorruptible's greatest weapon, kept only for extremis.

The world grayed out under that assault, and the pain was everywhere.

Michael fell.

FIRST THINGS FIRST

The light roared through her, spreading in concentric rings, and the first surprise was how warm it was. Jenna's bare toes, the only part of her touching the ground, scraped carpet. Her arms were flung back, something in her chest dilating. An aperture like a camera's, only much slower than a shutter-click.

Then it stopped short and she was dropped in a jumble of arms and legs, her head bouncing against the floor with stunning force. She lay for a few moments, and it *hurt*, all over.

Her head was a tender pumpkin balanced on a thin stem, her hands shook, and when she could hear over the roaring in her ears there were sirens threading through distant traffic-noise. Jenna scrambled up to hands and knees, bracing herself against torn carpet and gouged wooden underfloor; a cold wind teased her bare shoulders and ruffled her hair.

What did I do? Whatever it was, it had worked. After all, she wasn't dead. Was she?

"Michael?" she whispered. The sound was very small after all the noise. Glass dropped from the window's margins, tinkling-sweet, and the entire building swayed.

She found him by touch amid the shattered corpses. Greasy ash lifted on the strengthening breeze. They were all dead, even the biggest one with its tangle of arms twisted into a rat's nest. Once her vision cleared, looking at where alien musculature joined the torso in bony arm sockets made her stomach revolve so badly tiny black specks danced in front of her. "Michael. *Michael.*" His wasn't burned to flinders, thank God.

But he was so very, very still.

It was hard work to roll him over. Her head throbbed, that strange warm light bleeding away. She *felt* it ebb, a sudden drop like blood sugar or air pressure falling before a storm, her body struggling to cope with a sudden loss. The smoke-fuming demon things were all dead, most of them with terribly scorched faces and chests. The light had all but cooked them, and the smell was eyewatering.

It's all true. All of it. Not that she'd doubted—well, she hadn't doubted *much*—but there was nothing like seeing the unbelievable right in front of you *twice.*

It was enough to make her wonder how many more times she'd see it.

Michael sprawled amid the tangled bodies. A hilt protruded from his chest, a terrible, twisted bony thing. Her hands closed around it, and a sudden sickening jolt up her arms made her cry out with weak revulsion. Still, her body knew better than she did and *pulled,* working the blade free. It grated on bone; she turned her head aside, a hot flood of bile filling her throat, and spat-retched. The blade slid free of his chest with one last sickening sucking sound, and Michael twitched.

He can't be alive. He can't be. Still, getting the nasty, twisted thing *out* of him seemed important. Jenna's sobbing breaths were very loud. The curved blade smoked, that weird steam-curling vapor sliding free in heavy droplets that sizzled when they touched the carpet. She dropped it and backed away, scooting on her hands and bottom, her new boxers almost pulling free of her hips.

Think, Jenna. Goddamn you, think *about what you're going to do.*

The noise. Someone would come, someone would call the police if they hadn't already. Did she want to be found here with dead, scorched bodies after vanishing from home? Trying to explain this was a bad move. Who would believe her, even if all the evidence was right there?

The things' bodies were sagging, floods of strange amber fluid drenching the floor. They were rotting in fast-forward, like bad special effects. Dim electric light from the hallway—good God, the door was now a hole, the walls on either side torn away—showed the great cracks and runnels developing on their surfaces. There might not be much evidence left when the police got here, except Michael's body. He was stabbed in the chest, and her fingerprints were probably on the knife now.

Would the knife rot too? It still looked awfully, nastily solid, except for the smoky stuff pouring off the blade.

Honey, listen to me. It was Mom's voice echoing in her head now, soft but firm and utterly practical. *Get your luggage, get the keys to the truck, and get out of here.*

Jenna let out a last soft, sobbing noise, swallowed the rest. Her legs shook so badly she had to use the bed to pull herself up. The truck keys. Michael's wallet—she'd need cash. Her luggage, such as it was. All she had left in the world.

The urge to simply crawl back into the bed, close her eyes, and pretend this was all a dream was overwhelming. Gooseflesh prickled along her legs and shoulders, crawled down her back. The big muscles in her thighs shook, and her arms were leaden. The bedside lamp was shattered; there was glass everywhere.

Shoes. She needed shoes first. Everything else could follow.

A slight rustling noise, a pained inhalation, and Michael rolled onto his side. He coughed, a deep, racking retch, and groaned. "Jenna..."

Oh Jesus. He was alive. She couldn't just leave him here.

Still, the idea was awfully tempting.

"Jennaaaaa..." He moved again, weakly. "*Lumina.*"

Shit. Shit, shit, shit. No, she couldn't leave him here. Damn her and her conscience, she just couldn't do it. Even if it meant she'd go to jail for...whatever she'd go to jail for, even if he was only dying instead of dead. She tried to figure out what they'd charge her with, but it was, as Rach would say, academic.

God, she missed Rach. And Sam. She even missed Bob, Amy and Sarah too.

Cautiously, Jenna edged towards him on shaking legs. "Michael?" A dry, cracked whisper—she fell to her knees beside him again, the jolt echoing in her shoulders, clicking her teeth together painfully.

"Jenna." He coughed, curling up like a pillbug. He was covered in the stinking goop from the demon-creatures. "We...we have to move." Hoarse, husky words. Were they the last he'd ever speak? "Truck...leave."

Oh, I know. Believe me, I'm one step ahead of you there. "It s-stabbed you." A scared little girl was using her voice, and a great pointless wash of anger boiled through her and away, barely recognized. *Jesus, this is insane.*

"Fine. Just need time." He coughed again, retched, and amazingly, he starfished instead of curling up, scrabbled weakly against the carpet and kicking the swiftly rotting things off his legs. Once he was free of their dead clutching, he rolled onto his side.

How was he still *moving*? "You shouldn't," she managed, reaching for his shoulders. "You...it *stabbed* you."

"Fine. I'll be fine." He coughed again. Muscle stood out stone-hard under her palms, and feverish heat scorched her fingers through thin T-shirt material. "Just...weak. Need to move."

How the hell had she ended up in a high-rise hotel room full of dead demons and a stabbed man? The sheer unreality of the situation threatened to knock the breath right out of her once more, but Jenna held on, grimly. "Okay," she said. "Okay." Her hands glued themselves to his shoulders; she began trying to help.

It took some doing to get him sitting up, but once he got his boots underneath him he surged upright and all but carried her along. He shook his head, swayed, and almost toppled; if he went down now she would land underneath him again. His boots crunched on glass and splinters; Jenna was suddenly aware she was half-naked in pajamas and it was cold.

Very cold. The broken window was a hungry mouth, sucking heat into the night sky.

"More." Michael coughed again, almost doubling over. She strained to right him, her bare heel slipping against nylon and that reeking amber goop. It was a miracle her feet weren't hamburger by now. "More soon. We have to move."

"All right." *I can handle this.* It was no different than moving out of your apartment once your boyfriend was safely in jail and bail had been denied, Jenna realized.

You just picked the first thing to do, then the next, then the next. Not easy, certainly, but very simple indeed.

"All right," she repeated. "I'm gonna get you to the bed. Then I'm going to get dressed."

THE HARDEST THING was hefting his bigger black canvas duffel; thank God his smaller one was in the truck. Whatever he had in the big one—weapons, clothes, whatnot—weighed a goddamn ton. Worse, he wouldn't let them take the elevator, so it was lugging both him *and* the duffel down twenty flights while praying nobody would be coming up. The hotel hadn't wasted any aesthetic cash to soften the stairs, and their footsteps echoed loudly.

On the bright side, he swayed and veered drunkenly but largely managed to keep on his feet, and he dragged her rolling suitcase behind him with several thumps and bumps. At least she wasn't going to lose all her clothes this time. And if she hitched the duffel onto her back, it wasn't too bad, just clumsy. Her legs trembled and her knees weren't too steady, but she could manage.

Barely.

The brightest news of all was the stab wound on his chest closing up, its edges raw and pink. He still looked green under the stairway fluorescents, and Jenna's head still ached, but nowhere near as badly. "How is it doing that?" She almost regretted wasting breath on the question; her arms and legs were burning.

"Legion," he said, clinging to the banister. His torn T-shirt flopped, crusted with who-knew how many kinds of drying ick. "Hard to...I'm hard to...kill. Plus...*you*. Grace." Another deep breath, filling his lungs, and he straightened. "So much light," he continued, wonderingly. "You saved us."

"Yeah, well." *I'm glad it worked, whatever it was.* All the same, if it made her feel so weak and shaky she'd prefer to never do it again, thank you very much. "How did they find us?"

"Don't know. Yet." He paused for a moment, hanging onto the metal banister covered with thick chipped paint. He was deadly sallow, two bright spots of color high on his cheekbones, and his blue gaze was a hawk's fierce glare. "When I do..."

You know, I'm pretty sure that should frighten me. "Let's just get out of here first." She hauled him back as he overcorrected, both of them almost tumbling down the concrete stairs in a heap. There was scurrying motion and banging doors above and below them, but they were left in a bubble of solitude—which was great, because she didn't know what to do if someone saw them. "Okay, so I did something. What did I do?" *And can I do it again, if they come back?*

"Light. In sliptime." Michale coughed again, spat a wad of something tinged with bright crimson aside, and straightened as if he felt much better. "Beautiful."

I'm gonna count that as a good thing. "All right." She told her legs they were just going to have to deal with the current situation and tugged at the duffel's strap cutting her right shoulder. "Come on, only ten more floors."

By the time they spilled into the back end of the soaring, marble-sheathed lobby, Michael's shirt crusted and sticking to his broad chest, he was walking more or less in a straight line. A flurry of activity at the front desk said someone had indeed noticed the ruckus twenty floors up, but all they had to do was get down a short hall to the parking-garage elevators.

"Stairs," Michael gasped. "Too easy to get trapped."

"Forget it." Jenna was having none of *that* bullshit anymore, so help her God. She took a firmer grasp on his belt and the duffel's strap. "Come on, someone will see us." The security cameras would definitely see them, but she couldn't do a single blessed thing about that, so she decided not to worry about it.

It would ordinarily have been nice, she reflected grimly, to find something that *wasn't* her problem to deal with.

"Jenna..." For a man who had just been stabbed, he certainly seemed about to argue with her. So she ducked under his arm, aiming them both at the end of the hall. Her reflection in the silver elevator doors was a sight—mussed hair, her jeans hastily buttoned and her parka slipping sideways as Michael's heavy arm dragged at the shoulders. He slumped as if after a long night spent drinking, blinking bloodshot blue eyes, and thank God there was nobody in this hall to see them.

The elevator was mercifully empty as well. She pulled him inside, hit the P4 button, and almost dropped his duffel. The only thing keeping it on her back was the idea of having to heft the damn thing again once they reached their floor.

"There could be more," he said as the elevator slowed. He blinked rapidly, his eyes watering, and tiny bits of broken glass glittered in his hair. Thin tracks of clean skin on his stubbled face showed where tears had washed the guck free. "Let me go first."

"What, so they trip over you?" She should have been too terrified to risk using sarcasm on a man much bigger than her, but she was also tired, and that strange light—the *clarity*—still bloomed around them both. It was a warm comfort, and she figured she needed every scrap she could get. "What a great idea."

He glanced at her, his dirty jaw stubborn-set. "I can fight."

"I don't think there are more of them." She blinked, remembering the most important thing of all. "Keys. Give me the truck keys."

"Jenna—" Was it *pleading* in the single word? Wonders never ceased.

"You just got *stabbed*, you're not driving." If he passed out or wavered, they could end up wrecked. Well, even more wrecked than they already were.

He still wasn't convinced. "I can—"

"Michael." Good God above, she was tired of pleading, especially with men. Jenna's feet throbbed; she wondered if she could lean the duffel against the wall. "Give me the fucking keys. Please."

"Yes ma'am." He hung his big blond head, swayed, and dug in his pocket. "But I'm telling you—"

"I know how to drive." She exhaled, shakily. At least he wasn't like Eddie. He'd see reason, and she was fairly sure she wouldn't pay for daring to disagree later. "You just, uh, get better." *Oh, my God, what a thing to say.*

But the stab wound was definitely closing up. It wasn't even bleeding.

"Easy." Michael didn't lift his head, but he did hand over the keys. "You're so much grace, *lumina.*"

"Uh, thanks." *Isn't that nice. I wish I knew what the fuck he was talking about.* She supposed she did—the light, that crazy-ass *light.* Where had it been every other time she needed it?

The elevator dinged again; the doors opened. Michael tacked away, only a little unsteady, peering at concrete, empty parking spaces, a few cars desultorily waiting for their owners, and the faded red Dodge truck, a welcome sight.

"Clear," he said, and beckoned. He made it almost the entire way to the truck without staggering, and she hurried to grab his elbow.

"See?" An *I told you so* lingered behind her lips; she swallowed it. "You're *not* driving."

"Yes, *lumina.*" His eyelids had fallen to half-mast, and he was still feverish-warm. The red blotches on his cheeks had faded, though. "Tired."

"I know," she soothed, propping him against the side of the truck and unlocking the passenger door. Everything on the Dodge was manual except the transmission; he was an old-fashioned sort of guy. "I just need to know where the fuck we're going now."

"Another hotel. Just not here." He leaned his head back, his Adam's-apple bobbing as he swallowed. "Sleep, then I'll be all right."

"Great." She wrenched the door open, almost overbalancing under the duffel. Getting the damn thing off her back would feel like a vacation. "Get in. Let's go."

LUCK AND GRACE

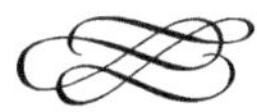

JENNA DROVE CAUTIOUSLY, obeying every traffic law to the letter. She even halted twice at stop signs, and clearly considered the speed limit to be just that—an actual limit, not a minimum goal. It was like watching a mortal pick a scab, but Michael was exhausted enough to find it somewhat amusing, especially when she swore under her breath at a white Corolla riding the truck's tailgate.

Besides, if she was driving, he could study her all he wanted, hurriedly looking away when she glanced nervously in his direction or grimaced as if her head hurt again.

"You could speed up a little," he managed. His chest was full of the slow flame of healing, and with her nearness flushing his marks with grace it would take far less time than usual. Still, he was more than uneasy.

He was, in fact, flat-out perturbed. A *hazazel*, with enough *diaboli minori* to overwhelm a legionnaire? Add the spider-unclean at the window, and you had a concerted, planned attack, not just a few unclean stumbling across an Incorruptible's trail.

And that should not have happened. At least, not so soon, in a city full of enough mortals to provide the white noise of cover for a single Incorruptible.

Jenna's mouth tightened, her lower lip compressing. "I hate back-seat drivers." Her pretty hands, filthy with decaying ichor and stripes of drying blood—all Michael's, thank the Principle—rested exactly at ten and two o'clock on the wheel, and her knuckles were white.

What could he say to put her at ease? "Technically I'm in the passenger seat."

"Driver picks the speed, passenger shuts his pie-hole." She touched the brakes, and the truck rolled to a stop precisely before a white painted line. The stoplight threw a rubescent glow into the cab, and there was precious little traffic at this hour. The Corolla had turned down a side street, probably relieved to be free of impediments.

"Yes ma'am." Why was he smiling? Probably because she was, a tight curve of her pretty lips that filled him with a different heat. A fresh flood of grace filled him toes to hairline, and he luxuriated in it. "Any place will do, Jenna. Just find us another hotel."

"I'm *working* on it." A welcome flash of irritation, much better than fear. She freed a hand to push her hair back. Silken strands clung to her fingers, and he longed to touch them as well. "You crushed my phone, or I could find one in two shakes."

Was she still angry? There was a lump in his throat. "They'd track your phone."

"Looks like they're tracking us anyway, right?" She glanced at him, a quick flicker of dark eyes, but the light turned green and the truck rolled forward again.

"Not sure." It wasn't a lie, he told himself. He wasn't *completely* sure, he only suspected, and besides, she didn't need anything else to worry about right now. His chest ached, the marks clustering the wound and re-knitting unmortal flesh.

"You're not sure? What was *that*, then?" Her irritation was blessedly natural, reaction setting in. The battle was over, now it was time for the fallout.

"I don't know yet, *lumina*." Michael sagged against the seat. It was the first time someone else had driven his truck, and they were a tiny red beetle crawling between stacks of concrete, caught in a tangle of one-way streets. "I'm sorry."

"I didn't mean it that way. If they're not tracking us, how did they—"

She was bright in more ways than one. "They sense Incorruptibles like we do." Michael touched his chest, wincing slightly. A *hazazel*, and he'd survived—and she'd had the presence of mind to pull the blade free. Otherwise he might still be there, pinned like a butterfly. "It could just be bad luck." He didn't want to tell her his other, darker imaginings.

Not yet.

"Great," she muttered, stopping at yet another white line, rolling forward, stopping again as she peered to the left. At least they'd made it out of the parking garage before the cops showed up. Scrambling the security cameras on their way out had taken a great deal of his waning strength. "Pretty much the only kind of luck I have, anymore."

"I wouldn't say that." From where he was sitting, it looked they were doing unreasonably well, considering the circumstances. "We're still alive. And you threw light in sliptime. That's pretty considerable."

"If it makes me feel like this, I'd probably rather not." She was *still* smiling, but her mouth was much softer now.

He was lucky, to be able to see as much. The Principle was kind, and she was doubly so. It probably hadn't even occurred to her to leave him behind, or to leave the knife in him. He would have returned to conscious motion as soon as the thing was extracted, but fighting free of a morgue and tracking her down in a *diaboli*-infested city wasn't the best way to make a good impression. "Next time, you just run. Run as far and as fast as you can, I'll find you. But you can't stay if I'm put out of commission, Jenna."

"Oh, so I should have just left you there with a demon knife in your chest? Duly noted." She winced, pushing her hair back, her left hand still clutching the wheel. "Good thing this is an automatic. Manuals hate me."

"Duly noted," he echoed. By all rights he should be driving, letting her recover from the shock. She was running on adrenaline now, and the crash would come sooner or later. "I'm serious, Jenna. You have to stay alive and reach L.A."

"I'm not going anywhere without you, Michael. I've been running all my life." She exhaled sharply, spotted a freeway sign, and stepped on the gas. "Hallelujah. Do me a favor and just start looking for hotel signs, okay?"

"Yes ma'am." He sagged in the seat, fingering the crusted, ragged hole in his T-shirt. Pinned on ruined carpet, hearing her sobbing breaths but unable to move—that was hell, and he was grateful she'd stopped to take the spike out of his chest. She was saving him instead of the other way around, and that wasn't good. He'd never make centurion, or even stay as her legionnaire once they reached Los Angeles, if this continued.

They might not reach the last Eyrie in North America at *all*, if he kept fucking up. But a *hazazel* with a hunting party? Coming right to their door instead of working a hotel floor-by-floor to find their prey?

It was easy enough to figure out *how*. He just didn't want to believe it, and that was dangerous.

Michael settled himself to the work of healing, drawing as much grace as he could from the volcano in the driver's seat. His marks prickled, sang, filled with slow fire-honey. She had the Breath, so she was slightly more durable, but still, she shouldn't have had to attack at all. She should be safe in a plush suite in the Eyrie already.

Why hadn't they arranged a helicopter or a private plane? Did the Legion not have the means it once had?

Forget about that. Figure out how to keep her safe. He would have to hope the planned rendezvous tomorrow wasn't a trap. And, more importantly, he had to plan.

Just in case it was.

Dawn was clear and chilly, the mercury plunging and weak sunshine unable to do much more than gild a few edges through a Motel 6 parking lot in Aurora. The wound on his chest was fully sealed, the scar shrinking hourly, and he was only hungry. Fueling the healing was hungry work, and one of the few times a legionnaire outright required mortal food. Even the amount of grace she emitted couldn't bring him back to full capability fast enough.

Jenna, however, was having a little difficulty. She examined the pink scar over his heart, the bandage she'd insisted on taping down last night innocent of any stain. Her dark, liquid gaze stuttered to his face and Michael suffered it, hoping he had an appropriate expression on. They'd never told him what to do when a tank-top-and-boxer-clad Incorruptible insisted he take his shirt off and sit on a closed toilet. The first-aid kit she'd placed solicitously in their shopping cart several towns ago rested on the bathroom counter under high-glare fluorescents, the red cross on its blue cover a reminder of other battles.

Mortal battles. Now he was engaged in other ones.

The tank top hid nothing; her legs were long, smoothly muscled, and *incredibly* distracting. "That's so freaky." Fascinated, she extended a fingertip and touched one end of the scar.

Michael's jaw set. The contact was electric, grace spreading in hot, concentric rings. Cool air mouthed his bare skin, every nerve tingling at her nearness. It was exactly like waking from a dream of victory to find his body behaving like a mortal's, and he gripped both sides of the plastic seat with aching fingers.

It wouldn't do to lose control now. Of course they told you about the effect an Incorruptible could have on a legionnaire, but feeling it was something else.

In all senses of the phrase.

"I heal fast," he muttered. It made sense that he was... *receptive* to her. Who wouldn't be? She was flat-out gorgeous, stunningly kind, and so brave it could break a legionnaire's heart, let alone a mortal one. How could any of them, even with their dulled senses, been unkind to her? "See? I'm all right."

He didn't want his *lumina* to move away. In fact, the only thing he wanted was to lay his hand over hers, flattening her palm against his bare chest to bathe in that warm, forgiving grace, and it was the thing he couldn't do.

You did not force an Incorruptible's touch. It was a gift to be accepted, not sought and definitely not stolen.

"Yeah." Thankfully, she took her hand away, gazing at his face. Her worry taunted him, turning her dark eyes sad and highlighting the shadows underneath. Her hair was a soft, glorious tangle from restless sleep on one of the sagging double beds. A cheap motel was no place for her, but of course she wouldn't complain. "So, we're meeting up with more of your guys today."

Hopefully. If I'm wrong. And I'd love to be wrong. "Yes. That means you'll be safer." His hands tingled, throbbed, ached with the craving to reach across a bare few inches of space, maybe close around her soft, fragile wrist.

She straightened slowly, nervously gathering her hair with both hands and backing away as far as limited space permitted. Her hip brushed a stack of white towels on the counter. A fresh set of clothes for her were on the other side of the sink, neatly folded, but she refused to clean up until he was taken care of. "What if they don't show?"

Then I know I'm right. But he didn't want her worrying about that. Not yet, not for as long as possible. "We keep driving. They'll catch up." Another statement that was only partly an untruth, but an acceptable one, he hoped. The calmer she was, the better. "You want a shower now?"

"My hair'll probably freeze. But yes, I should." She drew away, busied herself fussing with the unnecessary first-aid kit. A tiny tremor ran through her arms, barely visible, but her hands were steady.

"Funny, huh? I can deal with demons and bad dreams, but you getting stabbed and it closing up... that's a little, you know..."

"Troubling?" Would it reassure her to know she was handling this far more gracefully than most mortals? The Legion protected the Incorruptible from humanity's howling, cheated jealousy, but mortals were masters at not-seeing the darkness or the weird until forced, and then deconstructing as soon as it was thrust upon them.

"And comforting, I guess." Another one of those small, sipping glances, checking the emotional weather on his face. He longed to find the man who ground that habit into her, and wrap his hands around the mortal's throat. "I guess you're tougher than you look."

"I hope so." It would be easy to reach out, touch her arm, the back of her bare hand. To feel that drugging, drowning grace again... oh, the temptation was amazing, and he didn't have the strength to keep it at bay for much longer.

So he did the only thing he *could* do, pulling his cheek in and biting down, savagely. The pain helped center him, and he tasted mineral blood. His was still thin and red as a mortal's, not the thick amber ichor of the twisted and unclean. It hadn't occurred to him to be grateful until now; if he was bleeding clean, he had not deviated.

Oddly, Jenna laughed—a soft, nervous sound, tightening his skin and brushing velvet along his shoulders. "You're a very funny fellow, Michael."

"Yeah." He searched for something else to say, some way to amuse her, steady her. "I'll, uh. Just go get dressed. Packed. Yeah."

"You do that." She closed the kit with a snap, and when he unfolded, he was very aware of how small and slim she was, and how close in this small space. She glanced at him, hunching her shoulders, and Michael moved past an inch at a time.

He had to say something. Anything. "If you get a headache again, tell me." He made it to the door without grabbing her arms *or* burying his face in her long dark hair to inhale the scent of the Principle clothed in warm, beautiful mortal flesh. "I think you're sensing them."

"At least I can do *something* useful." She turned, extending the kit in both hands like a gift. "Here. I...thank you, Michael. I was really scared."

"I know," he mumbled. He should have told her she was *more* than useful, that she'd saved him, but the words tangled in his throat. "I'm sorry." He took the kit and fled while he still could, shutting the door, and didn't move away from the thin pasteboard and cheap, locking doorknob until he heard the water start in the tub.

Thinking of her sliding her pajamas off and climbing under a shower's warm flow wasn't calculated to help him stay calm, either. So he retreated, step by step, and set himself to repacking his duffel.

It was going to be lighter today, because he was going armed with every mortal weapon he had, as well as grace.

STRICTLY HUMAN

WHAT DID you talk about with a man who had just been stabbed in the chest? Nothing in Jenna's life had ever prepared her for this particular situation. Fortunately, Michael was monosyllabic once she got out of the shower, and she glimpsed a shoulder holster under his hip-length, high-collared leather jacket. She even him tuck a knife into his boot, and he pushed the hem of his jean-leg down over it without glancing at her.

He'd turned completely businesslike, but he didn't seem angry. Still, Jenna kept a weather eye in his direction. He piloted the truck through a coffee shop drive-thru and ordered tea and a cranberry scone for her, then pointed them at a McDonald's and paid in cash for a truly staggering amount of fast food. One of the employees had to bring out two armfuls of paper bags, almost staggering under the weight.

"Need to fuel up," Michael said, and began to eat. Jenna watched, fascinated. He didn't seem to get much pleasure out of his breakfast; she nibbled on the scone while he chewed and swallowed mechanically, bolting a cup of coffee doused with creamer and several sugar packets for good measure.

Finally, though, she had to say *something*. "Good Lord. Do you even like it?"

"Cheap calories. The healing takes energy." He slanted her a somewhat sheepish glance, taking the turn onto the freeway with one hand on the wheel and the other holding yet another breakfast sandwich. "Oh. You probably want something nicer, huh?"

"I'm good, I like scones." *Though I wouldn't mind a hash brown or two.* "I just don't want to get in your way." A joke lingered on the tip of her tongue, but she throttled it.

She didn't think he'd take it the wrong way, but better safe than sorry.

The truck rocked slightly, its engine purred, and acceleration held them both in its weightless grip again. Michael checked over his shoulder and merged with light early morning traffic, still chewing. "I can order more—"

"I'm *kidding*, Michael." She shouldn't expect him to guess, though. "Sorry."

"No, I'm just pretty focused." His nose was a little too long and his cheekbones a little too wide, but when he relaxed, the effect was a good one. Shaved and in fresh clothes, there was no sign of last night's haggard, staggering man with a giant hole in his chest. "We have a little time before the meet. Figured I'd fuel up and get us onsite early. If there's setup I want to see it."

It was comforting that he was trained for this, but it was doubly comforting that he was smart. Jenna took a bite of scone, relishing the tart sting of cranberries. "Like a spy movie, right?" She swallowed hastily. *Don't talk with your mouth full.* "Whoever gets there first gets the jump on everyone else?"

"So to speak." A pleased smile lit his face and he swallowed the rest of his sandwich with only two token chews. "We swung by it yesterday, too."

And I didn't even know. Jenna watched a few cars up, where a light pink sedan had forgotten to turn off its left blinker. "You like to be prepared."

"I don't want anything to happen to you." He crumpled a McMuffin wrapping, tucked it into the bag holding nothing but empty, greasy paper, and reached for another one. "Better I prepare, the less chance of you getting hurt."

"I can't argue with that." A shiver worked up her back, and she wished her tea would cool down. Some caffeine would make this a lot easier to deal with.

"It'll likely be a ten-man team." He took another giant bite, barely chewing. "Four's the bare minimum for moving an Incorruptible even in safe territory, so they should send more. In any case, they'll have comms and linkups with Los Angeles and we'll get out of here fast. They may leave me to drive decoy and take you—"

"No." It was out before she could stop herself, a bark of refusal almost spraying scone-crumbs all over the dash. Jenna swallowed hastily. "I'm not going anywhere with strangers. I don't care if they're like you."

"Jenna—"

"No." Being carried along like a doll was just fine with monsters running around, but something about the prospect of being spirited away from the only halfway-familiar person she had left called up a strange, panicky feeling behind her breastbone. "You're coming along. Someone else can drive your truck, right?" *Great, Jenna. Just assume he'll leave his car behind.*

Michael didn't sigh, but he was silent as he consumed two more sausage sandwiches with big, efficient bites. His throat worked, carrying the last of them down, and he finally spoke. "Jenna, I'm just a grunt, I'd just be in the way. They'll be a good team, high ratings, to pick up an Incorruptible. They won't want me in the mix."

"But *I* do." She stared at her tea, wincing a little as the truck curved through an onramp and hot liquid sloshed inside the paper cup. He knew where he was going, at least. If he was going to get mad at her for disagreeing, now was the time. "I trust you, I'm not sure about anyone else."

That was the heart of it. She did trust him. It was hard *not* to, especially when he'd thrown himself protectively on top of her not once but twice, fought off monsters, and even kept his hands to himself the whole time.

"If you insist they'll take me along." He hit the turn signal, merging with traffic going northeast and reaching for a fresh bag. "But, Jenna—"

"I plan on insisting, then." Her stomach had closed up. Good thing there were only crumbs left of her scone. The pink sedan peeled away to the left, its blinker still going, tick-tock. "Unless you'd rather not be saddled with me." Which could very well be the case, she admitted.

Once she wasn't hanging around, would the demons leave him alone? It was a helluva consideration, as Dad might have said.

"It's not that." Michael shook his head before digging out a hash brown patty. Anyone else might look distracted, eating while driving. He, however, looked incredibly alert for someone who hadn't even slept last night as far as she could tell—just stood near the window, watching, while she tossed and turned. Maybe he slept on his feet. "I just want you safe, that's all."

"Well, I'm not sure about these guys. But I *am* sure about you. Okay?" She tried a sip of tea, burned her tongue. "Ugh. I do have a question, though. How do they know to pick us up?" *Yes, I'm an idiot, I only now worked up the courage to ask.*

But she still didn't have enough to ask if the monsters would leave him alone if she wasn't around. The Subaru in front of them hit the brakes but Michael, observing a safe following distance as usual, only had to let up on the accelerator too slow enough.

"I called in." He glanced at her again, a worried blue flash. "Burner phone. I'll toss it once we're picked up."

"Oh, so *you* get to have a phone." The tea was burning her fingers through the cup. If there was magic in in the world why couldn't it do something useful, like making sure she didn't get scalded?

Michael let the Dodge slow further. Traffic was knotting up. "They could track *yours*."

"I know." She swallowed a burst of uncharacteristic annoyance. "What's to stop them tracking yours?"

"It's a *burner*. The only thing I've ever called on it is the Legion drop-line." Was it mild irritation in his tone, or did he just have too much McMuffin in his mouth?

"It was a rhetorical question." *Mostly*. Or, really, it wasn't. She was just...well, this was a road trip, and you couldn't have one of those without at least one small argument. Human beings trapped in a small moving box for hours got cranky.

But was he strictly human? Or just human enough?

"Sorry." The thickening traffic still moved at a good clip, and he veered between lanes seemingly at random, never slowing. Spaces just opened up for the red truck, a bubble of free pavement. At least that was a practical magic. "We're close. Any headache?"

"Nope. Just a burned tongue from my tea."

"Oh." But instead of looking relieved, his face fell, and he continued chewing.

THE RENDEZVOUS POINT was another motel, a middle-sized Golden Inn near the airport. The Rockies frowned in the distance, a huge change from the plains and very welcome. She'd read about people going mad with all the space and grass, but hadn't really believed it until now. Being chased by nightmare monsters certainly broadened the perceptions.

Michael drove through the parking lot with excruciating slowness, eyeing the lobby and the corrugated tin awning in front of its double glass doors. "Room 303," he said, finally. "Looks like a good call, plenty of exits. Airport's close too, so they'll probably hustle you out there and load you on a chopper."

"A helicopter?" *Get on the choppah*, an old movie actor barked inside her head. She couldn't remember who, only that Dad had loved the line and used it at every opportunity. "Or a bike?"

Thinking about Dad didn't make her think of Mom and the accident, for once. Instead, she wondered how Rach and Sam and Kitty and Belinda and Evan were handling her disappearance. Maybe they didn't even notice; she wasn't anywhere near the center of their tight-knit group. Just an orbiting particle on the fringes, especially after Eddie had finished, patiently but ruthlessly, cutting everyone out of her life.

She hadn't fought too hard, already suspecting she was bad luck they were better off without. Now she knew, and she hoped her friends were oblivious to her absence.

It seemed kinder that way.

"Helicopter." Michael pulled into a parking spot, still gazing out the windshield. He didn't *look* like a man who had just eaten sixty dollars' worth of fast food. There weren't even any crumbs on his navy T-shirt or dark jacket. "They should've sent one for you right away, I don't know why they waited."

"We can ask." Jenna's fingers were cold, despite the tea cupped in them. It was a drinkable temperature now, so she took another hasty swallow and almost swallowed air with it.

She couldn't do *anything* gracefully. Some days were just like that.

"*You* can, once we reach the Eyrie." He peered at the block of concrete, brick, and sloped roof to shed snow in the winter. Any trace of amusement or uncertainty had fallen away, and he looked like a man contemplating a complex and potentially dirty chore. "It's pretty quiet. Let me get out first, okay?"

"Sure." *You're such a gentleman.* It would have sounded snide, though she meant it. It would be difficult to find a more fitting illustration of *chivalrous*; they should just put his picture in the dictionary. "Should we take our luggage?" A regular, prosaic, everyday question, probably ridiculous, but she couldn't stop talking.

Jenna realized she was afraid of what silence might bring.

"Uh, we can get it on the way out if you want." Michael's gaze moved over the motel, jumping from one point to the next. He reached for the door handle. "Once we land they'll get you everything—clothes, a new phone, you name it. You're a *lumina*, they'll get you anything your heart desires."

Was it nervous chatter? Maybe he didn't like the quiet either.

"Sounds too good to be true," she muttered, but he was already out of the truck.

At least they didn't have to go through the lobby to reach the rooms. Instead, there were concrete staircases at both ends of the building; he climbed first, almost going sideways and glancing behind them frequently. It wasn't until they passed Room 302, the brass numbers on its door corroded, that he stiffened and Jenna shuddered, realizing what he was looking at.

The door to Room 303 was open, just a fraction. It creaked as Michael pushed it wide, and Jenna peered over his shoulder.

"Oh, God," she whispered.

Looked like they weren't the earliest birds, after all.

A TRUE DEFENDER

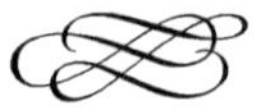

THIN PITILESS SUNLIGHT made a rectangle across cheap carpet, and Michael had to blink a few times before he could distinguish how many bodies were in the room. Looked like a four-man team, and now he could see a star of breakage on the inside of the double storm windows, invisible from the parking lot because of the angle. There were holes battered in the walls on either side, too—*diaboli* tunneling in or the team trying to escape, who could tell? He wasn't here for forensics.

"Come on." He grabbed Jenna's arm, drawing her into the uncertain cover of the room. His boots made a heavy sound against sodden carpet—ichor and blood, splattered everywhere. They hadn't been satisfied with a hit-and-run, no, this was a vengeance raid. The legionnaires, all of them in standard black-tac gear, were dismembered, scattered across two twin beds. The antique television on a heavy graceless dresser was a shell of itself, its innards exploded from sliptime flex. One of the team had made a stand in the bathroom and lay spilled in that doorway, the body savaged and the head missing.

It took some doing to overwhelm four legionnaires. Hadn't they posted a guard on the roof? Not that it would have done much good, with this many *diaboli*. Had a *hazazel* been here, too?

That wasn't the only strangeness. There should have been more legionnaires—if it had been a full extraction team, where were the rest? Also, there wasn't nearly enough ichor, and what bits of rotting unclean he could see were inconclusive.

Think, Michael. Think. What he did next was important, and it had to happen fast. It was no longer enough to move. He had to move quickly, and well.

Jenna had gone transparent-pale, her lips slightly parted, and she stared at the bodies with wide, uncomprehending dark eyes. "*Lumina*." She didn't look at him. Was it shock, or were the *diaboli* moving in? "Jenna, listen to me."

She probably didn't even hear him. Her expression had a dreamy, wandering quality he didn't quite like, either; she should never have to see something like this. She should already be in an Eyrie, wrapped in silken safety, listening to the legionnaires tell her how beautiful she was, how valued.

"Jenna." He had to get her attention off the carnage. "Stand right there, okay?" He grabbed her other arm, too, and quelled the urge to shake her. "*Jenna*!" Here he was, practically yelling at an Incorruptible.

What was going *on*?

"Michael?" She focused on him, blinking, and a little sense stole back into those huge, wounded dark eyes. "What...who..."

"I don't know," he said, grimly. "But I'm going to look for ammo. Do you have a headache?"

She shook her head, the slow motion of a woman in nightmare's grip. Her parka's hood brushed her shoulders, a thin rasping sound. "N-no. I...Michael, these...these people..."

"Legionnaires." He didn't mean to sound curt, but these were his brothers, and their fate a reminder of what could happen to him in a heartbeat. Or—unacceptably—to her. "I'm getting ammo and whatever gear I can. I need you to be a lookout and tell me if your head starts to hurt."

He didn't really need her keeping watch, but it was better for her to look at the parking lot, the door, anything other than this. He backed her against the wall out of sight, and pointed at the walkway. "Watch that," he repeated. "Don't take your eyes off it, and if you feel *anything*, even the tiniest bit of a headache, say something. Okay?"

She nodded, her lips moving soundlessly. She'd gone chalky, and shivered. Michael turned away and began searching.

That was when he found out their tags were gone. *Diaboli* didn't often take those, they settled for simply savaging the bodies—so the legionnaires couldn't heal and rise again—before scurrying away into the dark.

I don't like this. He stared at one corkscrewed body, attempting to make the wounds match a *diabolo*'s claws or teeth, and came up blank. He'd be sure his eyes were fooling him if not for the missing tags, and the persistent, aching feeling of *wrongness*. That sensation had been his unwelcome companion since the beginning of this trek, growing larger and larger.

Now it was a monster, strong and vicious.

"May the Principle keep you," he said, finally, doing one last sweep to make sure he wasn't just overlooking the damn tags. There was another wrongness—their ammo was gone, as well as anything he could use. Michael let out a shaky sigh and rejoined Jenna, who had shut her eyes and slumped against the wall, one hand on the open door's knob, clutching like she'd fall over if she let go. Her knees trembled visibly, too. "*Lumina*. Let's go."

"They're all dead," she whispered. "Right?"

"But we're not," he reminded her, grimly. "And I'm gonna keep it that way."

"What do we do now?" When she finally opened her eyes, the open, aching vulnerability printed on her face made his entire chest seize up as if he'd just been stabbed again. Even with the parka's bulk, she was so small.

I do not know, my lady. But he had to decide. *He* was the one trained for this, *he* was the Legion's only presence here, and *he* was going to keep her safe. "We drive."

"Okay." Her chin rose slightly, and it hurt to see that fragile bravery. "We drive." Her gaze moved past him, and he moved with thoughtless, twitching speed to block it.

"Don't." He shouldn't bark a harsh command at an Incorruptible, but he had no choice. "Look at me instead."

She did.

"It's going to be all right," he lied, bending slightly over her, making sure she couldn't see. It was an outright falsehood, and worrying that it might twist him away from the true path of the Principle was a waste of time and energy. "I'm not going to let anything happen to you."

"That's nice." Her tongue crept out, dabbed her chapped lips, and a bolt of something hotter and sweeter than grace went through him. "But you might not be able to stop it."

"The hell I won't." He straightened his arms—why had he taken her shoulders again, and why was he holding her at arm's length? He didn't want to.

What he *wanted* to do was lean forward and touch those chapped, pale lips with his own. Fold her in his arms and hold fast, hoping his heat would warm her. He realized his palms were slippery and his body was taking notice of her nearness in the most pleasantly uncomfortable of mortal ways.

It was official. He *was* deviating from the Principle, just when she needed a true defender most.

"Look." He was hoarse, his throat full of something too dry to be anything but fear. "We've done all right so far. We'll keep moving, and they won't catch us." More lies. More *deviance*, and he was helpless to halt either.

"Okay." Those big dark eyes swam with hot salt water and a single tear welled out, tracing the soft curve of her cheek. "Okay, Michael."

He couldn't tell if she believed him, but that was beside the point. He had work to do. The first step was getting them back on the freeway.

The second, he decided, was just as simple. He dug in his pocket as he ushered her through the door, closing his fist around plastic and thin glass with a heart of circuitry.

He made a fist as he checked the parking lot, and on his way down the stairs, he crumpled the burner phone like a wad of paper, dropping it in a corner. Jenna perhaps didn't notice, stumbling behind him with her hand pressed to her mouth, and it was just as well.

KINDNESS DOES

THE HEAT WAS TURNED up as high as it would go, but Jenna couldn't stop shivering. I-70 began to climb with a vengeance, and by the time she remembered she had tea, it was stone-cold. The morning commute was well underway but they had escaped the city's confines early, and by the time the sun was directly overhead the truck was taking long shallow curves between rising foothills. Clearcut slopes alternated with thick timber, and Michael drove with his eyebrows drawn together and his hands tight on the wheel.

He said nothing. If he was angry, it didn't show, but she thought it was possible he was furious.

Very possible, indeed.

Each time Jenna shut her eyes the motel room rose before her, full of twisted, shattered bodies, blood and that nasty amber stuff smeared on the broken walls. How had nobody *heard* it? Or was there nobody left in the entire motel? Had the monsters gone room to room, a murderous housekeeping?

Her imagination just worked too goddamn well sometimes. "How did nobody hear that?" she managed, after taking a huge gulp of cold

Earl Gray with cream. It wasn't pleasant, but she needed the caffeine. "Why weren't the cops there?"

"Whatever happened, it was fast." Michael glanced at her. His jaw was set, and muscle flickered in it during his long silences. "Could be there's nobody left in the entire motel. We didn't check the lobby."

Well, hearing her own thoughts spoken aloud didn't help the squirrelly, panicked feeling under her ribs. "Oh. Yeah." She took a deep, shuddering breath. "Did you know them?"

"No. But they were legionnaires." He paused, maybe weighing the advisability of explaining corpse identification methods to her dumb ass, maybe struggling with grief, she couldn't tell. "We're all brothers."

"I'm sorry." And she was. The whole thing was hideous. "It's my fault, you know. I'm bad luck."

"What?" That earned her a very blue, very startled glance, and the Dodge wavered slightly as if the steering wheel had trembled. "Why would you say that?" He reached for the heater knob, but it was turned up as far as it would go.

How could she explain? First Dad, then Mom, then...everything afterward, a round-robin of disappointments, failures, derailments. The only commonality among them was *her*, and she knew it. "If it wasn't for me, you'd still be safe at home." She cradled her tea, gently, as if being careful now would change anything.

That earned her another sideways glance, but he had to return his attention to the road in a hurry. He did twist the knob for the fan, turning it down. The windshield was clear again, and some feeling had begun to creep back into her fingers and toes.

"You're Incorruptible," he said, finally, settling into the bench seat. "Things are drawn to you, but it's not your fault, you didn't ask for it. The Principle seeks to order and to heal."

Was *that* what it did? "It doesn't do a very good job." She looked out the window as another town flashed by, spreading from the interstate like a tumor. The mountains, patiently standing, waited for waves of time and people to wash over them. The truck engine kept up its steady humming, finding little difficulty in taking the hills. Really, whatever was under the hood sounded like a beast. Michael was a fantastic mechanic, to add to all his other talents.

Jenna could wait tables, work a dancer's pole, tell a Mondrian from a placemat, write a paper on French revolutionary pamphlets, and take a punch from a small-time hood of a boyfriend. Nothing even remotely useful among *her* skills, no sir.

"You don't know all the people you've helped." His shoulders relaxed a little, then a little more. "I saw you at work, you know."

Now she had to think about the crushed, ravaged SunnyTime. Strange, now she could remember all the crumpled bodies, not just the trucker's. In fact, she suspected she'd see them again, in Technicolor, as soon as she fell asleep tonight. Assuming, of course, that she was alive when the sun went down.

Sooner or later it would catch up. The monsters had numbers on their side, and they didn't get tired or cold, did they? She'd probably get Michael killed too, and here he was calling her *kind*. "Waiting tables isn't going to save the world." She longed to roll her window down and toss her tea into the slipstream, caffeine withdrawal be damned.

Might as well. What was the point of anything, anything at all?

"But kindness does, every day." How could such a large, well-armed man sound so naïvely certain? It boggled the mind. "It matters, Jenna. And you're kind. You can't help it."

"Like you're not?" After all, she had to admit he'd been nothing less than stellar so far. And what had he gotten for his trouble? Stabbed, and now his friends were dead too. His brothers.

"Not usually." Another shallow curve, the interstate rising swiftly along the face of a foothill. The trees began to rise as well, clearcut scars even more glaring because they were more infrequent. "We'll drive as long as we can today. If that's all right with you."

"Of course." She held her cold, useless tea and stared at the ribbon of dry gray pavement, bright and innocuous under pale winter sunlight. Great stacks of cloud peeked over the foothill-shoulders, and this road was probably a bitch later in winter. Still, there was a steady stream of traffic, and Michael's truck kept pace with smaller vehicles, passing semis like a loping herd dog at the edge of a flock. "I can take a turn at driving, too. You don't have to do it all."

"I like driving." A small, tight smile tilted the corners of his lips. "Just rest, Jenna. Try to sleep or something."

How could anyone possibly sleep after seeing so much carnage? Jenna dropped her gaze, staring at a white plastic lid, and decided to keep her mouth shut. Who knew when he'd get angry?

After all, she deserved it, and that he hadn't so far was a miracle.

Lunch was more fast food, but she didn't have much appetite. The place was full of other travelers, the drive-thru was packed, and Michael ordered for them both, saying he didn't need a bathroom stop. Splashing her face with cold water didn't help her mood, and she was glad to be back in the truck's relative quiet afterward.

She just couldn't stop imagining what one of those monsters would do to the crowd.

He set a drink container between them on the bench seat. "There's weather ahead," he said. "I got you some more tea. It's not Earl Gray, but—"

"It's fine. Thanks." Getting back on the freeway absorbed the next few minutes. This town nestled along a river wasn't the largest, but its smug little houses and brightly painted business buildings had the comfortable look of old slippers. Solid, dependable, boring, *safe.* What she wouldn't give to live in a little house like that, maybe with a husband who didn't get angry. Maybe even with a couple of kids she could drive to soccer practice and sit on tedious PTA committees for. "Michael?"

"Huh?" This time he was chewing thoroughly as he consumed his sandwich, and much more slowly.

"Do these luminous things, the thing you think I am—"

"Incorruptible." There was no sharpness to the correction, just quick interest. "And I don't think, Jenna. I *know*."

"Okay." She decided her stomach could handle a few more French fries. It was proof that she was a horrible person, really—a decent human being would be unable to eat after seeing such horrible things. Besides, it was a stupid question, she'd been about to ask if Incorruptibles could have kids. She had her period each month except for when the stress got too bad; thankfully, she'd just finished so she wouldn't have to worry about tampons for another little while.

Being chased by demons while on the rag was a final indignity, one she was glad to be spared. It couldn't take more than a couple days to drive to L.A. now, right?

We won't get there. You might as well face it.

Mom's optimism had all but deserted her. And now that she thought about it, Mom had been *different*, too. *You and your crazy ideas*, Dad used to say, with varying levels of exasperation or fondness. Jenna was in high school before she realized other people's mothers didn't feed every stray in the neighborhood or stop to listen to beggars' hard-luck stories with genuine attention, didn't almost got frostbite because they gave their coat to a homeless person.

Dad loved her, sure, but he also thought she took it a little too far. *If there's a sad sap within fifty miles, Jen, your mom'll find him and give him her wallet.* He sometimes joked about being her guard dog, and Mom would laugh. *My own Doberman*, she would tease, and ruffle his hair. Sometimes they'd even kiss, and young Jenna might make retching sounds.

Now, she'd give just about anything to see either of them again. Maybe she'd see the strange clarity, what Michael called the Principle, around Mom.

Wouldn't that be a trip. But why didn't Mom tell me, if she was like this?

They rejoined the interstate, traffic now much sparser. Painted poles along both sides of the freeway—gauges for snowplows, she thought—flickered by like lazy eyelashes.

"What were you going to ask?" Michael was well on his way to demolishing a bacon cheeseburger. He still didn't have any crumbs on his shirt, not even the cornmeal dusting the underside of the bun. It was ridiculous.

"Nothing." She stared at the mountains, eating mechanically, and the hum of the engine along with the rumble of tires was a lullaby. It was pretty scenery, especially if you imagined what it was like to be a tree getting ready for winter, retreating inside its trunk, pulling up the blankets, turning down the lights. There were aspen groves, too, shaking quivering fingers painted with the scraps of bright autumn.

"I'm gonna try to make Las Vegas tonight," he said, finally. "We'll stop there so you can sleep."

"Okay." It was on the tip of her tongue to point out that driving while fatigued was dangerous—but then again, he'd recovered from a stab wound to the *chest*, for God's sake, and he didn't seem to need much in the way of rest. Maybe a sleepless road trip was small potatoes. "What about you?"

"I could go straight for L.A., no problem. But you need rest, and—"

It probably wouldn't help, but she could try to be just as tough as he was. "Straight through is safer, right?"

"It's a good sixteen, seventeen hours." He frowned, clearly undecided. "More, because we'll have to stop for gas."

"Can you drive that long?"

"Yeah."

Of course he could. Why had she even asked? "I can also drive, and you can nap." Jenna examined the unbitten half of her chicken sandwich. It was gross, and she couldn't wait for a decent salad. Brown rice. Some fruit, even. To go into a grocery store for something to cook at home seemed the height of luxurious normalcy right now. "Right?"

"I just don't want to mess up." He took another huge bite, gave it a more-than-token chew, and down his throat it went in a wad. "When we get there and you're exhausted, they're going to think I didn't do everything right."

Good God, he's an overachiever. "Then I'll tell them otherwise. Right?" As if they'd listen to *her*. But maybe, just maybe... God. The whole thing was crazysauce.

It really sucked that she couldn't even think she was insane. If hallucinations were shared, they weren't delusions anymore, or were they? She hadn't gone for a psych degree.

Maybe she should have.

"Okay, Jenna. Anything you like." He went back to eating, halting only to flick the ancient radio on and spin the dial. The AM weather report began, a comforting drone.

She stared out the window, watching great hoods of stone rise along the continent's spine, fabric made of dark trees slipping down their shoulders. A kind of trance swallowed her, engine-hum and heatless sunshine mixing, and when she closed her eyes, a soft inner certainty bloomed behind her breastbone. It was warm and kind, and if it was the Principle he was talking about, she breathed deeply, wiped at her brimming eyes, and hoped it would stay.

SENT FROM ELSEWHERE

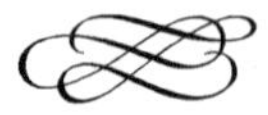

SHE WAS asleep by the time the Eisenhower Tunnel swallowed them. Asleep or in the deep healing trance of an overstressed and powerful Incorruptible, since her damp eyelashes fluttered and the outpouring of grace intensified. The truck's cab was too small to contain such beauty; the clarity moved outward in rippling rings. The mountains themselves were probably singing to her, overjoyed to feel the Principle's conscious presence in their stony arms.

The tunnel was a long, fluorescent-lit umbilicus, and a subliminal pressure eased as soon as they plunged into its glare. Jenna moved uneasily, her half-eaten sandwich resting in her lap along with cold fries. She wasn't getting enough nutrition—well, an Incorruptible needed better food than roadside grease, really. Maybe they *should* stop in Vegas and get her something decent, let her sleep in a bed.

The sensation of danger sliding away intensified. Not only that, but the truck's engine-sound changed too, and once they burst from the tunnel's westward mouth into yet more sunshine, they were on the downhill slope. The relief was almost physical, and Jenna made a small sound.

Moving cautiously, Michael fished the sandwich and fries out of her lap, stuffing them in the wrapper-filled bag holding the remains of his own meal. They still had the cooler, full of fresh ice from the last gas station. Something in there was bound to tempt her, she'd selected everything herself.

Utah and Nevada were next, and after that, California. It was probably even a pretty drive, when you weren't worrying about *diaboli* chasing you or an Incorruptible's fragile health. Still, his instincts were good, even if he hadn't listened to them enough.

"That's gotta change," he murmured, as the weather report fuzzed on a band of static. He flicked it off—heading downhill, he didn't need to worry as much about a freak storm miring them on the eastern side. The truck sped up, happy to be rolling with gravity rather than against it, and Michael's thoughts turned to the mystery of four legionnaires torn to shreds in a hotel room with their tags gone.

His own small metal tabs, along with their chain, nestled in his jacket pocket—which was against regulations in a big way, just another sign of how much he'd deviated in long years spent alone. He'd put the gorget on at their next stop, but from here on out he wasn't going to call in. They could afford to stop in Vegas long enough for her to get some sleep, but then he would drive, and drive, and drive until he saw the L.A. Eyrie.

And he would take her in publicly through the front door, making as much noise as possible. He hadn't been able to halt long enough to find a public computer, but that was probably for the best —even searching the address might trip a wire or two.

If what he suspected was true—and it probably wasn't, he was only a stupid grunt, there was likely a reasonable explanation even for this—she was safest that way. But even if he *was* stupid or wrong, he wasn't going to go against his instincts ever again.

Even if he deviated, even if he became what the Legion fought, he would protect her. They could kill him *after* he brought her in safely, if that was necessary.

His jaw set and his eyes burning, Michael Gabon drove.

SHE ROUSED an hour and a half later, stretching in the seat. "It's beautiful," she breathed, and a fresh flood of grace almost dragged his hands aside. They stayed nice and steady, though—at least he was still Legion enough for that.

It *was* beautiful. Traces of snow scudded away as they descended, and a stark landscape of less-thick forest and deep rocky gorge swallowed them. Michael would have viewed it strictly as terrain, rating each hill as defensible or why-bother, but Jenna leaned forward, a soft disbelieving smile turning her radiant.

"You like mountains?" It was a stupid question, one he regretted as soon as it left his mouth. But her smile widened, and if it made her even a little happier, he'd ask all the dumb questions in the world.

"Mountains are good. I like the sea more. But..." She bit her lower lip, rubbing at her eyes. "It feels like something's changed. It feels lighter. I don't know how else to put it."

"It has." Now he wondered for how long and by what small increments the Legion had retreated, leaving him stranded. He hadn't noticed the slowly rising waters because they had been gradual, low heat under a cold pot—and the lobster inside. "The closer we get to L.A., the better it'll be. More Legion means fewer unclean."

"Then that's good." She stretched again, hands clasped and legs stiffening. Once the desert arrived she'd be able to shed the parka, at least during the day. "Can I ask you something?"

Curiosity was a good sign; it meant relaxation. He couldn't make the traditional gesture of acceptance and attention, so he just nodded. "Of course, *lumina*."

"Please. It's just Jen." She didn't know that an Incorruptible's name was a treasure not to be taken lightly; still, it warmed him. She took a swig of her cold tea and sighed with what sounded like satisfaction. "I wanted to know... you said all the Legion are brothers, right?"

"Yes."

"What about sisters?"

Well, there's the Authorities. But that answer would just muddy the waters, he decided. "We mostly choose maleness. Female forms have more flexibility, more endurance, but a legionnaire has to be brutal. We're not subtle weapons." *Not unless we have to be.* Uneven tracts of scrubby brush flashed by, and he kept an eye on a semi ahead getting way too close to the edge of his lane first in one direction, then in another.

It was a little too early to be drunk, but maybe the driver was on a stimulant at the end of a long haul. Or simply fatigued. Mortal flesh had its weariness.

Jenna absorbed this. "You *choose* maleness?"

"Yes. Before we're sent." He paused, thoughtfully. She was far more alert to nuance than the average mortal. "Or so we're told."

"Sent from *where*?"

Sooner or later, every Incorruptible asked, so he gave the standard answer. "Elsewhere. An Authority could try to explain it; I'm just a soldier." He expected her to ask about the Authorities, but she surprised him again.

"Do all your brothers look like you?" Something about the question—a little too fast, a little too much stress on the final syllables—warned him. This was what she truly wanted to ask, for whatever reason. "I mean, blond, blue-eyed, the whole Kansas cornfed thing you've got going on?"

"No." *I look like Kansas corn?* He wanted to ask for clarification, but answering an Incorruptible took precedence. "We're all sizes and colors. We have to be, we're in all different mortal lands." The Principle occurred where it willed, and only the cultural trappings of it defense varied. The *diaboli* often took their shapes from mortal imaginings, and each country—not to mention each century—had its mortal protectors, who the non-mortal ones often copied in structure and organization. A guest followed the rules of his host, after all. "Or at least, we were. I don't know what's happened, or why the entire eastern continent is crawling with unclean and no Eyries. I was just supposed to keep my head down and do my job."

"Which was?" A faint shade of dissatisfaction colored her tone, hopefully not with *him*.

The semi ahead drifted to the right, its tires vibrating on rumble strips. Michael hoped the noise would wake the driver up long enough for the Dodge to safely pass. "Look for Incorruptibles, guard them, take them to the closest Eyrie." The most overriding duty. Then, in descending order, he could list the rest. "Kill the unclean, keep their numbers down. Avoid notice."

"Oh, is *that* all?" She played with her parka's zipper tab, a series of small, thoughtful tugs. "I guess I can see why you don't want anyone knowing about this, now. People would probably freak out."

Among other reasons. "Yeah. Anyway, the Eyrie's in Los Angeles; they don't call it that for nothing." He meant to make her smile, but there was no sign of amusement from the other side of the cab, so he hurried to continue. "At least not anymore. We're almost there."

"Oh." She studied his profile, her attention a warm forgiving weight. His marks were bathing in the grace, tingling as they worked deeper. How had he lived without that balm? "Are there any... are there any guys with red hair? Legionnaires, I mean?"

Now why would you ask that? Maybe she had a phobia. "I don't think I trained with any, but that was a long time ago." Just how long, he was hoping she wouldn't ask—mostly because he didn't remember anymore. It was a single road, all of it—awakening, training, long years of vigil in different places, moving when ordered to, fighting when called for, killing when necessary. A continuous, taut thread, ending the moment he looked up from the grill and saw a pale, tired Incorruptible tying her apron.

She'd given him too many easy questions; she went straight for the difficult one next. "How long ago?"

"A long time, Jenna." The truth was, he'd lost count of the years. He'd only been half-awake, plodding along from one day to the next, for quite possibly decades, and the only break in the monotony was the eruptions of violence when the unclean grew too bold. "It doesn't matter."

"You don't look a day over thirty."

"Thank you, ma'am. It's clean living." Why was he still trying to *joke*, of all things? At best, an Incorruptible would regard a clowning legionnaire with icy silence for daring to presume.

But this time, Jenna laughed. It was a gentle sound, flushing the entire truck cab with warmth, and Michael found himself smiling, the consciousness of having amused her salving some deep ache. It was good to hear an Incorruptible laugh; it was even better when it was *his* Incorruptible.

That's a dangerous thought, Michael. He sobered.

"I guess." Finally her chuckles faded, and she wiped at her eyes with a leftover napkin. "You don't even swear."

Of course not. "Not in front of a lady, at least."

She seemed to find that funny, too, which puzzled him, because it was only the truth. But Jenna sagged in her seat, laughing until tears slicked her cheeks, and Michael found himself mystified but laughing as well, shaking his head slightly.

Ahead of them, the semi slowed, and exited two miles later. The red Dodge continued, riding towards the far-off sea.

A NORMAL REACTION

UTAH ROLLED BY—ROCKS, sage, trees, widening patches of semi-desert. The wilderness birthed towns every once in a while, and by afternoon Jenna was hungry, her bladder was stretched, and even the new feeling of liberation and safety could take a backseat to a decent meal and the chance to stand up and walk a little. She didn't want to say anything, but Michael kept glancing at her and finally pulled off at the next rest stop, a bleached concrete cube set on an arid, windswept plateau. Dust danced across the parking lot, swept by a brisk breeze, and the foothills around them all but vibrated. At first Jenna thought it was freeway noise, but the humming remained when she shut herself in a dank, grimy bathroom stall and was faced with the prospect of hovering over a toilet seat.

Her legs ached already, and Vegas—not to mention L.A.—seemed an eternity away.

When she emerged into a dry chill breeze, Michael was bent over a road atlas spread on the truck's dusty red hood, frowning. His shoulders swelled under his jacket as he shifted, and Jenna halted at the top of the slight hill to the parking lot, examining him.

It was normal to feel pretty damn charitable towards a big-shouldered man who threw his own body over yours when the world exploded. It was predictable, really, and it didn't help that he was so diffident, so obviously pleased when she laughed at his infrequent jokes, or so carefully gentle. Eddie would have already popped her in the arm once or twice, telling her not to get fresh, and would have insisted she drive while also running down and critiquing every moment and movement while she did. The marks on Michael's arms and chest didn't so much say *felon* now as they shouted *strong*, and he seemed to know exactly what to do at any given moment.

It would be nice to be that certain.

She felt clearer now, almost lightheaded. Maybe it was all the mountain air, or maybe it was just that the low-level dread and creeping terror had fallen away. She hadn't realized how that slow, poisonous gas had filled her days and nights back home, slowly suffocating every inch. Of course, there were different things to fear. Her nightmares were real—the question of whether they were simply warning her or if she'd been locked onto some crazy mental wavelength and actually witnessing demon-murders was pretty academic at this point.

More troubling, and getting closer all the time, was San Francisco. Not the town itself, but the question of just what she'd seen crouching on the flaming wreckage of her mother's car.

Come on, Jenna. You know what you saw.

His brothers came in all shapes and sizes, Michael said. Jenna shut her eyes, that terrible day unreeling under mental fingertips, swallowing her whole.

The flames were greasy orange, the smoke billowing black, but the shape on the crumpled hood of her mother's Volvo was red. Jenna, bleeding on painted concrete near the shoulder, stared past the man dragging her away from the car as the shape unfolded, hearing horns blare as cars further back, not caring that the world had just ended, protested the sudden stoppage.

Tall and male, the shape was deceptively lean, and his long nose and strong chin reminded her vaguely of Eddie. Or Eddie had reminded her of that day, and maybe that was the feeling of familiarity when he'd twisted her arm during an argument, hissing be careful, honey, you'd better stay on the straight and narrow.

She'd tried. God, how she'd tried.

The man on the hood of her mother's car had a shock of red hair—not carroty but crimson, an angry starburst. Blood hair, and her own bloody hand, lifted as the sounds coming from the gouting smoke and licking flame were swallowed up in roaring...

"You all right?" Michael was suddenly right in front of her, the sunshine turning to gold in his hair and along his stubble; Jenna suppressed a flinch.

"Fine." Her voice wouldn't work for a moment, so she coughed, cupping her hand over her mouth to catch it for politeness's sake. The air was almost crystalline out here, despite a tinge of exhaust from the freeway's nearby drone. "Just thinking about old ghosts."

"They can't hurt you anymore." He squinted a little against sunlight. The sunshine picked out blond tips on each individual eyelash; his stubble was dark at the roots. His chest was ridiculously broad, and she had the sudden urge to put her palm flat against his T-shirt, covering the stab-scar, feeling the solidity of muscle and that strange, steady heat. Her palms all but itched with the idea, so she put her hands behind her and dropped her gaze to his throat, the Adam's-apple strangely vulnerable. "I'm here."

It was a nice thought. She opened her mouth to deflect, to keep some distance, but what came out instead was a plaintive question. "They won't send you back home, will they? When we get to L.A.?" It seemed kind of like the military, where you were posted to wherever and just had to deal with it.

"Not if you ask for me." He leaned forward slightly, and his own hands dangled at his sides, palms turned slightly forward before he pulled them back. The cold didn't seem to bother him. It would probably get warmer, though; that's what *desert* meant. "If you, uh, request me as your guard. They'll try to talk you out of it, because I'm just a low-level grunt, but..."

"I don't care." The obstruction was back in her throat. She was about to make a gigantic fool of herself, and couldn't stop. "We can find work in L.A., right? A place to live, and maybe we can—"

"You'll live at the Eyrie." Did he look, of all things, shocked? "You won't ever have to work again unless you want to. You're an Incorruptible, Jenna. You've got more important things to do than some dead-end mortal job."

Oh, how I wish that were true. "Too good to be true usually is, Michael." Was it still too good if there were demon-monsters lurking in the shadows? How many of the strangenesses or the nightmares, how much of the bad luck, had ever been *normal*?

She kept thinking of little things, like how Mom always knew who was calling when the phone rang or how Jenna had sat up in bed, not afraid but *expectant*, and suddenly known that her father, struggling in hospice care, had stopped breathing at last? The clock had said 3:47 a.m, and that was the time on his death certificate.

"I know it sounds that way." Endlessly patient, Michael just *stood* there, watching her. "At least you can come and see, right?"

The breeze was trying to shove her hair into her face, and she hadn't thought to dig in her purse for an elastic. Maybe she was cracking under the strain, the way some in the family whispered Mom would after Dad...

Jenna returned to herself with an internal thump she was surprised didn't echo. "It's not like I have much of a choice." She sounded prissy and spoiled, she realized, and stole a glance at his expression.

Thankfully, he didn't look angry, or even mildly perturbed. Just thoughtful, and he held his thumbs near the outer seams on his jeans like a soldier waiting for orders. "I know. I'm sorry about that."

"Why are you so nice?" It finally burst out of her, and she squashed the tiny internal voice that was trying to tell her to *calm down, don't rock the boat, you don't want to be left alone at this damn rest stop, do you?* "Why don't you get angry and tell me to mind my own fucking business or shut up?"

His jaw actually dropped a few fractions, and his eyes widened. "I would *never*." He rocked back on his heels, and that helped—it meant he wasn't looming over her, it meant she could *breathe*, but at the same time, she felt oddly bereft. He was a good windbreak. "I know you're had it rough, Jenna, okay? I know—"

"What do you think you know?" *I'm not angry. Why am I yelling?* It wasn't like her to raise her voice; she tried to push the unsteady, explosive feeling swelling inside her ribs away, corral it. It didn't want to be corralled. "I didn't ask for this! *I never did*!"

"I know." He didn't get angry even then, just took a cautious step back, putting his toes down first and rolling through, a cautious, catlike movement. Not as if he was afraid—Christ, he outweighed her by an order of magnitude—but like was was giving her room. "Go ahead, get mad. It's all right."

"Jesus, can you *stop being so nice?*" Jenna's voice broke in the middle of the high-pitched, forlorn cry, and she almost clapped her hands over her mouth, horrified at herself.

Because she was angry. She was *furious*, and she hated the feeling, because it was only a short step from there to Eddie Rayburn, wasn't it? bad enough to have monsters chasing her, but to become one was even worse.

"Anger's a normal reaction." The corners of his mouth twitched. "Besides, you're beautiful when you're angry."

Oh, for God's sake. She stared at him, speechless. What was *with* this guy? Of course, he wasn't, well, *human*, right? Nothing human could recover from a stabbing in mere hours. Maybe that was it.

And if he wasn't human, he might not be exactly safe, either. But if he wasn't, why would he have protected her this far?

"You're crazy." It was the only thing she could say, and it popped out of her mouth like a word balloon in a comic strip.

"I don't think I am, but they'll check at the Eyrie. Psychological testing's part of the package." He was *still* absolutely level, serious as a heart attack. He looked human enough, right down to that stubble and the faint asymmetry of his face. "I mean it, Jenna. I'm glad you're a little angry. It means you think I'm safe, so you can afford to let it out."

Was that the problem? "I guess." All the hot prickling under her skin went away and her shoulders sagged all at once. "I'm sorry." Now she was abruptly conscious that she'd been yelling at the one person who probably didn't deserve it in this fucked-up situation.

Maybe Eddie *had* rubbed off on her. Or maybe, just maybe, she couldn't tell what was reasonable anymore, because she was being chased by *monsters*, for God's sake. Or maybe both, a rough knotted snarl she didn't know how to begin untangling.

"You don't have to apologize." He gave the empty parking lot a once-over; there weren't even semis in the truck half.

Given the state of the restrooms, she didn't blame them. Nobody would stop here unless they absolutely had to. The landscape was beautiful, but it had a strange sterility, too. Almost as if it had been drained, except for tiny flickers of life hiding below the arid, inhospitable surface.

"Yes," she said, heavily. "I do. I guess we're getting back on the road, huh?" *I wouldn't blame you if you left me here.* She could sit on the curb and wait for the monsters—inhuman or otherwise—to show up.

It might even be safer, she decided. For him.

"Yeah. You hungry?" And to top it all off, he *still* didn't look angry. Just hopeful, with a small, pleased smile. His blue eyes kindled and his mouth was kind, and his hands weren't tense at all. He just stood at the edge of her personal space, the breeze combing past both of them, and waited for her to make up her mind.

Fine. Sure. Whatever. What does it matter, anyway? "I am." Surprisingly, it was true. Her stupid body kept demanding nourishment and sleep no matter what else was happening. There was a certain comfort in the fact. "You?"

"Yeah." He extended a hand, its palm cupped to catch sunlight, and waited some more.

Jenna laid her fingers in his. Warm skin, rougher than her own.

He didn't squeeze or pull, just turned, threading his fingers through hers. He was so warm. No wonder he had to eat so much, his metabolism was probably a locomotive engine.

"There's stuff in the cooler," he said, tentatively. "We can eat while we drive."

SOMETHING RIGHT

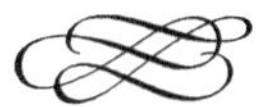

There was a whole lot of nothing and more mountains to get through before stopping again, but Jenna put the cooler between them and started making sandwiches. It was a good idea—a package of rolls, a package of deli meat, a package of cheese, a dab of mustard from a well-shaken container, and *voilà*, you had road-food. She didn't say much, but the sudden sharp spike of irritation in the parking lot had comforted Michael immensely. Feeling safe enough to lash out was better than her former numb, cautious politeness. It cleared the air, and he felt a lot lighter than he had on the other side of the tunnel.

It was almost like being on vacation. Not that legionnaires *got* vacations, or felt very comfortable attempting them—ease and peace were dangerous, they drew you away from the Principle. Training and routine were much firmer guardrails.

The road curved back and forth, sometimes just a little, sometimes in great swinging arcs. What forest there was turned dusty olive instead of the dark green of firs, and the open spaces were full of sand and sage instead of rolling grass. Towers of stacked stone eroded by time and wind abrasion stood chimney-sentinel, and as the afternoon wore on Jenna began to make soft remarks about the landscape, pointing out strange and whimsical things.

She didn't ask about the Legion, or about the unclean. Rather, she seemed to crave normality, and he did his best to give her some. It didn't hurt to pretend they were...somehow, in some way, friends. Or perhaps more.

Well, he was taking her to safety, so it kind of counted, right? He could imagine, inside the secret chamber of his skull, that they were together by choice instead of simply thrown into a rolling metal rectangle by an outer threat.

The land changed again, smudged peaks in the distance resolving clear and sharp, and they plunged into national forest land as the sun sank. A redgold glare filled the windshield, and when they finally hooked south to begin the descent to Las Vegas she had fallen into a deep reverie, watching the country roll by.

Michael drove, listening to her soft breathing, and let the fantasy fill his head.

A VOLCANIC ORANGE glow stained the desert night, drowning stars and a nail-paring moon. It was Vegas, the dame of the desert herself—not nearly as beautiful as an Incorruptible, especially if you knew what lingered under her skirts. Michael found a gas station before the city proper and got them off the freeway; as soon as their speed dropped Jenna woke with a gasp, her hands leaping in the cab's gloom like small frantic birds.

"It's all right," he said immediately. *Orient and comfort, that's the first step.* "We're getting gas. We're right outside Vegas."

"Really?" She rubbed at her eyes, her breathing quick and light. "Oh, wow. I dropped off."

"You need the rest. It's another five hours or so to L.A." Michael hit the blinker and piloted them diagonally across three lanes—oncoming and the middle turn lane—and over a bump into the parking lot. Fluorescent light drowned out orange city-glow and stung eyes used to watching a dark ribbon starred with headlamps and brake lights; Jenna rubbed at hers again. "But it's late. We'll stop for a little while."

He meant to be comforting, but her face fell. She'd slipped out of her parka, its extra bulk no longer a necessity. "Shouldn't we get there as soon as possible?"

"I scrapped the phone, nobody knows where we are. Might as well get some rest in a good hotel." He cut the engine and found himself looking across the cab at a woman with sleep-mussed dark hair and a shy smile. Her T-shirt, tucked neatly into her jeans, all but clung to her, and his mouth was suspiciously dry. "Besides, how often do you get to Vegas?"

"I've been here once in my whole life. My mom and I got a couple rolls of quarters apiece and played the slot machines." Her smile widened, and she looked around with interest, as if they could see the Strip from this far away. The gas station's fluorescent glow reached her hands and knees but not her face; her eyes were soft gleams. "It was fun."

Michael suddenly wanted, very badly, to keep that smile on her face. "Why don't we stop somewhere nice, then? Get a room, do some gambling." It wasn't hard to tickle slot machines *or* make a roulette ball fall where you wanted it, and he'd played his fair share of poker in army barracks across the years. He didn't think she'd be much good at *that* game—everything she felt was written across her soft, pretty face, underlined and in neon.

"We probably shouldn't stop to..." She realized it was a joke and shook her head, still smiling, but a thin shadow of fear lay under the amusement.

Well, he was clumsy as usual; he should just stick to his duties and nothing more. "Next time we can gamble. This time we can just rest for a little bit."

"Either way, it sounds expensive." A question lay under the

words, and she reached for her door, pausing and pulling her hand back as she remembered the drill.

He could feel good about that, at least. "Money's easy."

"Oh, really?" An arch inquiry as she stretched, pointing her toes, obviously eager to get out and use her legs. "Besides, if they can track a phone, they can track credit cards."

"I've got clean cards." It might have irked him, that she didn't think he had that particular matter well in hand. "And more than enough cash."

"I don't want to know how you got it," Jenna muttered, folding her arms and all but fidgeting. Of course, she probably had to use the little girls'.

Michael reached for his own door. "Standard procedure to keep a fair amount of liquidity in case you need—"

"I said I didn't want to know." But her smile remained and even strengthened, bathing him in the Principle's forgiving warmth. "You're really funny, Michael. Let's go, I need the restroom."

A half-hour later they were deep in a tangle of brightly lit streets, circling. He'd studied his faithful atlas that morning, so he had a good idea of the city layout by the time they got to the Wisteria Hotel, its front alive with creeping vines watered assiduously morning and night. Masses of flowers hung in carefully trimmed color-blotches, and the pillars along the front porch as well as the two massive glass revolving doors sparkled with self-satisfaction. Bands of tourists and those longing to fleece them thronged the wide sidewalks, and the entire place throbbed with light even at this hour. More than that, though, instinct told him it was comfortable and there was a vacancy, the Principle arranging matters now that a legionnaire was attending one of its bearers.

"It's so tacky." Jenna pushed her fingers through her hair, attempting to curb the waving mass. It was the first time Michael had seen her outright *grin*, and the sight threatened to take his breath away. "I love it."

Then so do I. He couldn't say it, of course, but he could think it all he wanted. "I'll get us a room."

"Does this place have a pool?"

For a moment he thought she was seriously asking, but then he caught the light, amused lilt in the question. "We're in the desert, baby." It wasn't a bad Elvis impersonation, even if he did say so himself. His mouth curved up into a half-smile. "They *all* have pools."

Her laughter dipped every inch of him in electric honey. It felt so good he almost missed the turnoff, but at least he was doing *something* right.

Or at least, so he hoped.

HUNDRED OTHER CONSIDERATIONS

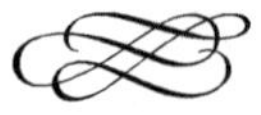

Whatever credit card Michael had must've been a good one; as soon as the middle-aged woman at the massive old-growth front desk got an eyeful of the small black plastic rectangle they were immediately treated like royalty. It was sheer heaven to walk again, not to mention hear something other than engine-hum and the weather report. It was even better to drop onto an over-pillowed king bed and stretch her limbs in every direction, as if she was eight and making a grass-angel in the backyard again. The place was just so bizarre, thick blue carpet patterned with golden fleur-de-lis, frosted glass wall sconces with gilded edges, wallpaper with stamped golden roses on an indigo background—completely over the top.

Mom would have loved it.

"I don't even want to gamble," she said to the ceiling. "I just want to walk around and find something to eat that isn't fast food."

"There's no shortage of options." Michael glanced at the suite, closing the door behind the well-tipped bellhop. Maybe working as a cook had taught him to be generous. "The casinos generally have good restaurants to keep everyone inside. The longer you stay, the more you spend."

He didn't unpack, and she only did so enough to take a shower. Desert dust had worked its way into the truck, and her hair took to extreme dryness just the same way it took high humidity—as an excuse to rise up in rebellion. What clothes she had left from their shopping trip were basic, but blessedly clean. It was a good thing Los Angeles was close, she was going to run out of panties at this rate.

It was a town built to disorient, but she was already so far away from the familiar it seemed almost normal. The sensation of a world slipping away underfoot, of regular rules not applying, turned everything—even the cheap plastic and tacky glitter—into a strange, gem-studded wonderland. It felt both exotic and blessedly mundane at once to step into a streamlet of people ambling in front of the vine-choked hotel, Michael looming at her left shoulder. Jenna could be completely anonymous in a crowd that didn't care she was being hunted, or that she'd been a down-at-heels waitress a few days ago. And when she reached down, blindly, to grip his hand, suddenly she was part of a unit, boy-and-girl vacationers walking the Strip.

Michael didn't seem to mind. In fact, his fingers laced through hers and he was smiling pretty much ear-to-ear when she stole a glance over her shoulder.

Happiness looked good on him. He let her set the pace, let her wander without continually tugging for her attention or squeezing brutally when he wanted to stop. In fact, he seemed more than content to simply follow along, occasionally leaning forward to look at something in front of her. Tall and buzz-cut, with his high-collared, hip-length leather jacket on even on a relatively balmy desert night, he looked like off-duty security, a cousin to the beefy men in suits and earpieces at almost every door. They tipped their chins at him, a salute he returned each time with a tiny, tight nod.

The casinos swallowed them. Everyone she passed seemed to be smiling, some bemused by the glitz and others delighted by the alcohol and flash. Employees hummed around in different crisp uniforms, and *they* were smiling too.

Funny, Jenna didn't remember everyone in Vegas being in a good mood last time. Far from.

It didn't matter. There were the glowing slot machines, the serious players with their good-luck objects and drinks arranged according to strict rules, and the heady ratcheting sound of the roulette wheel. Sometimes she could almost hear Mom's delight, pointing out the unexpected or hilariously garish—fantastically costumed employees or hustlers, gaudy machines from franchises that died decades ago, a blown-glass chandelier in violent vile colors dangling over a fake marble foyer, an honest-to-gosh Venetian *canal* trapped inside a building. Drinks everywhere, a laughing knot of college kids on some kind of break, grannies with reading glasses dangling on their chests and the grim demeanor of soldiers battling for a lost cause, Michael a solid warm wall when she stepped back in a hurry to avoid a slinky-gowned blonde cocktail waitress with a full tray and a mission.

He caught her waist, gentle fingers all but humming with leashed strength. This close, she could almost feel the marks on him moving, lines tickling as they ran through skin and flesh.

No, there was no *almost* about it. The waitress switched away on a pair of impossibly high red heels, and Michael's breath ruffled Jenna's hair.

She should have been afraid. She should have been downright *terrified*, this close to a big male so obviously used to violence. Instead, she felt a strange comfort like in the early days when Eddie was sweet and attentive, before breathless tension filled every corner and everything she did irritated him. Safety washed over her, a feeling so novel she almost closed her eyes to soak in it.

"You all right?" Michael's voice rumbled in his chest, and Jenna let out a shaky exhale. She nodded, watching the blonde reach a crowded roulette table and start distributing drinks with high speed and a certain bored, habitual style that shouted professionalism. Cocktailing was good, there were great tips as long as you could put up with the harassment.

"A little overwhelmed," she said, and his hands tightened a fraction. "Just...it's pretty crowded."

"Want to go back, get something from room service instead?" He breath tickled her ear—of course, he didn't want to shout. "Or takeout?"

She tried to figure out if *he* wanted to, or if he'd be angry if she said yes, or any of a hundred other considerations a woman had to take when dealing with a man. "Yes?"

"Then we will." But he didn't let go of her immediately. His touch lingered, and he held her hand, again, on the way back to the Wisteria.

THE LOBBY WAS DESERTED except for two bellboys joking at the front desk with the same middle-aged woman who had checked them in. A bright dart of unease lodged in Jenna's throat, and she looked hurried away.

"Everyone's smiling." She wanted to fold her arms defensively, but couldn't with him holding her right hand. "It's kind of weird."

"They can feel the closeness of the Principle." Michael looked down at her, his right arm out to hold the elevator door even though there wasn't any need. It was an old-fashioned gesture, and caused a funny flutter in her chest.

Thank goodness he didn't insist on climbing the stairs; he said the elevator was *safe enough*. Funny how two little words could be a comfort, or none at all. Her stomach flipped as he touched the button for their floor, and she should probably reclaim her hand...but she didn't want to.

She didn't want to at all. "Michael?"

"Hm?" He glanced up as the metal box began to move. If he grew his hair out a little, it would look a lot better than that short, angry chop-cut, but there was no way to tell him so without sounding bitchy. "What do you feel like eating?"

"I don't..." She blinked, her eyes watering. Her unease crested, more than a small sharp dart. Now it was a cold, greasy flood, and her heart began to hammer. "That's weird."

His shoulders stiffened. The elevator's lights flickered, and his fingers, still warm and safe in hers, tensed. "Jenna?"

"Ugh." Her temples ached, her neck suddenly too tight. It felt a little like heatstroke, but that was ridiculous; desert nights were cool and they'd just come from the mountains, besides. "Maybe I'm just dehydrated."

"Headache?" The elevator slowed, and he pulled her aside, so gently she barely realized they were moving. He had her tucked in the back corner of the elevator now, and the fuzzy realization that it was in case the monsters had found them threatened to turn her stomach fully upside down.

Ouch. It took concentrated effort to nod, the pain a sudden spike rolling down railroad tracks inside her skull. "Yeah. I...it's sudden—" *I should have known. Nothing good ever lasts.*

"It's all right." Michael dropped her hand, leaving her bereft, and stepped in front of her, facing the doors. "Everything's fine, *lumina.* All you have to do is stay where I put you."

Funny how even *that* bit of chauvinist bullshit sounded reasonable and entirely rational when he said it. Tears welled, tracking down her cheeks, and her shoulders hunched as her head gave an amazing flare of pain. "I shouldn't have gone out," she gasped. "They find me, right? I *knew* we shouldn't—"

"Don't *worry,* Jenna." Maddeningly calm. "We'll get our stuff and go. Might even be best."

"You paid for the night." God, why was she worrying about *that*? Her head gave another amazing, pounding flare of pain, but she straightened, breathing through it. She'd had tons of practice, after all. "Ouch."

"We don't *have* to sleep here. I just thought you could use the rest." The doors opened, and he beckoned her into the hall. "Relax, *lumina.* You're with me."

That's great, but what if you get stabbed again? She wasn't sure she could scrape up whatever-it-was that had saved them last time again. She didn't even know what she'd *done.*

The room was just as they'd left it; Jenna cast a longing glance at the huge bed and hurried to grab his large duffel. Michael took it from her, though, lifting as if it weighed nothing and slinging the strap diagonally across his body. He grabbed her rolling suitcase, too, tugging the zipper closed the rest of the way and locking it with a swift motion. He glanced at her, nodded, and headed for the door, beckoning her along. "Stairs."

Great. She tried a pale smile. "How did I know?"

"I can carry you if it gets bad."

It wasn't so much the idea as his patently serious tone that wrung a small laugh from her, ending on a gasp as her headache mounted. It was all so *sudden.* She hurried after Michael, the duffel like a familiar fellow soldier riding his back, and the stairwell echoed with their footsteps—his deliberate and almost soundless, hers a terrified pitter-pat.

It was only four floors, but then they had to go through the lobby to reach the entrance to the parking garage. Halfway across that echoing expanse, her head turned into a volcano and she halted, staring, as the bellhops at the front desk both turned in unison, tiny trails of black steam-smoke rising from heads and hands and toes. Behind them, the woman at the desk raised her chin, her face a pale somber moon instead of a broad, laughing apple-doll's. The fumes wrapped around her as well, and her nametag glittered uneasily.

Three gazes swiveled unerringly in Jenna's direction, and it took her a moment to figure out what was wrong.

All six eyes were tarry black from lid to lid; Jen's feet tangled with each other. The almost-fall snapped her gaze aside, and it was a good thing—Michael told her later that those black gazes could hypnotize. It was, she later learned, how a Corruptor kept a new host still for long enough to infect it.

Or, if it could not, long enough to kill.

WOULDN'T MIND WINNING

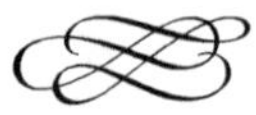

IT WAS a good thing they'd gone out; if Michael kept her in the room they might have been trapped again. Especially with a Corruptor on their trail. The hissing stench-beasts made wonderful trackers, slipping from one host to the next, sniffing their way along their quarry's trail, and driving their mortal shells mercilessly. This one was mid-grade, its fumes thinned by division of control among three soul-eaten corpses.

Jenna almost tripped; his hand closed around her elbow and he righted her gently, absently. The Corruptor's gaze glanced off his marks and their invisible bolstering of muscle, skin, sinew; Michael snapped a glance at the walkway to the parking tower.

Clear enough. Maybe the Principle had arranged a chance at escape, too.

Three no-longer-mortal mouths moved in unison, giving birth to a peculiar, distorted hiss. "*Sssoftling,*" it said, a chorus of moaning and feedback lingering under the word. "*I ssshall sssuck you dry.*"

"Jenna." His hand found the truck keys, pressed them into her warm, soft palm. "Go."

"Michael..." His name rode a small breathy sigh. She winced

again as the Corruptor flexed, the two bellhops stepping away from the desk and the woman behind it sinking down. The woman was preparing to leap the over the obstruction, that much was obvious, and the bellhops were moving with the dreamy twitching of the unclean. At least a Corruptor couldn't use sliptime until it stopped riding host bodies and coalesced.

There still remained the problem of how it had come in the front door. That meant there was a fourth mortal somewhere nearby, possibly dead but most likely held in reserve to overwhelm a legionnaire—or strike at the *lumina* who reeled unsteadily, clutching at a handful of sharp metal keys. Her old, battered leather purse swung daintily; he hoped she didn't have anything in the suitcase she couldn't stand to lose.

"Jen." Her name filled his mouth, sweet as apples. "Go to the truck. Now. Drive out of here." Michael's back was alive with gooseflesh.

"I can't leave you," she whispered.

He was the only familiar thing in her world anymore, so it was only to be expected. Still, her reluctance warmed him all the way through. "I'll find you, *lumina*." He took a step, another, testing the weight of his duffel—easy to fight even with that, it wasn't as heavy as armor. His hands flickered, and the gun-butts filled his palms. 9mms would barely make a dent in most unclean, but if he could kill each mortal host and isolate the Corruptor, he could force it to take physical form.

And *then* he could kill it with something else, something sharp and glowing with grace.

"*Sssoftling*," it hissed again, all three mouths moving in a chorus of sticky, sickness-laced satisfaction. "*Look at me. Look upon your doom.*"

"Go," Michael said, hard and loud over the siren song. "Don't look back. Just drive."

Jenna's trembling threatened to infect him. "I *can't* leave you." It was a thin, croaking whisper.

He gently shouldered her aside, every nerve alert. Where was the fourth host? It couldn't be in the parking tower, that was too far away for the Corruptor's control.

"*Look at usss,*" the Corruptor repeated, and the middle-aged woman leapt atop the front desk, muscle and bone creaking as it obeyed an inhuman imperative. "*The Legion has forsssaken thee!*" A whine under the words carried a note of desperation, and Michael saw what he'd hoped for—a pair of wingtips lying like stuffed sandbags behind the swinging half-door that blocked off customer space from the employee realms.

Ah. The Corruptor had driven its last host right behind the desk, and dropped the corpse to jump into the woman. "Go," he said again, fiercely. "*Go,* Jenna!"

She stumbled away, making a beeline for the walkway to the parking tower as Michael leapt, both guns tracking the bellboy on the right as the Corruptor concentrated, its fumes distilling into deadly smoke. He fired twice, the bellboy on the left hissed, showing blunt human teeth warping into filed points as the Corruptor yanked on cell structure and muscle-strings to turn mortals into something closer to its natural form. Right Bellboy screamed, a long cheated howl as bullets tore flesh, tumbled off bone, and exited in a splatter of steaming, blackened chunks. "*Run!*" Michael yelled, and landed hard, snapping a shot at the woman atop the desk to keep her from springing at Jen's trail. The Corruptor drove the woman's body down, Left Bellhop streaked for Michael with unholy speed, and he did not have to win, he only had to hold them long enough.

I wouldn't mind winning, though. Time to go to work. Two bullets in the Left Bellhop, not enough to put him down since both were glancing shots, the thing was streaking forward not in sliptime but with the hysterical, spooky speed of a berserk mortal. Most of all, he didn't mind the casualties. The mortals were already dead, the Incorruptible was not going to join them if he could help it; he was just glad she wouldn't see this.

Straining, boots leaving black marks on the faux-marble lobby floor, he skidded aside and snapped off another shot at the thing on the desk. The woman's body was swelling obscenely, poison gathering in mortal flesh, and long training averted his gaze just in time as its mouth opened and a jet of slippery smoking ectoplasm bulleted past him.

The toxin wouldn't kill him and any blinding by venom was only temporary, but it still hurt like hell and more importantly, could not be permitted to slow him down. Dodging the splatter, he met the remaining bellhop with a crunch, driving it down as the thing sought to scurry past him and onto Jen's thin sparkling thread of cleanness and clarity cutting through the stink of mortal flesh turned to unclean will. A quick hard stamp, the thing's sponge-rotten skull breaking—pushing the cells to behave unnaturally without the Principle's light touch weakened them past easy repair—and the Corruptor howled, suddenly forced into one body instead of three.

He could have finished it then, if he'd been fast enough. Just as Michael was turning, though, an inopportune tour bus docking in front of the Wisteria's doors had begun discharging its cargo, and a group of travel-weary, excited mortals pushed through the revolving doors, chattering excitedly.

The Corruptor let out a hideous barking laugh, and the corpse behind the front desk began to twitch. It hadn't been dead at all, just waiting in reserve.

And now the thing had several fresh mortals to infect, as well as weight of numbers to pull Michael down.

BIG FAT NOTHING

JENNA'S FEET thudded painfully against concrete, and she tried desperately to remember where Michael had parked. It was a good thing he hadn't let the valet take the truck; she saw a familiar yellow parking pillar, its paint chip-cracked in almost-random patterns, and let out a barking sob of relief. There was the red Dodge, the back of its familiar canopy watching her with two windows and a small door.

What if it doesn't start?

She told the perpetually worrying part of herself to take a hike, clipped a parking pillar, glancing off as her shoulder flared with numbness, and scrambled for the driver's side. There was only one key big enough on the ring, but her fingers were clumsy fear-sausages. She rammed the key home on the third try and heard someone swearing at a husky, monotonous clip. Pretty creatively, too, stringing together obscene syllables with furious invention.

I sound like Rach. Her friend could swear a blue streak. She was probably never going to see Rach again.

Jenna twisted the key the wrong way, let out another cry of frustration—thank God the thin metal strip didn't snap—and turned it the opposite direction. Fluorescents overhead dimmed, fuzzing out, and she climbed into the driver's side in a wild tangle of arms and legs.

Now all she had to do was remember how to drive. "OhGod," she whispered, over and over, jamming the key at the ignition. The engine turned over, caught with its familiar buttery purr, and she let out another sobbing string of relieved invective.

Thank God it's not a manual. She dropped into reverse and hit the gas, narrowly avoiding sideswiping another damn parking pillar, and stood on the brake. The jolt shook her back into sense; she fumbled for the gearshift and the little orange bar moved over to "D". *Now don't hit anything, Jen.*

She generally used public transportation; her driving was rusty at best. There was Eddie's Camaro, of course, but he would no sooner let her behind the wheel than he would admit to any wrongdoing, especially when he was in a petulant mood. The truck handled well but it was still a barge, and she cut the turn too close as the whale-swimming vehicle slid sideways a fraction in front of the panted walkway to the lobby doors. The passenger-side mirror took a hit, dangling forlornly as she roared past a pillar, and something hit the back of the truck with a crunch.

Just keep going, he'd said. Jen was completely unaware of screaming as the back end fishtailed. The tires bit and she slewed onto the street, barely registering the giant silver bus disgorging a crowd of weary travelers in front of the Wisteria.

Boy, are they gonna get a surprise. She should stop to help, but what could she *do*? A big fat nothing.

As usual.

Thankfully, she didn't hit anyone, but a glare of headlights and blaring horn told her it was close, so close. White-knuckled, staring, she jammed the accelerator down, and might have considered praying if she hadn't been so busy. *Freeway, find the freeway, got to find the fucking freeway. Which one, which way?*

She didn't care. Any direction would do, as long as it was *away*.

Something big thudded on top of the cab and she cried out again, the truck jumping like a live thing as the wheel twisted. She all but stood on the brake, whipping the wheel to the right, and for a long aching second the vehicle yawed as physics took down notations, peered over her glasses, and decided what to do with so many hundreds of pounds of truck moving at whatever speed on a much-mended surface street. Tires jumped the curb, pedestrians scattering, and Jen stamped on the accelerator again, pushed past terror and into the clear prickling flood of survival adrenaline soaking every tissue. Her fingers gentled, her grip almost loving on the wheel, the truck leapt off the curb back into the street, and she skidded through a yellow light, narrowly avoiding a collision with a blue semi that locked its brakes and blatted.

More thuds and thumps overhead. Something was *on* the truck, and she saw a blue freeway sign, half-blasted by flying sand and just barely readable. Thankfully it held an arrow, pointing the way she was already going.

Don't stop, Michael had said. *Drive.*

So she did, flooring the accelerator again, and the engine barked once before swallowing fuel and translating it into wild acceleration. She was pressed back into the bench seat, Michael's hollow worn in its cushioning too big for her, and her foot almost slipped free of the gas. *God damn it.* "Fuckitall *move!*" she yelled.

Rattling, bucking, she ran two red lights before the onramp to 515 South opened up on her right, and she jerked the truck aside as more thumping and thudding smashed through the canopy and into the bed.

Shit shit shit... Gasping, eyes wide with terror and every inch of her leaning forward as if to will the truck on, Jen's breath turned to short puffs of vapor. The sudden, unnatural cold burrowed into hands, feet, heart, and she knew with miserable certainty that the thing in the bed was one of the demons; at long last they were going to get what they really wanted.

Her.

LIFE IN HIM YET

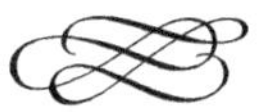

The last corpse-mule died hard, the Corruptor spending force recklessly, but Michael had arms and legs wrapped around the bucking, heaving mortal shell and a quick movement sheared the cervical column with a greenstick snap. Rattling, bumping, swaying, cold metal under his back and the thing's clawmarks slicing across the ancient circuitry-map on his skin, he gave an extra wrench to make sure there was no remaining avenue for the Corruptor to force growth along. Blood, already turning to thick amber ichor, sprayed in a high-tension jet; he'd almost taken the thing's head clean off.

May the Principle receive you, he prayed for the mortal who had been eaten, but there was no time for more than the brief pained thought because the Corruptor was coalescing, stealing heat from the air to power its transition as it found all other avenues cut off. It could not infect a legionnaire unless he had fallen away from the Principle, and even then only fitfully—but it could try digging its smoky claws in and scrabbling to find purchase, tearing Legion flesh as it sought blindly for continuance.

It took shape above him, malformed smoke building an obsidian skeleton, and he untangled himself from the corpse with a violent scrabble. His fists blurred upward to break glass-crunching bones, his lips skinning back as noisome shards fell like daggers. The trick was to cause so much damage the thing could not heal itself quickly enough, draining its swelling infection from the fabric of the mortal world until it vanished in a puff of mist.

Unfortunately, with the thin metal floor under his back bucking plus the cold screaming wind tearing at anything not nailed down, not to mention bits of careening equipment knocked free by the struggle, a few of his strikes didn't land with as much force as necessary. The thing fell upon him, its thin pointed nose-tip against his cheek and its glassy teeth snapping together as it lunged, claws sinking into his legs and arms to provide traction, attempting to open his jugular.

Michael let out a coughing roar, the wine-sweet rage of battle filling every vein to bursting, and for a moment he felt them again, the weight and bulk behind his back swelling from shoulderblade to hip, muscles twitch-working to provide motion to the two appendages lost when he *arrived* in this cold thankless hell of a mortal world and was set to long years of fruitless, murderous watching.

The thing howled, a spiraling falsetto drilling through eardrum and brain at the same time. Its teeth snapped like a good clean break on a billiard table, and Michael's own fingers turned clawlike. Grace poured through him, fractionally sweeter than the rage, and at the center of that flood was a thin thread of coolness, straight and pure. It had Jenna's voice, sweet and soft.

Don't forget, the Principle whispered. *You fight to protect, not to conquer.*

His fingertips ached as the knives flashed into being, golden circuit-chased metal stabbing and twisting, shredding the Corruptor's bones and showering Michael with yet another crop of stinging needle-slivers. He slashed, again and again, and when the thing broke and was sucked into a screaming, dancing pinpoint, its long dying cry was another sliver, desperately seeking to lodge in a mortal ear unprotected by golden light.

It winked out, the hideous scream fading into nothingness. Michael sagged on cold metal, his ribs heaving, and smelled his own copper-hot blood. Wind whooshed and rattled, pouring over him in clean, stinging waves, and he let himself close his eyes for a few bare moments. Grace stung his fingers, his toes, settled against the marks and burrowed inward. It even, for a single weightless instant, made the invisible memory of feathered things trapped underneath him flex and fill again; a sweet piercing pang went through him, crown to soles.

Then it was gone and the truck drifted to the side, running over stutter-strips cut into concrete to jar a fatigued driver back into temporary alertness. Michael lunged upward, but the driver's correction tipped him at the wrong moment and he had to stamp, his right boot slipping then holding as his knee flexed, and the resultant thudding made the truck swerve nervously again.

She was probably terrified. There was a hole in the canopy roughly the size of his own body, and the wind of eighty miles-per snatched and fingered at every surface. He racked his brains, trying to figure out how to get into the cab without frightening her any more and possibly sending them both off the road in a tangle of metal and glass. He could, he supposed, shield her from enough of the shock to keep her alive—*if* he could get close enough to the driver's seat the moment things went wrong.

The engine gulped at fuel, a subtle knocking developing in its steady cycle. Nothing to be worried about yet, the old beast had plenty of life in him yet.

I hope I do, too. He moved, slow and steady, bent almost double, until he was as close to the driver's seat as he could get. The back of the cab was a solid wall, and he'd added the bulletproof sheet to it himself back at the warehouse. It was a shame. He was going to miss his garage, every tool neatly in its place and the big red engine-lifting hoist gleaming over its hand-dug central well.

The marks of the Corruptor's claws were slow to close. He crouched and bled silently, alert for any sudden change in direction or speed. Could she feel his nearness? Would she know what it meant?

Michael told himself to stop wondering useless things, but more questions crowded in with the wind's persistent belling.

The unclean lied, for amusement or to cause pain. You could not trust a single barbed word, even if dipped in honey. But why would a Corruptor bother to say something any legionnaire would never believe?

Why, in the name of the Principle, had it said...what it did?

The Legion has forsaken thee.

CAPPER ON EVERYTHING

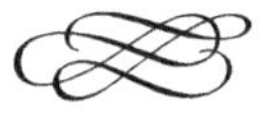

THERE ARE VERY few things more terrifying than a slope of pavement unreeling down a slight hill to rejoin the interstate while you roll to a stop somewhere vaguely southeast of Las Vegas, dust dancing in headlights and someone else's truck with a smashed camper silent as a grave.

Whatever had been bumping around back there had gone still, and Jen's head didn't hurt anymore. Her shoulder did, though, badly enough that the stupid, sunny optimism she'd been fighting for years was pretty much effectively canceled. All it took to get rid of that bullshit was a demon-infested road trip, apparently.

Was there something hideous in the back of the truck, just biding its time? She had to *think*.

No headache was a good sign. She put the truck in park and stared at the headlights cutting a white cone in the night. She'd have to fish out the road atlas, look at where she was. The truck had three-quarters of a tank, she would have to figure out how to get more. She had her purse, and the demons could track credit cards. Her bank account might even have a freeze on it, if they thought she was dead.

L.A. was as good a destination as any. Or she could ditch the truck back in Vegas and hope to find some kind of work before the monsters hunted her down.

One problem at a time, Jen. That's how you survived Eddie, and that's how you'll survive this.

She was beginning to get the sinking feeling that perhaps surviving wasn't an option. "Okay," she whispered, looking at her hands on the wheel. Her knuckles weren't white anymore, but it was close. Her throat was dry as the cold, still desert sand, and her knees trembled. "Okay. First thing, Jen. What's first?"

Well, that was simple. Finding out where she actually was and looking for her next stop. She had to unclench her fingers and look for the road atlas. It should have been on the seat near her right hip, but God only knew where it had ended up during the wild bucking ride out of the parking tower.

What was the point? They were going to hunt her down anyway. Was Michael all right? Maybe her first move should be going back and looking for him.

I'll find you, lumina. Well, that was nice, but if he could find her, the demons could too, right? So the first thing was *definitely* to look at the road atlas. Still, she couldn't just leave Michael behind in Las Vegas with a bunch of demons. And getting any further away from the city meant she could run out of gas and be stranded on the side of the freeway.

Wouldn't *that* just put a capper on everything. How much worse could it—

Something drummed on her window and Jen started wildly, half-swallowing a scream and throwing herself sideways. Her foot slipped off the brake, but the truck was in park so it merely settled a fraction, pointed downhill and longing to obey gravity.

"Jen." A familiar face streaked with blood and grime peered at her through dust-speckled glass, two fierce blue eyes in a mask of splattered, drying goo. "It's me. It's all right."

OhGod. Relief crashed through her. She scrabbled at the seat belt's release, then at the door. It opened, heavy metal swinging; she slid out, throwing her arms around his waist and hugging as hard as she could.

Michael winced but hugged her back, gently but definitely. He was tall and warm and tattered, blood-crusted flaps of his T-shirt crushed between them, and Jen swallowed tears. "Michael! Oh, my God, are *you* all right? I didn't know it was you, I thought it was one of those things, and then I didn't stop and—"

"You did right." He rested his chin atop her head. "Exactly right, *lumina*. You did perfectly."

It was good to hear, though she didn't quite believe him. Still, with her cheek pressed close, listening to his heartbeat under the words rumbling in his chest, she felt, well...

Safe. Unreasonably, completely safe. Again.

A chilly desert night breathed around them, sand hitching a ride on dry crackling wind, and Michael took a deep shuddering breath. She hugged him again, fiercely, and realized he was battered and bloody. "Shit." She tried to loosen her arms and step away, but he didn't let go. "You're hurt. We've got to get you..." *To a hospital*, she wanted to say, but that was ridiculous, wasn't it? "...some help," she finished.

"It's fine," he said into her hair. "You're all I need, *lumina*."

It was ridiculous, the way her knees went weak. It was doubly ridiculous that she couldn't just step away, couldn't think of anything to say that wasn't silly or prim. She simply stayed still, her eyes shut tight, listening to that heartbeat, until he moved.

"Let's get you somewhere safer," he said, and pushed her gently back into the truck. "I'll drive."

WEIGHING OPTIONS

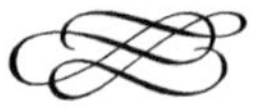

THEY WERE POINTED southeast on 515, and Michael decided that was as good a direction as any. It was a five or six hour drive to L.A. if they swung west on 40, longer if they took the old Route 66, and he longed to go straight through without a single stop. He thought it over while he settled into the driver's place and Jen huddled on her half of the bench seat, shaking with exhaustion and adrenaline, a ring of white around her dark irises and her hair a wild glory.

He still felt her slenderness against him, fitted close like she belonged there, her arms resting on bruises, scrapes, and slowly seeping claw-marks. The Corruptor's poison slowed his healing but couldn't halt it entirely; still, he was glad of the dark so she wouldn't see the extent of the damage. It was good to be in the cab instead of the back, and doubly good to hear her breathing, reassuring him she was alive and unwounded. She looked a hairsbreadth away from shock, but on the whole, they'd gotten off lightly. Luck or the Principle, he didn't care as long as it kept him whole enough to fight.

"How did it find us?" she finally asked, after a few miles had unreeled under the tires. "It was stopping, right? That's what did it. Stopping and going out walking. I shouldn't have—"

"There's only so long you can sit in a car without needing to stretch your legs." The last thing he needed was his *lumina* blaming herself. "I should have thought that the Strip would be crawling with the unclean, there's good prey for them there. Just bad luck, that's all." The almost-untruth made him nervous, but on the other hand, what other explanation was there?

The Legion has forsaken thee.

It was impossible. Unthinkable. He'd even gotten rid of the phone, but of course, news of a traveling Incorruptible would spread like wildfire, and the unclean would pass it along every likely route. It did not have to be treachery.

And yet. Why would one of the unclean use those specific words?

"The only kind of luck I have," she muttered again. Both of them smelled of rotting ichor now, but he hadn't had the heart to push her away when she clung to him so desperately. "No, that's wrong. *You're* good luck."

It was nice to hear her say it. "Kind of destroyed your nice normal life, though." Even if he suspected there had been nothing nice about it. How long had he been wandering that city, a hairsbreadth away from her and unable to help? The idea chilled him right down to his reinforced bones.

She let out a trembling, shaky noise that was perhaps meant to be a laugh. "At least I don't have to worry about Eddie anymore."

"Was that his name?" He rubbed at his eyes, wiping away crusted blood and ichor, beginning to believe they were both still alive and their trail was clear for the moment. "I'd forgotten."

"Yeah." Jenna sighed, the clear glow of grace quivering as it spread. She was, incredibly, relaxing, as if she found his presence comforting at last. "He was nice in the beginning."

"They usually are." He suppressed the thin crimson ribbon of rage in his guts, thinking about what this *Eddie* had likely done to turn her into such a bruised, uncertain shadow. It would be satisfying to quietly find the fellow and mete out a little justice.

Once she was safe. That was the mission, and by the Principle itself, he was going to complete it.

"Are we going to drive straight through?" She shifted again, fidgeting. A ghost of metallic adrenaline soaked her scent, teasing at his control. "I was trying to figure out where to go."

You're smart, lumina. And brave. That bravery in such a fragile vessel shamed him even as it had saved her. "We'll stop someplace small." Their pursuers would be expecting them to ride hell-for-leather, and Michael found he didn't want them to be right about anything, much less their direction and speed. "Less chance of the unclean, they tend to gravitate to urban centers. More prey."

Her shudder was visible even in the dim glow from the dash. "Great."

"On the other hand, cities provide cover. It's just weighing the options, that's all." Headlights drenched the inside of the cab for a moment; he focused through the glare and kept the truck at a reasonable seventy. The knocking in the Dodge's engine was subtle, but it was there. "That time we were unlucky, but we're close to LA. Once we get to the Eyrie..." Michael couldn't bring himself to finish the sentence, even if it would comfort her.

His conscience wouldn't let him.

"I'll tell them you're a good guy, and that I want you to stick around." An eager student reciting her lessons, probably to keep the fear at bay. "Right?"

"I'd like to." He kept his eyes on the road. Fatigue-fog would be a danger; he needed a couple hours to let grace and the marks knit him back together. If they hadn't left the hotel room at precisely the right time, they might have been trap-bottled—the Corruptor could have been an advance guard or merely the front-runner of a hungry pack of unclean. "We'll stop someplace small and rest for a little bit, then go for L.A. All right?"

"Why ask me? I have no clue." Then, amazingly, she unbuckled her seat belt, slid across the bench, and began digging for the central belt. "Do you, uh, mind if I sit here?"

"Not at all." *I'd like that. Probably too much.*

Her hip settled against his. She was still trembling, slight movements communicating to his own muscles. And when she laid her head on his shoulder, the resultant flood of hot, sweet grace from the contact was enough to make a legionnaire drunk.

Michael set his jaw, and began looking for a place to rest.

NOT DIMINISHED BY GIVING

The sign read *Highwayman Inn*, and the place was a single low building with twelve room-doors marching in tired succession, its parking lot unraveling into gravel at the ends. The stars were out, rivers of jewels crossing the cold, remote desert sky; the air was so dry it tickled the nose, stripped moisture from lip-corners, and made every hair-end crackle with electricity. There was no traffic in this lonely place late at night, though the highway hummed in the near distance. You could see a pair of headlights coming for a long while before they reached you, and Jen liked the thought.

She also liked the thought that there were plenty of exits, though Michael probably knew more about that than she did.

It was the type of place that took cash and asked no questions, and with Michael looking the way he did that was a blessing. She hadn't realized how battered he was until he stepped into the weak circle of light outside the barred window that housed the office. His shirt was in tatters, his jeans were ripped all the way down his left leg, and the black crust at the edges of flapping cloth was dried blood, not to mention strange amber monster-fluid.

He might not be human, but he bled like one, and now Jen knew human blood looked black at night. She should have been the one going up to the window, but Michael just shook his head. *No,* he'd said, tight-lipped. *You'd be too nice.*

She couldn't quite figure out if that was one of his infrequent jokes, or a statement on her negotiating capabilities.

The full bed in the room was sagging, the carpet was dingy and starred with cigarette holes, but the linens were clean and there were two good towels. The lights worked just fine, too, and seeing the full extent of the damage to her traveling companion turned her cold.

"My God," she whispered as Michael tossed his duffel onto the bed. How he'd managed to retain it was beyond her; her own suitcase was gone with the wind. "You're really hurt."

"Corruptor," he said, pacing to the window and peering out through the curtains before yanking them shut with quick efficiency. He was moving just the same, a prowling, graceful glide, and he didn't seem that hurt despite the mess his clothes were in. "Takes a while to heal. I'm fine."

"You're *not* fine." Her throat was closing up, her arms and legs shook like a gelatin salad, and now that they were stopped all she wanted was to be back in the truck and driving again. "Those need disinfecting, and you need a bandage, and... you came back from being stabbed, but—"

"Looks worse than it is." He glanced at her before striding to the door again, looking at it like it had offended him. "I just need rest, and so do you. You want to get cleaned up?"

"No, I don't." Jen's hands curled into fists, released. This same unsteady, unhealthy energy had grabbed her right after she'd escaped Eddie and stood in the middle of her new studio apartment, listening to the almost-silence of a large building stuffed with people and shaking with the need to keep running, keep doing, keep *going*. "I want to get the first aid kit out again and take a look at you."

He fastened the door's anemic chain to a loosely drilled bar, and his shoulders relaxed a little. "I can't get cleaned up until you do, *lumina*."

"Michael." She found herself with hands on hips, drawn up to her full height, and her jaw clenched so hard she had to try twice before she could talk. "Come here."

He turned with almost military precision, walked silently in his boots—at least *those* weren't torn—and halted right in front of her, his hands stiff at his sides. He didn't look angry, but he was tall, and broad, and there was a certain gleam in his blue eyes she wasn't sure she could identify.

So she looked at his chest under the ruins of his navy T-shirt. The wounds had closed up, but they were angry red and looked raw. Blood crusted skin over sharp-tiled muscle and clung to curly, golden-tipped hairs. Vivid bruises marched across his ribs and belly, and his arms were so thickly crosshatched he must have been almost cut to ribbons. There was another bruise fading on the left side of his face, yellowgreen at the edges but fresh and deep black at the center, and both his eyes were slightly swollen.

He still said nothing. Jen's right hand lifted; she touched the most glaring gash on his left arm. He sucked in a breath, and the marks—still visible, and moving purposefully to cluster the damage—seemed to darken.

No, the ones closest to her fingertip *were* darker, and they yearned towards her touch. "Why do they do that?" It was a ridiculous question, but she couldn't help herself.

"Grace." He was hoarse. Maybe the desert was drying him out, too. Or maybe it hurt, and here she was, poking at the wounds. "It... the Principle. It strengthens us. The marks drink from it."

"Drink from it. Okay." She pulled her hand away, fascinated as the marks returned to their business. "Like I'm a battery?"

"Not quite." His Adam's-apple bobbed as he swallowed. "You won't run out, though it could burn you from the inside if you aren't... cared for."

"Oh." *That sounds unpleasant. At least, the burning part.* She wanted to ask about the rest, but he didn't let her.

"It's a gift not diminished by the giving, we say." His jaw set, almost angrily, but the rest of him didn't look upset. Just tense, his shoulders iron-hard and his hands stiff.

"That's a nice way of putting it." It was, after all, what gifts should be, though so many people used the word to mean *something you'd better pay back when I decide I want you to.* She liked his saying better. "So it helps you heal?"

"Yes." One clipped, professional syllable.

Well, *that* was good. Jen looked up, full of more questions, but his chin had dropped and he was leaning forward. She realized what was happening just in time. Most guys mashed your lips against your teeth or tried to shove their tongue past your uvula. Michael's mouth, however, halted just a whisper away, and the hesitation gave her the opportunity to deflect, step away if she wanted to.

She didn't. Jen went up on tiptoes, and there was an awkward moment that made it clear he hadn't done this much. He was a quick learner, though, and his hands cupped her shoulders with exquisite gentleness, holding her steady while her knees and pretty much everything else turned to liquid.

Everything else—the desert, the monsters, the residue of terror lurking under her heart and inside her bones, even the coppery fear-taste left from the wild, careening escape—vanished. There was only Michael, tall but not threatening, solid but not hurtful, his thumbs moving against her shoulders in tiny circling caresses. She almost forgot to breathe, and when he broke away she gasped to find herself separate.

Their foreheads rested together, his feverish-warm like the rest of him. Her fingertips had slipped into his belt loops, and the urge to pull him forward was almost irresistible.

"You don't have to," he whispered. "Jenna."

It almost stung, before she realized he didn't mean it unkindly. "Do you not want to?" If he said no, she would go find out how cold the shower could be. She'd need it. It had been a long, long time, and even the prospect of embarrassment if he found her unattractive was fading under the assault of sheer, idiot we're-still-alive hormones.

"That's not the problem." He inhaled sharply as she tensed, tugging gently at the ruined denim loops. She wanted him closer. "I'm afraid you'll regret it."

Oh, for fuck's sake. You can't be any worse than my last lay. A jagged laugh shook her on its way out. "I like you," she whispered. "And I'm interested, but if *you* aren't, that's okay."

The mortifying thought that he might not be built, well, like a human male occurred to her a bare fraction of a second before he kissed her again, and by the time the backs of her legs met the side of the bed she'd forgotten it as well as every other blessed thing in the whole wide world, as one of her fellow dancers used to say back before she met Eddie. Marie had been a lot of fun, but they'd lost contact.

But she didn't have to remember that. She didn't have to remember *anything* right now, and it was a relief. Michael tore the remains of his shirt in the hurry to get it over his head, and Jen began to laugh. He did too, a surprised chuckle that sounded nice even when they had a mouthful of each other.

Jen squirmed out of her own jeans, and the tangle of arms and legs was sweetly awkward, reminding her of high school and eager hands too young to know any better, kisses stolen on hot spring days with the sweet smell of cut grass. His mouth turned hungry, a greediness she matched, and Jenna, for the first time in a very long while, stopped worrying.

A PLEASANT ACHE

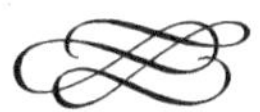

He couldn't say what it was like. Oh, he knew what was to be done, certainly; soldiers everywhere in the world spoke about it incessantly, whether complaining, bragging, or reverentially listing specifics. He'd even suspected it was pleasant, judging by the time mortals devoted to its pursuit, but you could say the same for cigarettes once they had been invented.

But Michael Gabon could not describe even the bare particulars of the act without stopping, lost in confusion.

The closest thing to it was flying, or breathing deep after a battle was won. But there was more—unalloyed tenderness, the hot salt-sweet scent of a pretty woman's sweat, a shattering of mind and heart at the same moment prolonged until something like soft, longed-for death swallowed him entire, all of it shot through with the singing of the Principle and the consciousness that it was *Jenna* in his arms, fragile warmth and strength that shamed his in its intensity.

It was another gift that did not diminish when shared, and an invisible buffeting swelled from his naked back to comb the air, twin curved scars ridging from shoulderblade to hip alive with singing ecstasy. Lassitude swamped him, and when he surfaced into conscious thought again he was kissing down her throat, pleasant shudders and twitches flooding his nerves. Best of all was her relaxation, and her fascinating, maddening softness. She demanded further investigation, just as soon as he could catch his breath.

"Shh," she soothed, fingers kneading, her heels clasped at the small of his back. "It's all right."

Everything was. Riverine peace filled him to the brim and he sagged, propped on his elbows and careful not to crush her. He wanted to say something, anything, but the words wouldn't come. So he worked his way back to her mouth instead, and tried to express at least a small sliver of his gratitude.

He could not bear to slide away, but he did the instant she made a restless movement. A few moments of arranging the covers and he had them both under the blankets, telling himself he'd only done so to keep her warm on a desert night. She didn't seem to mind; in fact, Jen lay her head on his shoulder and wriggled one of her long, lovely legs over his hips, which caused a pleasant ache at the core of his being.

"Just stay for a minute," she said, softly. "Please?"

"Of course." Michael found out his voice would work again, husky-dry with pleasure. "As long as you like."

"Look at that." Her fingertips skated up his chest, a pleasurable thrill following as his marks clustered like koi at a pond's surface, sipping at grace. Laceration and contusion had both vanished, leaving only the thinnest of white lines on mortal-seeming skin that would fade over weeks unless he chose to keep them as reminders. "They're all better."

Now he was only hoping he was mortal enough to please her. "Of course." How could it not be better? He rubbed his chin along her hair, gently, hoping the rasp of stubble wouldn't scrape her. Under a tang of hotel soap and the fading chemical bitterness of fear, she smelled of brunette spice, honey, and the wonderful warm note of the Principle in sweet flesh. He wanted to bathe in that scent; he took in deep lungfuls, storing it in memory.

Her fingertips played lightly over his chest. "How long are we safe here?"

She was worrying again, after *that*? "A few hours of rest, then I can drive again." Maybe it hadn't been as pleasant for her. Michael had to shelve *that* thought in a hurry, because naturally it would lead to wanting to do it again, and better this time. "Or we can stay until you've slept enough."

"No. I want to go. As soon as we can."

That was the safest option, but still, he was torn. She needed more than a few hours of fitful slumber. "We will, then. I'll wake you." It wasn't enough to merely reach the Eyrie. He had to show he'd done his job properly, and hadn't... taken advantage.

"All right." Her eyes were already closed. Her mons pressed against his hip, warm and damp, and the thought of what that fluid was made the aching tenderness in his chest even fiercer. "Michael?"

"Hm?" He propped a hand under his head, pushing the pillow away. At least the sheets were clean. Her eyes closed, lashes a sooty semicircle against her cheeks; she nestled sweetly against his side.

"Can you turn off the light?" A yawn swallowed the last of the question.

"As soon as I get up," he said, and listened to her breathing even out. She dropped into slumber without even a grateful murmur, and a single white feather drifted from the ceiling, seesawing lazily, until it found Michael's feet under the blankets and came to rest.

He stared at it, unblinking, until he was certain she wouldn't wake. Then, with infinite patience, he untangled himself by fractions, holding his breath every time Jen shifted restlessly. By the time he reached his feet, however, the downy white ship had sailed elsewhere, and he couldn't find the feather, even peering under the bed's squeaking metal frame.

Finally, naked in a California hotel room, Michael Gabon shook his head and opened his duffel. He took out his last clean clothes, turned off the light, and headed for the bathroom, carrying both guns with him.

A LOT MORE SENSITIVE

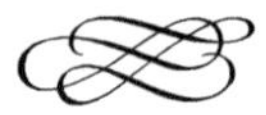

"JENNA." One quiet word, a familiar touch on her bare shoulder, and Jenna lunged into consciousness, her heart in her throat. Michael, freshly shaven and bright-eyed, snatched his hand back as if she'd burned him. The thin drapes were outlined with a gray dawn and a thread of gold showed under the room's door.

"Are they here?" She didn't have a headache, but it was the only thing she could think of to say. Her pulse galloped; she clutched the sheet to her chest, pushing herself fully upright.

"Nope." Michael shook his head, his hand falling to his side. "It's dawn, you've had a few good hours of sleep. We should go, unless you want to rest more."

God, no. Jenna scrubbed at her face, let out a shaky sigh. She twinged in interesting places, but at least her head was clear. Or so she hoped. "We should make L.A. today, right?"

"Six hours or so, depending on where we stop." That was good news, but he delivered it quietly, as if he expected her to protest.

She studied his expression, trying to figure out how he felt about... last night. She was going to have to roll back into the jeans and T-shirt she'd been in yesterday, and it had been a long, long time since her last one-night stand.

Well, what the hell, it can't get worse, right? She might as well ask. "Are you okay?"

"Of course." He straightened, his leather jacket creaking slightly. Now that she knew what was under those clothes, it was hard not to look. Aesthetic appreciation was just fine, or so Rach always averred, especially when she and Sam were on a break. "You?"

"A little nervous." Might as well be honest. Her mouth was full of morning-taste and a few parts of her were very pleasantly sore, and she was hoping like hell she hadn't given him a bad time. The dry, dust-freighted morning breeze rasped at the corners of the building, a subliminal song.

His eyebrows rose slightly and the tops of his cheekbones pinkened, which was either a good sign or a very bad one. "About last night?"

Of course, what did you think? She cast around for her clothes; at least she could get to her T-shirt on the floor without the sheet loosening. "Yeah."

"So am I." A slow, sweet smile bloomed on his face, and she was helpless to look away. "Was it okay?"

Not the worst I've had. But that would be damning with faint praise, and now wasn't the time for hilarious comments. "Yes." Her face felt strange—she was grinning back, mostly out of sheer relief. So she'd acquitted herself well, it looked like. "What about you?"

"Earth-shattering." He scratched at the side of his neck, ducking his head slightly. "Honestly."

"That's good." She couldn't ask what she really wanted to know, but she'd take the compliment. The space heater near the window was ticking; he must have turned it on. "Glad to know my technique's still on."

"I wouldn't worry about that, if I was you." He shook his head and his smile vanished, but enough of it lingered to warm her all the way through. "The water here isn't very hot, and the soap's not...well, it doesn't matter, we'll be at the Eyrie tonight and they'll have everything to make you comfortable."

Including you? It was on the tip of her tongue, but she swallowed it and slid her legs out of the warm nest. The pillow next to hers was dented, so at least he'd stayed a while.

Goosebumps crawled up her skin; the desert didn't hug any of its daily heat too closely, frittering it away into space all night. She didn't know just how warm it would get this close to winter, but maybe she wouldn't need the parka.

Hopefully he hadn't noticed she hadn't had a chance to shave, too. Her legs worked just fine; she fished around for her T-shirt and only then was able to let go of the sheet. Half-clothed, carrying her jeans, she picked her way across cheap carpet and was at the bathroom door, muscles twinging in unexpected places, when Michael spoke again.

"Jenna?"

"Huh?" She stopped, looking over her shoulder. Was he checking out her backside? Jenna decided it would be nice if he was, but he didn't appear to be. Oh well.

"I'm yours now." Michael had turned away, heading for the door. "You don't know what that means yet. Just remember it. Oh, and I checked your boots, but shake them out before you put them on. We're in the desert."

With that, he unlocked the door and was gone into the gray of early dawn, probably to check on the truck.

Jen, clutching jeans and socks to her chest, her bare legs roughening with gooseflesh, found her jaw suspiciously loose. She closed her mouth with a snap and headed for the bathroom.

He'd left her both towels.

THE CAMPER HAD a giant hole in the side; it looked like a wrecking ball had been dropped into the bed and there was a faint nasty smell lingering under the sand-spice smell of a desert morning. There was no sign of whatever he'd been fighting, and Jenna didn't want to know. The thought of him heaving a demon body out of the truck while she was driving was unappetizing in the extreme. He just got back behind the wheel as if nothing had happened, and Jen, her hair damp from the shower and rising in rebellion once more, scooted across to sit in the middle seat again.

Michael didn't seem to mind. He pointed them south, and the truck bounced up onto the highway like it hadn't been dragged through hell last night. The passenger side mirror, now lashed into place with duct tape and zip ties, was cracked, but other than that they seemed to have gotten off lightly.

Except for Jen's clothes, but that seemed about par for the course nowadays.

Breakfast was leftovers dug out of the coolers, awash with melting ice but still safely cold. No tea, of course, and there wasn't a coffee shop in sight. Still, the bright beautiful furnace of dawn rose at the eastern rim of the world, heat beginning to shimmer in the distance as the sun looked upon everything in a sandy expanse, driving life underground to wait for night.

She could *sense* it, just as she'd sensed the mountains' hidden secrets, small trickles hiding from the glare, things that crept or flew or slithered curled up in the shade and dreaming their alien, interminable dreams. Maybe it was just lightheadedness from lack of sleep and inadequate caffeine... but Jen didn't think so.

The strangest thing of all was closing her eyes and somehow seeing a tight, disciplined glow to her left, a column of angular light. It was different than sunlight, gold tinted with blue at its edges, and it brightened just before Michael spoke.

"You all right?" Did he sound tentative?

"I think so." She didn't mean to make it a question, but the sentence lilted up awkwardly at the end. At least her clothes weren't too dirty; she just felt like the end of a very long road trip, exhausted and hopefully pointed for home. If she could ever have a home again, that was. "I just feel a little strange."

"It's the Principle." He said it as if it explained everything, and maybe it did. "You have the Breath, you're going to get a lot more sensitive hanging out with legionnaires."

"Great." She kept her eyes closed. It was easier that way; she was still sleep-fogged. "It's not just you, though. It's everything. Even the rocks."

"Everything will wake up around you. Rocks, animals, plants." It didn't sound like he considered the prospect crazy or terrifying at all. "You're a blessing, Jenna."

"I'm glad you think so." Even Mom's silly optimism was back, forcing itself through the cracks like a weed. You couldn't kill it, you had to let it bloom and wait for inevitable disappointment.

Still...they were both still alive. And Michael seemed to like her, maybe just because she was this "lumina" thing. Did it matter if he liked that and not really, well, *her*?

"So when we get there, what happens?" Now was as good a time as any to ask. The truck achieved highway speed, engine settling into a familiar hum and the tires singing, happy to be turning again.

"I take you right in the front door, and it'll be busy for a few hours. They'll want to debrief me and check to make sure you're not injured or anything, and they'll ask you a lot of questions." He paused and she felt his quick movement to glance in her direction, even with her eyes closed. The truck rocked on its springs a little, cresting an almost-invisible rise. "Like if I was respectful, if I took care of you, what you need to be comfortable. They'll get you clothes and a suite high up in the Eyrie, and you'll be safe. You won't have to worry about anything ever again."

"There's always something to worry about." She decided she could scoot a little closer, her hip touching his. "Will you get in trouble because we, uh..." What euphemism was proper when you'd slept with a monster hunter? There should be a manual for these situations. Who would publish one? Who would *write* the damn thing, even?

Michael cleared his throat. "It just means I belong to you."

She waited, but he said nothing more. "You're going to have to explain that." *So I can tell whether to feel good about it, or scared out of my mind. Or both.* Last night had seemed like a good idea at the time, but then again, so had Eddie. So had working at the SunnyTime.

So had the trip to San Francisco that claimed her mother's life. All sorts of things started well and turned out badly. Then again, had this trip started well at all? Maybe it would end up great, but she didn't think so.

Jenna simply couldn't be that lucky.

"It makes me *angelus primus*, that's all." Maybe he realized she needed more, because he shifted slightly in his seat and continued. "Kind of like...oh, *consort*'s a good word, I guess. It means I'll set and command your guard detail, I'll order stuff you need or want, I'll do the planning if you want to go outside the Eyrie—"

Hang-a-loos whatsis? Consort? Her eyes flew open. *If I want to go outside?* "Wait." She should have picked the most important consideration first, but she was what Rach would no doubt call *too damn chicken*. "You mean I can't just walk outside if I want to?"

Michael's eyes narrowed against the glare, but he didn't seem a sunglasses sort of guy. Maybe she should suggest some. Did monster hunters get cataracts? "We'll just go with you if you ever leave the Eyrie, that's all."

Oh, that doesn't sound controlling or anything. "And if I don't want anyone going with me? Like, if I just wanted to go for a walk by myself?"

"You really want to run across one of the unclean alone?" He watched the road, chin dropped slightly and long proud aquiline nose just as forbidding as the sage-crowded rock formations rising in uneven clumps. His window was down, letting the slipstream fill the cab with fresh air, and he wore his jacket again despite the promise of heat later in the afternoon.

At home there might even be snow by now, but not here. "I guess not," she said, heavily, and wished she hadn't buckled herself in next to him. Maybe sleeping with her was just something he regarded as his duty.

He didn't turn the radio on and she didn't have anything else to say, so they drove in silence. They were touching, but Jen felt the new distance between them, sharp as prickly desert plants. Everything in this part of the country learned to protect itself, and she should be no different.

I suppose we'll see when we get there, she thought, bleakly, and blinked several times against the hot, swelling saltwater in her eyes.

UNCERTAIN OF AFFECTION

THEY STOPPED on the far edge of Klinefelter for fuel as well as drain and repack the cooler, but she was entirely too quiet for Michael's taste. Had he hurt her somehow, or was she regretting accepting him as *angelus primus*? It wasn't the kind of subject you could initiate with an Incorruptible, and his place wasn't to ask questions but to accept whatever she saw fit to give. Silent except for commonplaces, they swung west on the Needles, and for a long time the sun hung motionless overhead. It was the home stretch, and he should have been feeling relief and anticipation in equal measure.

Instead, his skin itched with tension and his *lumina* was back in the passenger seat, the freshly filled cooler a silent sentinel between them. She watched the wilderness change, mountains rising charcoal and blue on other side, approaching to swallow the truck, then receding. There was little traffic to speak of, and for long stretches the truck was the only thing on the road, a red beetle with a half-crushed wing busily trundling along. The heat built quickly despite the season, ovenbreath sighing into the cab along with sage-scent and a persistent faint note of burning. The knocking in the truck's engine wasn't a source of concern just yet, but when they got to the Eyrie he was going to request a tune-up.

And, possibly, a new canopy. That would be nice, if she'd approve it. He almost opened his mouth to ask, glimpsed her set expression and pale cheeks, and decided he'd better not.

He'd probably done something wrong. Hurt her somehow, in his stupid, clumsy way. He'd made a mess of everything else, why not that?

"Hey," he said finally, when Barstow was throwing its arms around the freeway, welcome spots of irrigated green breaking sere heatshimmer. They might even see farms soon, precious water dumped out to keep growing food clinging to the dirt. "You're quiet. Have I done something wrong?"

She twisted her dark hair up with her fingers, honey highlights shining in its rippling flow, and her neck gleamed with a fine misting of sweat. He wondered how the microscopic droplets tasted, and the thought of kissing that tender hollow right above the collarbone caused an interesting frisson up his spine. The speedometer's needle hovered just over seventy-two.

"I'm just thinking." A line between her dark, winged eyebrows, she stared at the city in the distance.

Traffic thickened, clustering, and his hands tingled with intuition waking up to lead him through any potential rush hour. "It's only a couple more hours. I figure we should stop on the other side of Barstow for gas just in case." His mouth was running, he couldn't stop it. "What are you thinking about?"

"Just things." She let go of her hair, and the tumbling waves made a halo. "A few days ago I was only scared of my ex showing up. Now I'm scared of demons eating me."

Maybe she needed something to tie her hair back with. A bandanna, perhaps? He'd have to dig in the small duffel. "They're not going to hurt you." *Nothing will. Not ever again.* At least, not if he could stop it.

"What about you?" As usual, she waited to broach what her tone said she was most concerned with.

Was *he* what worried her? Of course, he was larger, stronger, and had to be just as brutal as the unclean. He wasn't fit for gentler things, no matter how much he longed to be. "I'm not going to hurt you either."

"No, I mean, what if you get hurt?" She tucked her hair behind her ears, but it immediately sprang free again, refusing to be contained. Like grace itself, radiating from its vessels.

Oh. "I don't matter so much." Didn't she get that he was a lot more durable, and that *she* was the important one? "You do."

"You matter to me." Now she sounded sad, and turned her chin to gaze out the window. "I mean, I know it's not real, I know it's just heightened emotion and us being thrown together, but... I really like you, Michael."

A deep, painful rosette bloomed in his chest. "Do you?" How many empty years had passed, and now he had more than he ever dreamed of?

"I said it before, you're a good guy." Now she darted him a single, unsteady glance.

The strange, almost blasphemous idea that she might be uncertain of his affection tiptoed through his head. The junction with 15 was coming up; he took his foot off the gas and began reading signs. What was the best thing to say? He knew what soldiers joked about, but not what a woman—let alone an Incorruptible—would actually want to hear. He had to cough to cover his confusion. *Think fast, Michael.* "I adore you," he blurted. "You're brave and funny and kind." *And beautiful. So beautiful.* But if he added that, would she think he was just like those mortal men, perhaps even the one who had made her so uncertain? So afraid?

"Likewise." Now she looked at him, steadily, and he longed to return the favor but the road demanded his attention. "So... are we dating?"

"If you like, Jenna." He might have driven off the road if grace hadn't been tingling all through his marks, reminding him of duty. "Whatever you want, I'm all right with." Once they reached the Eyrie, his brothers would compete for the Incorruptible's attention. One of them might supersede him, but he would always be *angelus primus*, belonging to something other than the Legion, his place assured at long last. There would be no more uncertainty, his duties would be clear, and close to her, he wouldn't deviate from the Principle.

Unless he already had. That was a worrisome prospect indeed. So was the idea that perhaps another of his brothers would be better at keeping her safe, and wouldn't have made such a slipshod mess of extraction.

The soft warmth of amusement was back in her sweet voice. "I'm kind of high maintenance."

Is that what those mortal men told you? "I don't think so." He was grinning like a fool yet again, and the sudden easing of her tension was a gift all its own.

"You'd be the first."

"Honored to be so, *lumina*." He almost said *my lumina*, but that was a step too far. He could think it all he wanted, but an Incorruptible was not to be *owned*. Not by a blockhead grunt, that was for sure.

The silence returned, but it was different, easier, with no static-crackle of worry and awkwardness. And after they stopped outside Barstow, so close to safety he could almost *taste* it, she moved back into the middle seat. Her small, fragile hand crept to his knee, he carefully took it in his own, and for a short while all was right with the world.

VICTORVILLE SPRAWLED WIDE AND SUN-DRENCHED, traffic slowed, and they were almost clear of the urban tangle when Jen stiffened, a small sound escaping her mouth and her fingers tightening in his.

Her other hand flew to her head, and he felt the rasp of alarm along his own skin.

"It's them," she whispered, deadly certain. "Michael, it's *them*."

Of course the unclean would be watching the approaches to the city proper. Maybe Michael and his precious passenger could slip through undetected, but he didn't want to bet on it. "Just breathe." He kept his tone even and calm, though his hands wanted to clench. *Come out so I can kill you, diaboli.* "And tell me if it gets worse."

"They're not really close," she said softly, closing her eyes. Her attention sharpened; grace tingled along his arms and legs. "But they're here. I don't think they've noticed us."

"Okay," he murmured. "Good instinct, *lumina*. Don't focus too much on them, they'll be able to feel it in return. I'm gonna draw everything I can from you, okay?"

"Okay." Thankfully, she kept her hand in his; it was easier with the physical contact. Michael was glad they didn't have to stop for fuel and touched the accelerator a bit, nudging them into an opening in the thickening flow of traffic.

Now it was a race.

TORQUED AND TORTURED

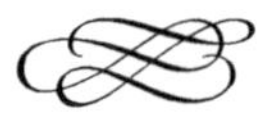

It would have been nice to enjoy the scenery. Instead, Jen held Michael's hand, her head pounding and sweat rising insistently all over her, alternately feverish and sickly-cold. When she peeked through her eyelids, glaring sunshine speared her tender skull, twisting like a blade, and the strange floating sensation as Michael piloted the truck into spaces opening as if by magic unmoored her stomach.

It was a good thing she hadn't wanted much in the way of lunch.

A painful, lurching half hour passed seamlessly under the Dodge's tires, canyons eventually rising on either side and greening in ridiculous defiance of the desert. The engine sound changed, a long downhill slope pulling them towards the sea, and another curious sensation began along her fingers and toes.

"Thank the Principle," Michael said, as soon as she noticed it. "Feel that? This is a Legion city."

"Is that what—" She gasped again as her head gave another pounding jolt, spearing all the way down her neck and spreading into her back muscles. Would others like him give her a headache? "*Ow!*"

"Anytime now," Michael muttered. "Anytime. Come on, guys. Notice me, I'm begging you."

"Michael—"

"Fine time to wish I had a phone." He probably didn't mean to sound so grim. "Just hold on, Jen. We're almost safe."

The pain in her head crested again, Jen let out a blurting, surprised cry, and the world turned over as something big smashed into the truck's much-abused canopy. Weightlessness swallowed them for a long, swimming second, and she had time to think *that's strange, it doesn't hurt anymore* before the fireball burst, a deadly beautiful flower, and for a moment she was bleeding under hot sunshine again, the red-haired man standing on the Volvo's hood and laughing as greasy gasflames licked him with kitten-playful tongues.

Gravity reasserted itself, the funnel of memory pinching closed, and a terrific jolt smashed the bright California afternoon. Flaming wreckage fell and she was rolling, her head bouncing hard on a hard-muscled shoulder and her terror raising a bright flaring ribbon of liquid gold, exploding like a firework in the smoggy sky above Rancho Cucamonga.

Later she thought she must have only been out for only a few moments, but it felt much longer—especially when the headache, furious that she'd slipped its grip even temporarily, returned with a vengeance. A spatter of loud reports was gunfire, and her head bobbled as Michael pulled her upright. His jacket was scuffed and torn, its back almost shredded to pieces, but the T-shirt underneath was curiously unharmed and his jeans were pristine.

The red Dodge, however, was a mangled mass of metal and exploding safety glass, great billows of oily black smoke rising skyward as it rocked to a halt on the interstate. Leggy, dusty-green sage and long withered yellow grass clutched at Jen's legs as she stared at the burning, wondering blankly just how in the hell either of them had survived the impact.

Mom? She shook her ringing head, the pain crunching all through her with vicious, serrated teeth, and Michael shoved her almost headlong into a stand of exhaust-stunted highway greenery. Crackling gun-reports were small next to the massive noise of the truck's shredding still ringing in her head; the sounds were coming from him, and the malformed, shadowy *thing* amid the hungry flames screeched as he shot it, tiny puffs of amber ichor exploding free as bullets punched home.

She rolled into a spiny mess of sweet-smelling sage, catching plenty of it in her hair, scraping her face and palms. Michael's boots landed on either side of her hips and he kept firing, sunshine pouring over his blond buzzcut and turning his eyes incandescent. Now she could almost-see what he called *grace*, a stream of cascading light spinning around her like cotton candy, swirling towards his hard geometric gleam. It was beautiful, and for a moment she stared slack-jawed, forgetting the pain of her riven head and the terror of memory. The scar along her left forearm flushed with gold; she sensed a massive dozing presence beneath her, the earth ignoring insects crawling on its surface as well as their constantly repaired webs of concrete, not-quite-roused from a baking nap.

They came from the other side of the freeway, fume-shifting shapes streaking between cars caught in a curious stasis. It was just like the diner, the entire world a bubble of stillness while they loped with that strange, *wrong* fluidity, and Michael was standing over her, his head down and his hands blurring as he holstered his guns.

Yes, it was just like the diner—except she could *move*. She wasn't trapped helplessly in a cocoon of hardened air. There was all the time in the world to look at the monsters, and a strange almost-pity speared her.

They crouched inside human bodies, but torqued and tortured flesh past repair with their fury. It would be so easy to help them—just a featherlight touch here, another there, helping each one to shake off the twisting so they could grow straight and true. All they had to do was let go of the anger and they could step out of the steam-wafting sickness, shedding it like a too-heavy coat on a warm day.

She longed to tell them as much, but something inside her—the calm, practical voice that had spurred her to simply walk away from Eddie's apartment after he was denied bail—spoke up.

They won't listen. You know they won't. Just keep them from hurting anyone else.

It wasn't right, it wasn't *fair*—but neither was life, and she wasn't about to let these monsters hurt someone she loved ever again.

Not if she could help it.

Somehow her hands were underneath her, and her knees. She scrambled lithely from Michael's protective closeness, levering herself upright with odd ease. Her head still hurt, her back threatened to lock up, and her left arm burned like it had just been sliced open again, but the pain was a sweetness, a spur instead of a warning.

"No." The word fell into the stillness like a rock, spreading ripples of brightness in concentric rings. "I won't."

Michael turned, a supple, fluid motion. His hands ran with sharp-edged, sparkling energy, and there was a shadowy suggestion of great soft feathered shapes behind him, held high and buffeting in great sweeps. He shot forward to meet the shadows, and any question she had about his durability was answered twice over. He met the knot of leaping shadow-creatures with a great cracking, and Jen watched, fascinated, as sound waves spread slowly from the impact. *Now* she saw why the entire SunnyTime had been smashed—they blinked through space, and displacement or expended kinetic energy spread all at once when the battle was done and the knot holding the physical world aside was sliced cleanly in half.

She also saw how to catch that spreading energy, shape it, and *use* it. Her mental touch was clumsy, unpracticed, but it was surprisingly easy. All she had to do was decide, and the world practically leapt to obey.

But only within narrow parameters.

Jenna tipped her head back, gazing at the infinite lens of the smog-touched sky, its blue broken by only a few high, fleecy clouds. *We need help*, she thought, as clearly and loudly as she could. *Please, if you're out there, we need help.*

Her mouth opened and a pillar of force broke free, pouring upward and blossoming into rosy gold as it hit the sky. It lingered, a second sun casting sharp inkspill shadows. Her hands fell back, her spine arcing, and one of the shadowed things crumbled as Michael swung a bright silver sword-length through its midsection, using the spin in the movement to carry him to the next hideous horned thing, its teeth champing and rank with venomous, dripping foam. A thin golden gleam scintillated around him, a shield she wasn't aware of fueling until she *felt* it as the flare from her lips died and she staggered.

Wow. The thought stuck in golden syrup, rotating lazily. *What the hell was that?*

Her chin tipped back down, her eyes widening, just in time to see a crafty, slinking shadow streak from her right, straight for Michael's back. It leapt and hung in midair, straining and fuming, and another cry gathered inside Jen's chest with the trembling heat of a star about to explode.

FRAGILE MORTAL FRAME

The half-dozen closest unclean were simply hunting hounds, fast and vicious but essentially brainless. The one streaking for his back was of slightly more concern, but he was ready to slip aside when it had committed to its final lunge, letting it drive itself into the knot of its fellows before him. He moved, and the thing clipped his shoulder, sending him spinning. Even that was fine, he could use the momentum, and he was moving so fast it didn't even hurt.

Then a warm, painless impact hit his back, pinning him like a dead, stretched butterfly. It passed *through* him, a ripple of force raying along patterns very much like his marks, and the pressure of many unclean massing for the real attack was pierced by multiple swords of light thudding to ground around him.

His brothers landed amid sliptime-stalled cars, their boots thumping on pavement, gravel, or yellowed grass eking out survival between the petals of concrete cloverleaf. Hurtful brilliance radiated as legionnaires sensed an Incorruptible and their marks pulled hungrily at her clarity. Bright blades clove unclean flesh, and *diaboli* shrieked. Michael found himself in the middle of a unit, falling into their rhythm as if he was at practice in the abbeys just after his long-ago awakening. It was good to fight with them again, good to sense their unity, their strength, their nearness.

He hadn't realized how much he missed it.

The unclean—reckless of them, to come out in daylight and in such numbers, but the prize of a semi-unprotected Incorruptible was too great—poured from the east and north, attempting to flank their prey. The alert had no doubt gone out in Victorville, putting a crowd practically on the truck's back bumper. The approaches had indeed been watched.

What is going on?

It didn't matter. Nothing mattered but the glowing core behind him, Jenna a volcano of force multiplied by each legionnaire drawing strength from the Principle enfleshed.

She's not ready. This much grace could burn a fragile mortal frame, and she had no practice regulating its flow.

Sliptime trembled like a soap bubble, and the release of combat-pressure was almost painful. These were not mere legionnaires but centurions, and Celeres too, their swiftness outpacing both legionnaire and unclean even in sliptime. There were three—a red and two blues—bulleting through the malformed ranks of unclean and slaying as they went; there was even a Decurion in heavy armor chased with the light of grace, every sweep of his spear shattering a rank of *diaboli*.

Michael was supposed to fight with the infantry, but he fell back, his place in the unit closing over like water smoothing sand. The battle was won, anyone could see as much—and that meant he had to reach Jen.

She stood, straight and slim as a young sapling, her chin lifted and her dark eyes flashing. Her hair was a halo again, honey highlights glittering in thick California sunshine, and the egg of clarity around her almost hurt even a legionnaire's eyes. He strained through sliptime as more of his kind thudded down on streaks of light, their appearance spreading ripple-circles; every car on the freeway was going to have a bad time when the battle was over and air, metal, glass, and other materials took their revenge.

He couldn't think about casualties now.

Michael's boots left the ground. He slid out of sliptime as his arms closed around her and they both flew, a hard shell closed around a tender inner core rolling through grass smoking just before it combusted from slip-friction. He took the shock of tumbling out of sliptime, a hideous crunching blow snapping half his reinforced ribs and also his left femur, a bright starry instant of pain before grace roared through him again, bathing hurts in electric honey.

Even now she was holding the gateway open, allowing the Principle to speak through her. If she didn't stop soon she was going to combust, and Michael would have failed at the last possible moment.

No. Please, no.

Rolling, tumbling, his flayed hand at the back of her head and silky hair tangling over his bloodied fingers, the marks howling with light as they repaired damage in swift merciless tugs, he swallowed a hideous barking cry and they came to a stop on the slight hillside with a bump. He lay on his back, arms and legs cradling his *lumina*, and a deathly gray doze threatened to swallow him.

Stay awake.

It was no use. He'd damaged himself, possible irreparably. The Legion clustered them both, Celeres streaking through sliptime and the Decurion giving a bell-like battlecry signaling disengagement. Battle-hardened hands used all the gentleness they could to lift the Incorruptible from Michael's shattered frame, and they bore her away while more of their kind arrived in waves to cleanse the stain of *diaboleri*—and, not so incidentally, to cover the retreat as legionnaires carried her uphill to a long black helicopter descending in defiance of municipal codes. The wind-roaring craft barely touched the ground before she was bundled in, and it had lifted free by the time sliptime broke, signaling the end of the battle.

The red Celeres halted next to Michael, whose spine bowed as the sudden absence of grace made itself felt. The officer looked down, a legionnaire with the characteristic high nose and sharp chin, his marks roiling at throat and wrist, covering the back of his hands, his gloves tattered and his boots smoking from sheer speed. The officer's hair stood up angrily, a short crimson ruff, and he stared down with dark, dead eyes until the two blues, their hair clipped so short you could barely see a cerulean sheen on their skulls, lifted Michael and bore him away as well.

DURING THE BREAKING

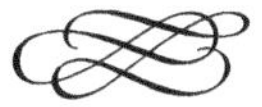

THE SUITE WAS QUIET, and soft, and smelled faintly of vanilla. The bed was big enough to swallow Jenna twice over, gossamer netting falling from a great hoop hung overhead and pooling on pale carpet on each side, high wrought-iron finials rising from every corner of the four-poster. Evening indigo filled wall-to-floor windows, gems winking as the whole of L.A. turned on its lights. Rivers of traffic moved along the streets and other tall buildings clustered close.

Everything looked different from this high up.

The apartment was gorgeous. A gas insert fireplace stood sentinel in the spacious living room with its white leather couch and broad chairs, a ginormous flatscreen hung on one wall; the open kitchen had granite countertops and sleek stainless-steel appliances, the bedroom held a walk-in closet the size of her old place. An extremely high-end sound system lurked in a cabinet under the flatscreen; it looked like a space-shuttle console. There was a big tiled bathroom with a clawfoot tub big enough to support an entire pond ecosystem, and a smaller half-bath near the front door.

Her legs were a bit unsteady but the devouring headache was gone, and she was ravenous. The capacious fridge held nothing, bare and white inside, but there was a brand-new, pristine filter pitcher on the counter next to the kitchen sink, and she found glasses standing at attention in one of the cabinets.

It was like a stage set. Well, she *was* in L.A., after all.

"We're having groceries delivered," Paulus said. He was the *really* thickset guy, even bigger than Michael, the wide lines of his tattoos moving slowly over his bare arms. A white T-shirt strained at his chest, and an observer might have thought he was Michael's cousin. He had the same high-prowed nose, and the same diffident way of moving, as if he understood his own size and furthermore that the world around him was fragile. "Is there anything special you'd like?"

She set the glass down, gingerly. "I don't know." Her stomach made a brief, unhappy sloshing noise. Good Lord, she hoped nobody ever dropped an egg in here. Granite was nice, but the cleanup was probably never-ending. And that white couch—who in their right mind would want furniture that easy to stain?

"It can be overwhelming." The bald one was Malachi, and his head-stubble showed a ferocious widow's peak. The stubble was also the exact color of blue raspberry Kool-Aid mixed with two packets of powder to only one ration of sugar, and his eyebrows were black with a tinge of cobalt at the ends. He looked a little like Michael as well, except for his deep-set eye-sockets and the tiny glowing pinpricks in his pupils. Little blue stars, caught in a round black sea.

Were they all related? Now *there* was a question, and one she didn't really think she wanted the answer to. They came from *elsewhere*, and she didn't think they meant Poughkeepsie, as Mom might have said.

"Where's Michael?" she asked, once more.

And again, they exchanged a Significant Look, like her parents discussing things little Jenna shouldn't hear. How much had Mom and Dad known about this? Anything at all?

"Gabon is resting," Paulus said, finally. "We have to make sure he's not..."

"Not *what*?" She restrained the urge to hug herself, but only halfway; she cupped her elbows in her palms and hunched her shoulders. They were bringing her clean clothes as well as groceries. Or at least, that's what they said.

"You have to understand, we didn't even know you existed until this morning." Malachi was the one who had lifted her onto the helicopter and held her waist while the thing lifted off, leaving Michael sprawled in the grass surrounded by those horrible things and the other legionnaires, all still fighting. "We got reports of *diaboli* activity coming down the road, and a trap-team got their hands on a few and questioned them. The unclean knew all about you, and we didn't."

It was one thing to hear Michael talk about this stuff. It was another thing to be bundled out of a helicopter and into a skyscraper full of expensive fixtures, whisper-quick elevators, and humming activity, and to hear a bunch of brawny, strange-eyed men saying the same things he had.

"That's impossible. Michael called in." She wished they'd just bring Michael to the room and leave her alone for a while. They'd been over this before, Jen's story jumping around in time as she tried to make them understand, words tumbling out of her all mixed up and crossways. "He had a laptop, he did it *days* ago after those things came into the diner and—"

They exchanged another glance, adults weighing whether to believe a frightened child. She was beginning to hate those little looks.

"It doesn't make sense," Paulus said, heavily. "If he's turned traitor, why did he bring her here?"

"You've got to be kidding me." She glared at him, wishing she knew how to use that invisible force Michael called grace to shatter something. Then she felt even more childlike. A tantrum wouldn't help, no matter *how* satisfying the idea. "Michael fought those things *off*. He kept us both alive. He's a good guy."

He'd also sworn that they'd listen to her, but it looked like he'd been a little optimistic.

"He may have deviated from the Principle." Malachi paced to the window, stood looking out. He almost vibrated with contained energy, kind of like Bob when he'd had too much over-boiled Sunny-Time coffee. *I'm a Celeres,* he'd said, with a peculiar little smile. *We run fast.* "But still... it doesn't make sense. You're right."

"I want to see him." She was very aware every single man here was bigger and stronger than her, and of the marks on these two moving hungrily. Something in her chest—a cork, a dam, a necessary stoppage—had been wrenched free, and the strange almost-glow hanging a few inches from her skin was a trip and a half. It felt like being near a power transformer on a sunny day, invisible and barely audible electric force just looking for a place to strike.

"We can't take you down there just yet, *lumina.* Every legionnaire in radius will be pulling at you." Malachi subsided when the bigger guy glanced at him.

"We're just lucky Gabon broke your contact so we could get you out of there, and that you weren't hollowed out. That's difficult to treat, we'd have to hospitalize you in the Baths." Paulus folded his beefy arms, leaning against the door to the outer hall. "Our first priority is making sure you don't get drained or injured. You need food, and rest, or the Principle will burn right through your mortal shell."

That sounds uncomfortable. It explained why Michael had tackled her. Saving her again, like always. "I want to see him. Can't he be brought up here?" He'd said they would let him stay if she insisted. Or were these guys on the monsters' side? She had her own reasons for suspicion, didn't she?

Good ones.

"Not until we know exactly what happened." Paulus's chin set, not stubborn but thoughtful. "You said he had a laptop?"

"He destroyed it after he told you guys about me, so they couldn't track us. But they did. They kept finding us." She'd already told them, why did they keep *asking*? Did they not believe her because she wasn't male? It figured. "He got s-stabbed, and torn up when that thing in Las Vegas—"

Malachi's frown turned him saturnine, and his fingers twitched. "He took you through Vegas?"

"There wasn't another route once we got to..." She trailed off. *I hate having to repeat myself.* Nevertheless, she tried again. "He said we had to get to the Eyrie in L.A., and then we'd be safe." She was beginning to feel lightheaded, and her stomach spoke up, rumbling. Of course it couldn't be simple or easy, even when they'd reached their destination. It would have been good luck, and God knew she didn't get much of *that*. "But it's not safe if he's not here."

"He could have been fostering a dependence," Malachi said softly, turning to regard the glimmering city spread below the window. "It's not out of the question."

"That's not the real issue, though." Paulus tilted his head, a listening movement. His boots were like Michael's, heavy black clodhoppers with thick soles. "Ah. Food will be here in a few minutes, *lumina*."

"Don't *call* me that!" For a moment she couldn't believe she was actually *yelling* at someone, but hot injustice filled her to the brim. She was so goddamn tired of this bullshit, the endless *male* bullshit. "*Michael* calls me that, and you bastards left him there to die!" The tears were coming, she couldn't stop them, but they were made of pure rage instead of hurt.

"We most certainly did not." Paulus didn't even blink, but he hunched his shoulders like Michael sometimes did when he wanted to appear less threatening. "He's in the Baths, *lumi*—ah, ma'am. He was badly injured. As soon as he can speak he'll be able to explain. Right now we don't know enough."

Badly injured was putting it mildly. And they put him in a *bath* to recover? Jenna opened her mouth, unsure what was going to come out.

"What's the real issue, here?" Malachi went up on his toes, dropped back, did it again. He couldn't bear to be still, it looked like, and he turned back from the window, both eyebrows lifted inquiringly. "You're the ranking officer, Paulus."

Neither of them were paying any goddamn attention. It was, Jenna thought, par for the fucking course.

"As soon as our lady Incorruptible is settled, I want you to go down to Records." Paulus glanced at her, a flash of dark eyes. At least his weren't blue. "Don't say anything to anyone, just go down and find Gabon's listing. I want to know why he was left out on the East Coast and not pulled back during the Breaking."

That made Malachi go still at last, examining the thickset man. "A lot of us weren't." Those strange pinpricks of blue light in his pupils flared and the invisible force thrumming through Jenna intensified slightly, a soft tugging at her chest.

"And we don't know why." Paulus folded his beefy arms, but his right-hand fingers tapped at his biceps in turn, a sign of deep thought.

"The Breaking?" Jen had the sinking sensation that they weren't going to tell her anything, but oddly enough, both of them returned their gazes to her as soon as her mouth opened.

"We used to have many Eyries," Paulus said, heavily. "But about a century ago, Incorruptibles started vanishing. Some said the Principle was displeased, that we had fallen away and grace was withdrawn. Thirty years ago, we realized there was just this one Eyrie left on the continent. We've lost contact with others in the world, and without an Incorruptible we can't bring more of our kind through. We don't have any Authorities, we don't even have any Principalities left; the last one was Gabriel Archer and he vanished during the Great Siege. We've been fighting a losing battle. Casualties can't be replaced. Gabon should have been recalled in the nineties, or even the mid-naughts. He wasn't, and I want to know why."

"He probably didn't want to come back, if he deviated." Malachi clasped his hands behind his back when Jen glared at him. "I apologize, *lumina*. I see treachery everywhere; it's in my nature."

"If you guys would have told him to come back, he would have." She realized it was true as soon as she said it. Michael wasn't here to defend himself, and she would be damned if she let these guys trash-talk him. "He's a rule-follower. He doesn't even break the speed limit unless those things are chasing us."

"That's good." Paulus nodded thoughtfully. Maybe she was getting through to him. "Nevertheless, we have to be sure. You may be the last Incorruptible on earth, ma'am, and if you are, it is *vital* we don't allow any injury to you, no matter how small. Now that you're here."

Oh, now that I'm here you're being a Monday morning quarter-back, aren't you. She bit back the words with an almost physical effort. *And if he'd been recalled, those... things, the demons, they would have eaten me at the diner along with killing everybody else.* A shudder worked up from her feet, shaking all the way through her.

It was a particularly gruesome thought.

"Did Gabon ever force you to do anything?" Paulus said it gently, but there was a glint in his eyes she didn't like. "Did he make you afraid, or hurt you at all?"

"Of course not." The very idea was ridiculous now, but she *had* been terrified. She took a step back, bumping the kitchen counter. It hurt, and she longed to see Michael, just to make sure he was really okay. "I mean, I was really...he had something he called a tacky-yum for a little while. It made me feel drugged. Otherwise I would have tried to escape and got my head bitten off."

Malachi leaned forward on his toes, back to vibrating in place with suppressed energy. "And how long did he keep you under *tacium*?"

"Just until we stopped the first night." She sounded like a hostage with an unhealthy attachment to her captor. But she could see the reasons for everything he'd done, now, God knew hindsight had absolutely *perfect* vision. "I know how it sounds, I really do. I just... I trust him. He even got stabbed protecting me against that thing that... it's crazy. It's *all* crazy."

"That's a natural response," Paulus said ponderously.

"Funny, that's just what Michael would say." She took a nervous step sideways, keeping the kitchen island between her and both men. A subtle change in the force flowing through her chest made her wince, swallowing a gasp.

"You see?" Paulus dropped his arms, spreading his hands like Bob faced with an angry customer to calm down. "That's why we can't have you around a large group of legionnaires until you've rested; they could injure you, drawing on grace. An Incorruptible must be cared for."

Malachi flowed across the room, cutting her a wide berth and heading for the door. "I'll go down to Records, then. With your permission, *lumin*—I mean, ma'am?"

"Go ahead," she said, numbly. "Knock yourself out."

"When you're finished there, I want you to go down to the Baths." Paulus's expression turned remote.

Malachi paused. "Oh?"

"It strikes me that Gabon might have something to say that someone in the Eyrie may not wish him to." Paulus's dark gaze rested on Jen, and now she *was* hugging herself, tightly. Squeezing as if she could find some comfort, though there was none to be found, and just then a faint knock sounded at the door. Jenna restrained a flinch at the last moment, and Paulus's expression said he'd noticed it anyway. "That's Bernard with the groceries. We'll stay with the *lumina*; I want a full guard detail on every floor. Let the city care for itself tonight, we have an Incorruptible to protect."

"Wait." *Care for itself* sounded dire, and Jenna almost cursed herself for opening her mouth again. Still, she couldn't help it. "What about the city?"

"It's full of the *diaboli*," Malachi said over his shoulder as Paulus moved away from the door; the bigger man moved in an arc to keep himself on the other side of the kitchen island. Nice of him. "Our main job is to protect the Incorruptible, but we also clean the streets to make it safer for mortals."

Mortals. Just the flat, humdrum way he said it was more chilling than any number of demonstrations.

Jenna decided she'd had enough. She turned sharply, almost hitting the counter again, and headed for the large bathroom. At least it had a locking door, and she sat on the closed toilet for a long while, listening to the rustling of grocery bags and a few soft murmurs. Sounded like they were putting things away.

Her stomach ached, her head was full of a strange whirring sound, and all she wanted was to see Michael again. Or, to be more precise, to crawl gratefully into bed and hear him breathing in the darkness, even if he was on the other side of the room.

It was, she suspected, the only way she'd ever feel safe again.

RATHER BE STABBED

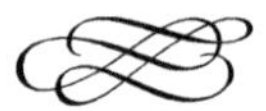

Floating, amniotic warmth cradled him, almost as kind as grace itself. Michael's eyes opened a crack, then slightly more. The green shimmer told him he was in a tank, and the thing clamped over his mouth and nose fed him oxygen. It was a far cry from the pools of his early training, where a legionnaire was wrapped in linen with a reed or similar hollow tube, held to his face with complicated fabric-twists, poking above the surface. The secret of the fluid's making was jealously guarded, and the Baths were only for the most grievously wounded of legionnaires.

Or the ones who needed to be held in narcotic stillness before summary judgment.

Am I really that hurt? Who's guarding her?

He had plenty of time to think while he floated, naked and twitching occasionally as flesh repaired itself, fingers slack and toes dangling a good foot above the bottom of the tank. Had he deviated from the Principle somehow? It didn't matter, she was safe.

I wouldn't be so sure, Michael.

Shadows moved outside the tank's glass walls. Were they filing past to look at one of the condemned, as was the rule? Or were some coming to look at a legionnaire who had brought in an Incorruptible? Was he being held up as an example, or a cautionary tale?

Wondering about that is useless. Think about what's really bothering you.

He didn't want to. He wanted simply to rest, and remember being in Jenna's arms. Remember the taste of her, and how she slept, her breath a warm spot on his shoulder and her dark curls tangled over a cheap hotel pillow. Remember the *feel* of her, grace and a hot, tight glove around him...

Michael stirred, again. Thick liquid rippled.

She's not safe yet.

It was simple, once he had some quiet time to piece it together. They hadn't moved to collect him and his *lumina* because someone didn't want them to. Of course the unclean needed her for their own purposes, but the break in the pattern, now viewed from above, was clear. Someone in the Legion—one of Michael's own brothers, sworn to the Principle—had simply told the local *diaboli* that an Incorruptible had been found, alerting the creatures it was his duty to hunt.

It was the only reading of events that made any sense at all. And now he was helpless, floating in a bath, while she was among the legionnaires who undoubtedly did not suspect one of their number of such a thing. Even the Celeres, with their noses for treason and divergence, had obviously not found the traitor.

Liquid sloshed again. He was fighting the sedation, struggling with its drugging hold on limbs and torso. Agonizingly slow, buoyancy lifting him by increments as he tensed, trying to semaphore his unease.

No, he wasn't being lifted. The liquid was draining.

Michael was lowered by inches, feet touching a tiled tank-floor, weightlessness sliding away until he lay curled on his side as if he had been descended to the mortal realm from *elsewhere* again, bright light stinging his eyes, the twin curved scars on his back oozing and his jelly-slick skin shrinking from the cold, thin dark marks scalpel-slicing their way deep and deeper, containing and reinforcing, healing and confining.

"Easy there, centurion." Someone sounded amused, and the rumble under the words told him it was a high-ranking officer. "Easy, you're not well yet."

Centurion? I'm just a legionnaire. Michael's eyes rolled and he scrabbled weakly at the face-mask. The tube in his throat threatened to gag him now that the relaxant in the fluid was wearing off.

Rather be stabbed than intubated. Ugh.

The strap at the back of his head loosened, and he coughed the tube free. The tank's door was open, a cold draft pouring over slick skin. Gooseflesh crawled all over him too, painful prickles turning into stabbing needles,

"Easy," the officer said again. "I regret I had to interrupt your upgrade, centurion, but I have questions."

So do I. He coughed, bringing up a clot of bile, and spat for where he sensed the drain was. The mask skittered away and was automatically retracted for cleaning. The tank would be flushed and sterilized for another poor wounded legionnaire, but right now Michael didn't care. He tried forcing himself to hands and knees, failed when both slipped and scrabbled weakly on jelly-slick tile, and tried again.

"Calm *down.*" It was a Celeres—one of the blues, the one with a sarcastic twinkle to his dark eyes and his feathery eyebrows tipped with cobalt. "She's with the Decurion and a Celeres, she's safe."

Not if one of them has deviated from the Principle. Who could alter records and override a Priority One message? Only a high-ranking officer, that's who. "Not...necessarily," he husked. "They knew we were coming. Even after I threw the burner away, they knew we were coming. Denver. They killed the team in Denver, had a Corrupter in Vegas." Now he could spit out his news, and he rolled half onto his back, examining the Celeres. The legionnaire almost vibrated with readiness, his fatigues well-worn and his marks flush with grace.

What if this one was the traitor?

"I know," the blue-haired man said, grimly. "I went looking in the Records Department. Someone overrode your initial call-in, and tipped everything from you afterward into a killfile. The legionnaires in Denver were coded as a recon, not as a pickup, and they were betrayed. There is *diabolerie* afoot, Michael Gabon." He paused, bending to offer a hand. "I'm Malachi. Malachi Pike."

"Principle guard you." Michael's throat was raw. "Where—" Another cough-spasm racked him. He was weak as a newborn kitten, but urgency gathered in his bones, beat under his heart. He couldn't even grasp the Celeres's hand; his arm was leaden. "Where is my *lumina*?"

"Fortieth floor. The heart of the Eyrie." Malachi regarded him almost sidelong, a sober, gauging gaze, but he left his hand in midair, patiently waiting for a grunt to gather his strength. "Whoever altered the records left very little trace. I think it's best I bring you to Paulus; he's the highest-ranking officer left."

What? "How many..."

"Not enough." A Celeres normally didn't look this set or grim; whatever else this Pike had found out, he was keeping to himself. At least if he was the traitor he wouldn't be telling Michael this, would he? No, he would just murder a helpless legionnaire in the bath, and it would be over. "That will change, with an Incorruptible here. Paulus is old, he'll probably be promoted to Principality when this is over."

"How do you know he's not the traitor?" He was well on his way to mistrusting every single one of his brothers, and that was a dangerous position to be in.

"I don't." Malachi's smile was knife-edged. "But we will soon, Gabon. Come, let us find you something to wear. Our *lumina* is waiting."

CHANGED MY MIND

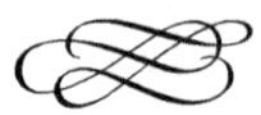

At least the bathroom was nice—too nice to pee in, frankly. The fixtures were all brand new, the sink had a lotus-shaped bowl, and every inch of it was clean as a whistle. The mirrored cabinet was empty and it looked like nobody had ever used the toilet. Even the big clawfoot tub was pristine, and the glassed-in shower glowed secretively.

Jenna stood near the door leading to the living room instead of to the huge bedroom, listening intently. There was motion in the apartment, and soft male voices exchanging cryptic terms. The fridge opened, closed, opened again; cabinet doors were opened and closed as well. It sounded like her parents come back from the store, exchanging soft snippets of information while they worked.

Her stomach rumbled again. Eventually, there was a tentative knock on the bathroom door. "*Lumina*?" It was the thickset fellow, Paulus. "There is an emergency elsewhere. Bernard is here, he'll take care of you."

Which one's Bernard? She cleared her throat, a small, forlorn sound. "Okay," she said, then repeated it a little louder. "Okay. Thanks."

A long pause, then the front door closed. A tense silence descended, and Jenna reached for the doorknob.

Don't. Panic gripped her for a few moments. *Don't go out there.*

It was ridiculous. She was safe here. Michael had told her so, but her hand wouldn't turn the knob. It simply refused, her fingers changed to ice.

"He's gone," another voice said, a light, amused male tenor. "You can come out, little *lumina.* I'd like to see you."

Something about the words turned her stomach upside-down. Or maybe she was just hungry and paranoid. Who wouldn't be, after all this?

Stop being such a coward. She unlocked the door and swept it open, decisively.

He stood in the kitchen, tall and broad-shouldered, and as soon as Jenna glimpsed him her mouth dried and her stomach stopped flipping, turning instead into a hard, roiling knot behind her breastbone.

Long nose. Arched, coppery eyebrows. A sharp chin. And that hair, a little longer than Michael's, standing up in a short, aggressive ruff.

Red hair. Bright red. His hair was, in strictest fact, *crimson.*

All the oxygen surrounding her vanished. She clung to the porcelain doorknob, staring wide-eyed as a kid on Christmas morning looking under the tree.

This present had sharp white teeth, bared in a lazy, twisted grin. "I must admit," he said, conversationally, "I never thought you'd survive. I visited the hospital but you'd already returned to the East Coast, and it was crawling with unclean. I thought it was only a matter of time, and surely you'd be collected and drained. Then, as the years went by, I started to wonder."

"You," she managed, a cricket-whisper. *Of course,* something whispered, deep inside her memory. *You knew this would happen. You knew, sooner or later, he'd find you again.*

"Yes." The red-haired man smiled, rather gently. Warm electric light made his hair a flame, glinted on his teeth, glowed on his white

T-shirt. Tiny red pinpricks danced in the center of each pupil, and they dilated as he returned her steady gaze. "They never even knew you'd been on this coast at all, once I tidied up."

"My mother..." Oh, God, this was a nightmare, and she couldn't *breathe*. She smelled gasoline again, and the sick, thick, sweetish smell of roasting. "You killed my *mother*."

"If it's any consolation, I was aiming for both of you, and you'll be with her soon." He took one step, another, flanking the kitchen island. "You're quite possibly the last of your kind, mortal bitch, and once you're gone, we can all go home."

Oh, great. Is that why? "But you chose to come here," she managed. Her lips were numb, and so were her legs, not to mention her arms. "Michael told me. You *chose*."

"Yes," the red-headed man who had crouched on the burning hood of her mother's car said. His tone didn't change—soft, reasonable, quiet. He kept moving, and he was almost around the kitchen island. Step by slow step, and once he was close enough he'd streak for her. She knew how *fast* they were, she'd seen it up close. "But, you see, I changed my mind."

He smiled, bright white teeth lengthening, and the clarity spilling through Jenna changed. It burned, spilling through parts of her still raw-sensitive from the earlier flood; she inhaled to scream, tensing to sweep the door closed. She could lock it, and there was another door into the bedroom. If she could reach that—

"Don't fight," he said, and he'd almost reached the corner of the island. "I'll make it quick and painless, if you don't fight me."

It was something Eddie might have said.

Jenna slammed the door, twisted the lock with sweating fingers, and bolted for the bedroom door.

VERY NAUGHTY INDEED

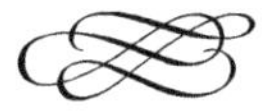

Maybe it was luck, maybe it was the Principle arranging things; Michael never afterward decided which. At the time, though, when the silver-shining elevator doors opened he was busy staying on his feet, weak from injury and the narcotic fluid of the healing-tank. His ribs were tender, his left leg was unsteady, and the body armor the Celeres had requisitioned for him didn't help.

Normally he wouldn't feel the weight, but at the moment it was a lead suit.

The Decurion was inside the elevator, frowning, and his mild dark gaze swung past the blue Celeres to Michael, who straightened automatically in the presence of an officer. If this was what promotion felt like, he'd almost rather remain a grunt.

Get out, he wanted to bark. *Where's my lumina?* But of course he couldn't say it.

"What are you..." The Decurion paused, then motioned them into the metal box. "Bernard said they wanted me in Control, and wouldn't tell him why. Where's Declan?"

"I don't know." Malachi put his arm over the elevator door, holding it open. "There's no emergency in Control, we just came from Requisitions. It's relatively quiet down there, they're just monitoring the city feeds—the unclean are furious, for obvious reasons." He took a deep breath. "Paulus, I went digging in Records just as you asked, and someone has been very naughty indeed."

The Decurion's expression shifted a critical few degrees. He was only relatively slow in battle, that change said, and not tardy at all above the neck.

Michael lost his breath. "Jenna," he said. *Hurry up. I don't care what you do, just get out of my way.* "Where is my *lumina*?"

"Come." The Decurion beckoned, a short, chopping motion. A flame had kindled in his gaze, slow to light but difficult to extinguish, the battle-rage of the most stolid and patient of Michael's kind. "Hurry."

At least they didn't have to climb stairs. Malachi laid out his findings in a few clipped sentences, and Paulus's face hardened into granite. "Treachery," he muttered. "There may be an explanation."

"But not a good one." Malachi, somber, glanced at Michael. "I'm glad I fished him out of the Baths early."

The lights fluttered, the elevator hesitated for a heartstopping moment, and every legionnaire on seventy-plus floors of Los Angeles skyscraper felt the burst of wild, spiking terror from the fortieth floor.

Michael's hands turned into fists. *Jenna.* He was stuck in this cable-dragged box, and she was in danger.

"Principle preserve us." The Decurion reached for the keypad and punched in a series of numbers, overriding all other functions. The doors slid closed and the elevator lifted with stomach-clenching speed.

"We could burn her, pulling too much force." The Celeres was pale, his blue stubble standing out in stark relief. Nowadays, mortals would simply think his hair dyed, but not so long ago hats and head-wraps were issued to keep their coloring from exciting suspicion.

Another burst of terror flowered above them, swelling rapidly as the elevator lifted. It seemed to take forever to reach the fortieth floor, and once the doors opened Michael didn't wait for the Decurion's signal or the Celeres's precedence. He turned hard left, sensing Jenna at the end of long, light-filled hallway, and ran.

The door was closed and quite probably locked, but he didn't care. He would simply go through anything in his path, one way or another.

All that mattered was reaching her in time.

HIGH DEFINITION

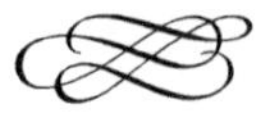

He was *fast*, streaking through their funny time-bubble trick and trailing fuming crimson. To make matters worse, he *pulled* at her, an invisible grasp tangling at her ankles, trying to throw her down. The pain was all through her, the glow they called grace a molten core in her chest; Jenna leapt over the bed, almost falling face-first on the other side as he bulleted past. She dropped instinctively, lovely pale carpet burning her bare elbows, and rolled.

The redheaded man swooped aside, moving so fast his feet skated over the trembling window, the rest of him almost horizontal. Hair-fine stress fractures bloomed on the glass. The redhead screamed, a high nasty cry like the demons' glassbreaking screeches, and she scrambled to her feet, caught in the syrupy stickiness of nightmare. She remembered *everything*, in stunning high definition, not to mention surround sound—the accident hadn't been the semi's fault at all, though that hadn't helped anyone. No, the redheaded man had simply dropped onto the hood of Mom's car, metal and glass crumpling and bucking wildly. Whatever chance had thrown Jenna free had also hidden her with a crowd of horrified onlookers, and now she understood the deep irresistible panic that had driven her from the hospital that evening despite the doctor wanting to keep her for observation.

She also remembered the flames coming not from the Volvo's ruptured gas tank or the semi's crumpled front, but from the redheaded man himself, and right now tiny burnt streaks followed him as he spun, found his footing, and leapt for her again.

Jenna scrabbled on hands and feet as the window shattered, sheets of glass exploding outward into a dry, keening wind. The roaring of altitude matched the noise inside her head, and if she could just get to the bedroom door she could run through the living room and maybe make it to the hallway outside—and then what? She didn't know the layout here, and she didn't think waiting around for the elevator at the end of the hall was going to be an option.

Stairs. There's got to be stairs. And wouldn't Michael be proud of her for thinking of them. God, she hoped he was all right—

All this passed through her head in a single, crystalline, adrenaline-soaked instant, and she all but erased the skin on her palms as she monkey-galloped for the door, the carpet burning with friction. Smoke rose; the redheaded man was beginning to fume like one of the awful demon things, smoke-steam trailing in curling ribbons as he charged again.

This time she didn't trip because she was already crawl-scrabbling. Instinct trumpeted inside her head and she went flat as he bulleted over her, a sharpness shearing the ends of her flying hair. Then she rolled aside and he crashed through the door to the living room, taking out a good chunk of wall on either side.

Go the other way. The bathroom again. Move!

Her head gave an amazing, razor-sharp flare of agonizing pain. A terrific, jolting crash shook the living room, and the building swayed.

"WHY WON'T YOU DIE?" he roared, and more glass shattered.

You know, at this point, I'm wondering that too. She gained her feet in a graceless lunge, cough-choking on fumes from burning carpet and scorched drywall. They were really high up, and it was *cold*—her breath puffed and she scrambled over the bed again, fighting through burning netting and drowning softness.

More crashing, and he must have guessed she'd try for the other escape route, because the bathroom door exploded. She tumbled back, drywall and wood splinters peppering the bed and making sharp little sounds when they hit sharp, toothy glass shards clinging to the window's edges.

The cleanup for this is going to be insane. She strained desperately to turn, to slither away, to do something, anything—but he was too fast, his booted feet sinking into the bed on either side of her hips. The redheaded murderer bent, claws prickling her upper arms. His face, sharp and once handsome, had twisted, suffusing with ugly purple-crimson.

He looked, in fact, very much like the thing that had stabbed Michael, but without the extra arms.

The redhead hopped off the bed with a jolt, carrying her with him. Black flowers danced in Jenna's vision as his left hand closed around her throat; something crackled near her larynx. Her feet dangled; she brought up a knee with hysterical strength and it sank in.

Hard.

The red-haired man howled right in her face, and he really did look an awful lot like Eddie, too. The echo was awful, and a great burst of clear, colorless fury flashed through her. *I hope that hurt,* she thought before he squeezed again, and she kneed him once more; at least she knew some of them were built like human guys. If he would just drop her so she could *breathe*—

He bellowed, and the world turned over. He did let go of her, but Jenna couldn't be grateful for that tiny mercy, because he flung her contemptuously through the broken window into a California night.

REJOIN THE PRINCIPLE

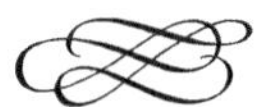

It was a beautiful suite, just the sort of cushioned light-filled nest an Incorruptible should have. Except now it was a smashed egg, windows shattered and smoke rising from smoldering streaks. The traitor was using his strength and speed ruthlessly despite the chance of discovery, and one lone, exhausted *lumina* had little hope of evading him for long.

One last high-octane burst of terror almost in front of him, and Michael tore diagonally through the living room for a hole blasted in the wall that had probably once held a door. Water sprayed from broken kitchen taps and the bathroom was alive with hiss-billowing steam, and there was the red Celeres, holding a small, thrashing woman by the throat.

Everything inside Michael Gabon froze.

The treacherous Celeres howled in her face; he was already twist-fuming with deviance from the Principle, his mask slipping aside. How long had he been working in secret, sliding away from righteousness?

It didn't matter. The Celeres gathered himself, sliptime trembling bubble-thin at its expanding edge, and *threw* her.

Michael bulleted past him, not even slowing to kill the traitor. The Decurion and the blue Celeres could handle that, should it need doing. He strained against his own weakness, his own too-slow, unwieldy, half-healed body, and lunged to catch her—anything, her wrist, her hair, her shirt.

Anything at all.

"*NOOOOOO!*" the traitor screamed, and something burst from Michael's back, twin arcs of singing pain slicing through cloth, Kevlar, and ceramic plate; the two invisible feathered things beat frantically to slow him as his clumsy fingers closed around her slim wrist. The jolt was immediate and he tried to dig his heels in, hoping to break enough momentum. Jagged broken-glass teeth sank into his belly with a crunch, and the pain was a fire-whip, goading him.

Thunk. The glass teeth tore down to his hips, stopping only when his pelvis arrested the motion with a shattering, crunching jolt. Her forward momentum halted, Jenna's legs flew out, and Michael braced himself.

This is going to hurt.

Oh, it already hurt, but he kept his fingers braced around her wrist as she curved to smack against wall or window below, letting out a furious, wounded cry. The red Celeres was behind him, and now was the time, if the traitor had his wits about him, for the foul one to spear him through the back.

Howling, crunching, high piercing screams. A hot wash of blood and great singing pain poured from Michael's violated belly but he ignored it, invisible feathered masses pumping furiously from his back as he grabbed blindly with his free hand as well, finding her wrist once more and latching on even more securely.

Now he had both hands locked on her; all he had to do was hold while the glass sank into his guts and Jenna's head tipped back on its fragile stem of a neck, vivid bruising already beginning to mar her beautiful, lucent throat. She stared up at him, dark eyes wounded and wild, and white feathers streamed into the draft, exploding from somewhere behind and above him as he held on, held on, held *on*.

He was losing blood and consciousness quickly, the sudden drop in internal pressure filling him with woozy, dozy alarm. He stared at Jenna, dangling by one wrist, and hoped her shoulder wasn't dislocated. Her eyelids fluttered, and she almost dropped her chin to look down.

No, he pleaded silently. *No, please, look at me. Don't go. Look at me.*

The darkness was coming. A massive grating noise behind him was a legionnaire's death, more crashing and snapping as the red Celeres was given the only mercy he could possibly hope for.

A swift end, yes, but not painless. Or so Michael hoped.

His hands were slippery, whether with sweat or blood he couldn't tell. If he passed out and his grasp loosened she would fall. The lights twinkling below would swallow her, the pavement breaking her fragile body. She would rejoin the Principle, and he would have failed.

Hot blood soaked his boots. The glass grated against his spinal cord, and it *hurt.*

Michael held on. It was simple; even if he bled out his dying bones would grasp her. They would draw her up through the hole, and now that the traitor was uncovered she would be safe.

Hands reached his shoulders, someone was shouting, but he stared at Jenna and hoped she could decipher his mute pleading.

Look at me. Just look at me, lumina, and hold on.

The darkness took him, but Michael kept holding on.

GOOD NEWS

Two DAYS later a long tiled room was a forest of vertical glass tubes, most of them clean and bare but a few full of vile-looking green liquid and indistinct, floating shapes. One, separated from the rest by a row of empties, held what they were looking for, and Jenna shivered as she halted before it, relief warring with fresh unease.

Her shoulder was tender, her throat was scraped, her arms and legs felt like someone had used them for batting practice, and her eyes were hot and grainy. To top it all off, the horrible draining sensation whenever she was near any of *them* was enough to make her nauseous.

Nevertheless, Jenna gave Malachi a pained, apologetic smile. "Thanks for this."

"No thanks necessary, *lumina.*" The blue-haired man stood between two rows of empty, cylindrical glass tanks, their doors hermetically sealed.

The one they wanted was full of that poisonous-looking fluid, moving sluggishly as it cycled from the top to a drain in the floor. Floating naked in the green goo, Michael bobbed gently, an insectile mask clasped over his face. He looked curiously small, hovering while tiny bubbles crawled through the thick goop, not quite obeying the laws of physics.

"He's a fighter," Malachi continued quietly. "He just needs rest, now. The fluid has antiseptic and painkiller properties, it encourages healing."

The tattooed marks moved all over Michael's body, just as sluggish as the drifting fluid. A garish scar sliced across his abdomen; you could see where the glass had almost sawed him in half and how it had dragged down his sides while Jenna dangled forty stories up.

She wasn't going to be looking out of any high windows for a while. Not without a shudder or two.

"That's good," she murmured, and reached up on impulse, spreading her fingers on cold glass. Condensation flowered around her touch, and Michael's marks sped up a little. They really did look like circuitry etched on his skin, following muscle-lines to protect and support, thicker over weak spots. Still, it was the body armor, shredded Kevlar and broken ceramic plates, that had stopped them both from tumbling out the window.

That, and maybe his stubbornness. They'd carried a screaming Jenna away to a fresh, beautiful suite on a lower floor, everything around her turning gray. *Shock*, they said, and *he'll be all right*, and *take this pill*, and various other things. She'd taken the sedative gratefully, not even caring that there might be one or two more of them with a murderous agenda.

If Michael was dead, why should she even bother? But when she woke up, Paulus had told her the good news—as far as they could tell, Bernard acted alone.

And as far as they could tell, Michael would survive.

"He's in for promotion, too." The Celeres sounded uncharacteristically tentative. "Once he's well, he'll be instated as the head of your guard, since you two are...uh, close." Was Malachi blushing? She didn't turn to check. "*Lumina*?"

She could have repeated *don't call me that*, but it was unfair. It was the word they had, so they used it. "Bernard," she said, the name echoing slightly off tile and glass. Whoever cleaned this place deserved a medal for both bravery and thoroughness. "He said he wanted to go home." Maybe Michael did too.

Maybe they all did.

"We all chose to come here." Malachi shifted uneasily. "To serve the Principle."

He wasn't such a bad guy. Neither was Paulus, who kept going pale and apologizing for not catching on to Bernard quicker. Nobody knew how long he'd been passing information to the unclean, and Paulus had said that once Jenna was well enough, more legionnaires would "come through" and a full investigation could happen. *It's a miracle you survived, lumina.*

Maybe so, but Jenna figured she was looking at the miracle worker right now. "Are you sure he's going to be okay?" The omelette she'd had for breakfast twitched a little uneasily in its new home, like it thought escape was an option. Michael stirred as well, his eyelashes fluttering as if he dreamed.

"He senses you." Malachi's tone was hushed. "We'd better go. He needs to rest."

Visiting hours are over. I get it. The new apartment was just as pretty as the first, but done in cream instead of white. She liked it better, but kept well away from the windows and dragged one of the dining-table chairs in front of the door each night before huddling in the bed, trying not to hyperventilate and achieving only thin, restless sleep. "I'll be back," she promised, softly. "Okay? You just get better, Michael."

He stirred again, the liquid moving with him. How long was it going to take?

Jenna decided it didn't matter. She let Malachi usher her away, wincing as the Celeres's marks pulled at her. In ones or twos, it wasn't so bad, but more than that and the awful burning came back. They told her it would get better. She just had to give it time.

Time was something she had, now. Michael wasn't kidding when he said she wouldn't have to work, though Jenna was pretty sure she'd probably go mad with boredom once the bruises and the hideous burning sensation faded. It was ridiculous, how much money these people had. Or maybe they weren't strictly *people*, but that was a question she could leave alone for a while.

She had plenty of questions. When Michael woke up, she'd ask them.

WONDER OF WONDERS

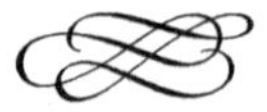

The light stung his eyes and he was sure some of the healing fluid was still coating his throat, but at least he was free of that drugging stillness and the fear shooting through his entire body whenever he reached for consciousness and the sedation dragged him down.

"You should have stayed in a little longer." The second blue Celeres—Declan, a little leaner in the hip than his brother, but slightly broader in the shoulder—shook his shaven head, watching Michael button his jeans and pull a standard-issue navy T-shirt over his head. "She's fine."

Michael made a short noise that could be taken as assent, unwillingness to disagree, or anything in between. His fingers were swollen-clumsy, it hurt when he bent to tug his boots on, and he was going to have to keep his belt tight enough to hold his jeans up for a while. He felt savagely stretched, ligaments and tendons still protesting, and he had to stop and rest for a few moments in the locker room's fluorescent glare, his breath coming hard and harsh.

Finally, he straightened. "How long was the red one—Bernard?" He glanced at Declan's brief nod before continuing. "How long was he deviant?"

"We don't know." Shame made the truthseeking lamps in the Celeres's pupils flare briefly. "He told the *lumina* she was likely the last, and when she was gone we would go home."

It sent a chill down Michael's spine. He should have listened to his instincts more, he'd *known* something was wrong. He'd even guessed it was a twisted legionnaire. It was unthinkable, that one of his brothers could have done such a thing—but he'd thought it, and he'd been right.

The Legion has forsaken thee. Even a Corruptor could speak the truth, if it served their purpose. Or half a truth. "And he could have had help?" It wasn't his place to question an officer, even if he was a centurion now, but Michael found out he didn't care.

All he cared about was getting back to work, and seeing if a certain dark-eyed woman was truly safe.

"Once the *lumina* brings an Authority through, I guess we'll find out." Declan didn't sound happy. Distrust was corrosive, and more than one legionnaire was probably eyeing his brothers with some trepidation. It took a long while for any breached trust to mend.

The unclean were massing, not quite daring to attack the Eyrie yet. If their numbers reached a certain point, would they seek to overwhelm the skyscraper and find the Incorruptible it was meant to shelter? He certainly hoped not—but he couldn't afford to rule out any possibility anymore.

No matter *how* outlandish.

Michael rolled his shoulders. He was weak, yes, but he couldn't float in the damn tube any longer. He'd heal just as quickly, though much more painfully, next to Jenna's bright, soft, welling grace.

As if his marks heard the thought, they twinged with heatless anticipation, and a door at the other end of the locker room clanged.

"—bring him up to you, you know." A familiar voice—Malachi. He'd been by to visit often, Michael guessed, having heard the Celeres's voice while he drifted in the tank.

"Oh, my God," Jenna replied. "Is this a locker room?"

"I told you." They sounded very friendly.

Michael's mouth twitched, wanting to smile. He dispelled the urge and tried not to notice how badly his hands were shaking.

She rounded the corner, ghosts of bruising lingering on her soft throat and cheek, her left arm still in a sling over a crisp white button-down. A pair of dark jeans on her long dancer's legs, and she wore the boots he'd bought her all the way back in New Paris.

She was *alive*.

Jenna halted between rows of metal lockers and stared at him, her pretty mouth slightly open and her hair falling sleekly over her shoulders.

Michael lost his breath again. She hummed with incandescence and his marks bathed in the flood, greedy for her. They studied each other for a long moment, and the insistent urge that had driven him out of the Baths and through cleanup, checkup, and dressing stopped between one heartbeat and the next.

There was nowhere else he had to be, and nothing else he had to do, if she was here.

Finally, Jenna spoke. "Hi." A shadow of uncertainty lingered in the word, or perhaps it was relief. Her dark eyes gleamed, and a single crystalline drop lingered on her right under-lashes before she brushed it away with a graceful, impatient movement. "They told me you were up, and I had to... I didn't mean to interrupt, I just..."

"It's no interruption." Declan grinned and brushed past Michael. "Come on, brother mine, I'm sure we can find something to do in the hallway."

"We'll be outside, *lumina*." Malachi's hand twitched as if to touch her injured shoulder as he turned, but she stood stock-still and he did not quite dare. "Don't stay in here forever, the damp is bad for you."

She rolled her eyes, but now there was a wan smile on her pretty face. It faded as she studied Michael again, listening to quick, light retreating footsteps. The locker room door swung open, closed with a rattle.

Now they were alone. The air conditioning kicked on, soughing cool air through ceiling vents, a soft whisper.

"They're treating you well?" Michael's mouth was dry. He was ravenous, too—he needed protein and carbs to replace lost muscle and fuel the deeper healing. The gel could only do so much, and drawing too much grace could injure her. His marks were greedy, sipping at her clarity.

"They're okay. I prefer you." She sucked in a breath, her cheeks coloring quickly. The flush made her even prettier. "I mean, Michael..."

"I'm glad to hear it." He gathered his courage, decided he might as well express his own feelings—or what he could of them, constrained by his position. A centurion couldn't demand from an Incorruptible; even an Authority couldn't. "I prefer you, too." Was it the right thing to say?

"We're home with your people now." She blinked, rapidly, fresh drops welling in her beautiful dark eyes. Was she unhappy to see him? Maybe he reminded her of things she'd rather forget. "So, uh, I wanted to ask..."

Michael waited, but she said nothing more. "Ask what?" He longed to touch her, and if a tear escaped to trace her beautiful cheek he would have to brush it away.

"It can wait," she said in a breathless rush, leaning forward on her toes. "It was selfish of me to run down here, I guess. I should thank you. You almost died, I still can't believe you caught me."

Neither can I. Miracles still lived in the world, and he had been granted more than his fair share of them after years of patient waiting. He could wait more, now, if he had to.

Michael took a step forward, impelled by her own leaning towards him. "I had to." That was the bare truth. "Either that, Jenna, or I'd have fallen with you. You know that, right?"

She shook her head, almost angrily, and wiped at her cheek again, denying him the chance. Protective of her wounded arm, she flinched slightly when he reached for her, his hand lifting to touch where

Malachi hadn't dared to. *If you're going to deny me, lumina, do it now.*

But he couldn't say that, could he? No legionnaire could. He was committing a blasphemy, helpless not to. He touched her cheek, running his damp-wrinkled fingertips over soft, delicate skin. "You should know." He tried to say it as gently as possible. "I'm not the brightest of my brothers, Jenna, but I'm yours."

"You suspected, didn't you." She gazed up at him, and the hope in those dark eyes was enough to level an Authority, let alone a simple legionnaire. Even if he was a centurion now, his marks thicker and his capacity enhanced. "I'd call that smart."

Yeah, well. He hadn't figured it out fast enough. "Thank you, *lumina*." He still couldn't bear to think of how *close* it had been. Had she let go or slipped free he would have fallen with her, but one lone, wounded legionnaire wouldn't have been enough to shield her from impact.

He would have tried, but it would have killed them both.

"I hate it when they call me that." Wonder of wonders, she leaned into his touch. "But from you, it sounds nice."

"Good." Grace spilled up his arm, pouring through his chest. He should have broken contact to avoid draining her, but he couldn't move. "It's traditional."

"And I... look, we were both under a lot of stress, and if you want to reconsider—"

Was that what she thought? "No." It burst out of him, the only time he'd dare interrupting her. "Not since the moment I saw you, Jenna. No reconsidering here."

"Good." Her chin tipped up, and he was hoping he was reading the signals right, because he was going to kiss her. It was a foregone conclusion. "I have another question."

He swallowed a brief flare of balked heat, but didn't straighten. Her breath was minty with toothpaste, and he was aware his was full of the odd petrichor unscent of healing fluid. "Okay."

"I've been thinking and thinking, and I just can't figure it out."

Heavy-lidded, she bit her lower lip gently, and he would have kissed her then, but she plunged onward. "Where did all the feathers come from?"

Oh. Michael lost the battle with tradition, with obedience, and with himself. He kissed her, and then he told her.

THEN, because he had to and he could, he kissed her again.

finis

ABOUT THE AUTHOR

Lilith Saintcrow lives in Vancouver, Washington, with the children, dogs, and cats who collectively own her, as well as a library for wayward texts.

ALSO BY LILITH SAINTCROW

The Complete Jill Kismet

The Marked

The Demon's Librarian

...and many more.

CPSIA information can be obtained
at www.ICGtesting.com
Printed in the USA
BVHW040225160919
558492BV00006B/50/P